THE CRUSHED FLOWER

And Other Stories

Leonid Andreyev

1ˢᵗ WORLD
LIBRARY
Literary Society

The Crushed Flower and Other Stories

Leonid Andreyev

© 1st World Library – Literary Society, 2004
PO Box 2211
Fairfield, IA 52556
www.1stworldlibrary.org
First Edition

LCCN: 2005901353

Softcover ISBN: 1-4218-1168-5
Hardcover ISBN: 1-4218-1068-9
eBook ISBN: 1-4218-1268-1

Purchase *"The Crushed Flower and Other Stories"*
as a traditional bound book at:
www.1stWorldLibrary.org/purchase.asp?ISBN=1-4218-1168-5

1st World Library Literary Society is a nonprofit
organization dedicated to promoting literacy by:

- Creating a free internet library accessible from any computer worldwide.
- Hosting writing competitions and offering book publishing scholarships.

Readers interested in supporting literacy
through sponsorship, donations or
membership please contact:
literacy@1stworldlibrary.org
Check us out at: www.1stworldlibrary.ORG
and start downloading free ebooks today.

The Crushed Flower and Other Stories
contributed by Tim, Ed & Rodney
in support of
1st World Library Literary Society

CONTENTS

THE CRUSHED FLOWER

CHAPTER I

His name was Yura.

He was six years old, and the world was to him enormous, alive and bewitchingly mysterious. He knew the sky quite well. He knew its deep azure by day, and the white-breasted, half silvery, half golden clouds slowly floating by. He often watched them as he lay on his back upon the grass or upon the roof. But he did not know the stars so well, for he went to bed early. He knew well and remembered only one star - the green, bright and very attentive star that rises in the pale sky just before you go to bed, and that seemed to be the only star so large in the whole sky.

But best of all, he knew the earth in the yard, in the street and in the garden, with all its inexhaustible wealth of stones, of velvety grass, of hot sand and of that wonderfully varied, mysterious and delightful dust which grown people did not notice at all from the height of their enormous size. And in falling asleep, as the last bright image of the passing day, he took along to his dreams a bit of hot, rubbed off stone bathed in sunshine or a thick layer of tenderly tickling, burning dust.

When he went with his mother to the centre of the city along the large streets, he remembered best of all, upon his return, the wide, flat stones upon which his steps and his feet seemed terribly small, like two little boats. And even the multitude of revolving wheels and horses' heads did not impress themselves so clearly upon his memory as this new and unusually interesting appearance of the ground.

Everything was enormous to him - the fences, the dogs and the people - but that did not at all surprise or frighten him; that only made everything particularly interesting; that transformed life into an uninterrupted miracle. According to his measures, various objects seemed to him as follows:

His father - ten yards tall.

His mother - three yards.

The neighbour's angry dog - thirty yards.

Their own dog - ten yards, like papa.

Their house of one story was very, very tall - a mile.

The distance between one side of the street and the other - two miles.

Their garden and the trees in their garden seemed immense, infinitely tall.

The city - a million - just how much he did not know.

And everything else appeared to him in the same way. He knew many people, large and small, but he knew and appreciated better the little ones with whom he could speak of everything. The grown people behaved so foolishly and asked such absurd, dull questions about things that everybody knew, that it was necessary for him also to make believe that he was foolish. He had to lisp and give nonsensical answers; and, of course, he felt like running away from them as soon as possible. But there were over him and around him and within him two entirely extraordinary persons, at once big and small, wise and foolish, at once his own and strangers - his father and mother.

They must have been very good people, otherwise they could not have been his father and mother; at any rate, they were charming and unlike other people. He could say with certainty that his father was very great, terribly wise, that he possessed immense power, which made him a person to be feared somewhat, and it was interesting to talk with him about unusual things, placing his hand in father's large, strong, warm hand for safety's sake.

Mamma was not so large, and sometimes she was even very small; she was very kind hearted, she kissed tenderly; she understood very well how he felt when he had a pain in his little stomach, and only with her could he relieve his heart when he grew tired of life, of his games or when he was the victim of some cruel injustice. And if it was unpleasant to cry in father's presence, and even dangerous to be capricious, his tears had an unusually pleasant taste in mother's presence and filled his soul with a peculiar serene sadness, which he could find neither in his games nor in laughter, nor even in the reading of the most terrible fairy tales.

It should be added that mamma was a beautiful woman and that everybody was in love with her. That was good, for he felt proud of it, but that was also bad - for he feared that she might be taken away. And every time one of the men, one of those enormous, invariably inimical men who were busy with themselves, looked at mamma fixedly for a long time, Yura felt bored and uneasy. He felt like stationing himself between him and mamma, and no matter where he went to attend to his own affairs, something was drawing him back.

Sometimes mamma would utter a bad, terrifying phrase:

"Why are you forever staying around here? Go and play in your own room."

There was nothing left for him to do but to go away. He would take a book along or he would sit down to draw, but that did not always help him. Sometimes mamma would praise him for reading but sometimes she would say again:

"You had better go to your own room, Yurochka. You see, you've spilt water on the tablecloth again; you always do some mischief with your drawing."

And then she would reproach him for being perverse. But he felt worst of all when a dangerous and suspicious guest would come when Yura had to go to bed. But when he lay down in his bed a sense of easiness came over him and he felt as though all was ended; the lights went out, life stopped; everything slept.

In all such cases with suspicious men Yura felt vaguely but very strongly that he was replacing father in some way. And that made him somewhat like a grown man - he was in a bad frame of mind, like a grown person, but, therefore, he was unusually calculating, wise and serious. Of course, he said nothing about this to any one, for no one would understand him; but, by the manner in which he caressed father when he arrived and sat down on his knees patronizingly, one could see in the boy a man who fulfilled his duty to the end. At times father could not understand him and would simply send him away to play or to sleep - Yura never felt offended and went away with a feeling of great satisfaction. He did not feel the need of being understood; he even feared it. At times he would not tell under any circumstances why he was crying; at times he would make believe that he was absent minded, that he heard nothing, that he was occupied with his own affairs, but he heard and understood.

And he had a terrible secret. He had noticed that these extraordinary and charming people, father and mother, were sometimes unhappy and were hiding this from everybody. Therefore he was also concealing his discovery, and gave everybody the impression that all was well. Many times he found mamma crying somewhere in a corner in the drawing room, or in the bedroom - his own room was next to her bedroom - and one night, very late, almost at dawn, he heard the terribly loud and angry voice of father and the weeping voice of mother. He lay a long time, holding his breath, but then he was so terrified by that unusual conversation in the middle of the night that he could not restrain himself and he asked his nurse in a soft voice:

"What are they saying?"

And the nurse answered quickly in a whisper:

"Sleep, sleep. They are not saying anything."

"I am coming over to your bed."

"Aren't you ashamed of yourself? Such a big boy!"

"I am coming over to your bed."

Thus, terribly afraid lest they should be heard, they spoke in whispers and argued in the dark; and the end was that Yura moved over to nurse's bed, upon her rough, but cosy and warm blanket.

In the morning papa and mamma were very cheerful and Yura pretended that he believed them and it seemed that he really did believe them. But that same evening, and perhaps it was another evening, he noticed his father crying. It happened in the following way: He was passing his father's study, and the door was half open; he heard a noise and he looked in quietly - father lay face downward upon his couch and cried aloud. There was no one else in the room. Yura went away, turned about in his room and came back - the door was still half open, no one but father was in the room, and he was still sobbing. If he cried quietly, Yura could understand it, but he sobbed loudly, he moaned in a heavy voice and his teeth were gnashing terribly. He lay there, covering the entire couch, hiding his head under his broad shoulders, sniffing heavily - and that was beyond his understanding. And on the table, on the large table covered with pencils, papers and a wealth of other things, stood the lamp burning with a red flame, and smoking - a flat, greyish black strip of smoke was coming out and bending in all directions.

Suddenly father heaved a loud sigh and stirred. Yura walked away quietly. And then all was the same as ever. No one would have learned of this; but the image of the enormous, mysterious and charming man who was his father and who was crying remained in Yura's memory as something dreadful and extremely serious. And, if there were things of which he did not feel like speaking, it was absolutely necessary to say nothing of this, as though it were something sacred and terrible, and in that silence he must love father all the more. But he must love so that father should not notice it, and he must give the impression that it is very jolly to live on earth.

And Yura succeeded in accomplishing all this. Father did not notice that he loved him in a special manner; and it was really jolly to live on earth, so there was no need for him to make believe. The threads of his soul stretched themselves to all - to the sun, to the knife and the cane he was peeling; to the beautiful and enigmatic distance which he saw from the top of the iron roof; and it was hard for him to separate himself from all that was not himself. When the grass had a strong and fragrant odour it seemed to him that it was he who had such a fragrant odour, and when he lay down in his bed, however strange it may seem, together with him in his little bed lay down the enormous yard, the street, the slant threads of the rain and the muddy pools and the whole, enormous, live, fascinating, mysterious world. Thus all fell asleep with him and thus all awakened with him, and together with him they all opened their eyes. And there was one striking fact, worthy of the profoundest reflection - if he placed a stick somewhere in the garden in the evening it was there also in the morning; and the knuckle-bones which he hid in a box in the barn remained there, although it was dark and he went to his room for the night. Because of this he felt a natural need for hiding under his pillow all that was most valuable to him. Since things stood or lay there alone, they might also disappear of their accord, he reasoned. And in general it was so wonderful and pleasant that the nurse and the house and the sun existed not only yesterday, but every day; he felt like laughing and singing aloud when he awoke.

When people asked him what his name was he answered promptly:

"Yura."

But some people were not satisfied with this alone, and they wanted to know his full name - and then he replied with a certain effort:

"Yura Mikhailovich."

And after a moment's thought he added:

"Yura Mikhailovich Pushkarev."

CHAPTER II

An unusual day arrived. It was mother's birthday. Guests were expected in the evening; military music was to play, and in the garden and upon the terrace parti-coloured lanterns were to burn, and Yura need not go to bed at 9 o'clock but could stay up as late as he liked.

Yura got up when all were still sleeping. He dressed himself and jumped out quickly with the expectation of miracles. But he was unpleasantly surprised - the rooms were in the same disorder as usual in the morning; the cook and the chamber-maid were still sleeping and the door was closed with a hook - it was hard to believe that the people would stir and commence to run about, and that the rooms would assume a holiday appearance, and he feared for the fate of the festival. It was still worse in the garden. The paths were not swept and there was not a single lantern there. He grew very uneasy. Fortunately, Yevmen, the coachman, was washing the carriage behind the barn in the back yard and though he had done this frequently before, and though there was nothing unusual about his appearance, Yura clearly felt something of the holiday in the decisive way in which the coachman splashed the water from the bucket with his sinewy arms, on which the sleeves of his red blouse were rolled up to his elbows. Yevmen only glanced askance at Yura, and suddenly Yura seemed to have noticed for the first time his broad, black, wavy beard and thought respectfully that Yevmen was a very worthy man. He said:

"Good morning, Yevmen."

Then all moved very rapidly. Suddenly the janitor appeared

and started to sweep the paths, suddenly the window in the kitchen was thrown open and women's voices were heard chattering; suddenly the chambermaid rushed out with a little rug and started to beat it with a stick, as though it were a dog. All commenced to stir; and the events, starting simultaneously in different places, rushed with such mad swiftness that it was impossible to catch up with them. While the nurse was giving Yura his tea, people were beginning to hang up the wires for the lanterns in the garden, and while the wires were being stretched in the garden, the furniture was rearranged completely in the drawing room, and while the furniture was rearranged in the drawing room, Yevmen, the coachman, harnessed the horse and drove out of the yard with a certain special, mysterious mission.

Yura succeeded in concentrating himself for some time with the greatest difficulty. Together with father he was hanging up the lanterns. And father was charming; he laughed, jested, put Yura on the ladder; he himself climbed the thin, creaking rungs of the ladder, and finally both fell down together with the ladder upon the grass, but they were not hurt. Yura jumped up, while father remained lying on the grass, hands thrown back under his head, looking with half-closed eyes at the shining, infinite azure of the sky. Thus lying on the grass, with a serious expression on his face, apparently not in the mood for play, father looked very much like Gulliver longing for his land of giants. Yura recalled something unpleasant; but to cheer his father up he sat down astride upon his knees and said:

"Do you remember, father, when I was a little boy I used to sit down on your knees and you used to shake me like a horse?"

But before he had time to finish he lay with his nose on the grass; he was lifted in the air and thrown down with force - father had thrown him high up with his knees, according to his old habit. Yura felt offended; but father, entirely ignoring his anger, began to tickle him under his armpits, so that Yura had to laugh against his will; and then father picked him up like a little pig by the legs and carried him to the terrace. And mamma was frightened.

"What are you doing? The blood will rush to his head!"

After which Yura found himself standing on his legs, red faced, dishevelled, feeling very miserable and terribly happy at the same time.

The day was rushing fast, like a cat that is chased by a dog. Like forerunners of the coming great festival, certain messengers appeared with notes, wonderfully tasty cakes were brought, the dressmaker came and locked herself in with mamma in the bedroom; then two gentlemen arrived, then another gentleman, then a lady - evidently the entire city was in a state of agitation. Yura examined the messengers as though they were strange people from another world, and walked before them with an air of importance as the son of the lady whose birthday was to be celebrated; he met the gentlemen, he escorted the cakes, and toward midday he was so exhausted that he suddenly started to despise life. He quarrelled with the nurse and lay down in his bed face downward in order to have his revenge on her; but he fell asleep immediately. He awoke with the same feeling of hatred for life and a desire for revenge, but after having looked at things with his eyes, which he washed with cold water, he felt that both the world and life were so fascinating that they were even funny.

When they dressed Yura in a red silk rustling blouse, and he thus clearly became part of the festival, and he found on the terrace a long, snow white table glittering with glass dishes, he again commenced to spin about in the whirlpool of the onrushing events.

"The musicians have arrived! The musicians have arrived!" he cried, looking for father or mother, or for any one who would treat the arrival of the musicians with proper seriousness. Father and mother were sitting in the garden - in the arbour which was thickly surrounded with wild grapes - maintaining silence; the beautiful head of mother lay on father's shoulder; although father embraced her, he seemed very serious, and he showed no enthusiasm when he was told of the arrival of the musicians. Both treated their arrival with inexplicable indifference, which called forth a feeling of sadness in Yura. But mamma stirred and said:

"Let me go. I must go."

"Remember," said father, referring to something Yura did not understand but which resounded in his heart with a light, gnawing alarm.

"Stop. Aren't you ashamed?" mother laughed, and this laughter made Yura feel still more alarmed, especially since father did not laugh but maintained the same serious and mournful appearance of Gulliver pining for his native land....

But soon all this was forgotten, for the wonderful festival had begun in all its glory, mystery and grandeur. The guests came fast, and there was no longer any place at the white table, which had been deserted but a while before. Voices resounded, and laughter and merry jests, and the music began to play. And on the deserted paths of the garden where but a while ago Yura had wandered alone, imagining himself a prince in quest of the sleeping princess, now appeared people with cigarettes and with loud free speech. Yura met the first guests at the front entrance; he looked at each one carefully, and he made the acquaintance and even the friendship of some of them on the way from the corridor to the table.

Thus he managed to become friendly with the officer, whose name was Mitenka - a grown man whose name was Mitenka - he said so himself. Mitenka had a heavy leather sword, which was as cold as a snake, which could not be taken out - but Mitenka lied; the sword was only fastened at the handle with a silver cord, but it could be taken out very nicely; and Yura felt vexed because the stupid Mitenka instead of carrying his sword, as he always did, placed it in a corner in the hallway as a cane. But even in the corner the sword stood out alone - one could see at once that it was a sword. Another thing that displeased Yura was that another officer came with Mitenka, an officer whom Yura knew and whose name was also Yura Mikhailovich. Yura thought that the officer must have been named so for fun. That wrong Yura Mikhailovich had visited them several times; he even came once on horseback; but most of the time he came just before little Yura had to go to bed. And little Yura went to bed, while the unreal Yura Mikhailovich remained with mamma, and that caused him to feel alarmed and sad; he was afraid that mamma might be deceived. He paid no attention to the real Yura Mikhailovich: and now, walking beside Mitenka, he did not seem to realise his guilt; he adjusted his moustaches and maintained silence. He kissed mamma's hand, and that seemed repulsive to little Yura; but the stupid Mitenka also kissed mamma's hand, and thereby set everything aright.

But soon the guests arrived in such numbers, and there was such a variety of them, as if they had fallen straight from the sky. And some of them seemed to have fallen near the table, while others seemed to have fallen into the garden. Suddenly several students and ladies appeared in the path. The ladies were ordinary, but the students had holes cut at the left side of their white coats - for their swords. But they did not bring their swords along, no doubt because of their pride - they were all very proud. And the ladies rushed over to Yura and began to kiss him. Then the most beautiful of the ladies, whose name was Ninochka, took Yura to the swing and swung him until she threw him down. He hurt his left leg near the knee very painfully and even stained his little white pants in that spot, but of course he did not cry, and somehow his pain had quickly disappeared somewhere. At this time father was leading an important-looking bald-headed old man in the garden, and he asked Yurochka,

"Did you get hurt?"

But as the old man also smiled and also spoke, Yurochka did

not kiss father and did not even answer him; but suddenly he seemed to have lost his mind - he commenced to squeal for joy and to run around. If he had a bell as large as the whole city he would have rung that bell; but as he had no such bell he climbed the linden tree, which stood near the terrace, and began to show off. The guests below were laughing and mamma was shouting, and suddenly the music began to play, and Yura soon stood in front of the orchestra, spreading his legs apart and, according to his old but long forgotten habit, put his finger into his mouth. The sounds seemed to strike at him all at once; they roared and thundered; they made his legs tingle, and they shook his jaw. They played so loudly that there was nothing but the orchestra on the whole earth - everything else had vanished. The brass ends of some of the trumpets even spread apart and opened wide from the great roaring; Yura thought that it would be interesting to make a military helmet out of such a trumpet.

Suddenly Yura grew sad. The music was still roaring, but now it was somewhere far away, while within him all became quiet, and it was growing ever more and more quiet. Heaving a deep sigh, Yura looked at the sky - it was so high - and with slow footsteps he started out to make the rounds of the holiday, of all its confused boundaries, possibilities and distances. And everywhere he turned out to be too late; he wanted to see how the tables for card playing would be arranged, but the tables were ready and people had been playing cards for a long time when he came up. He touched the chalk and the brush near his father and his father immediately chased him away. What of that, what difference did that make to him? He wanted to see how they would start to dance and he was sure that they would dance in the parlour, but they had already commenced to dance, not in the parlour, but under the linden trees. He wanted to see how they would light the lanterns, but the lanterns had all been lit already, every one of them, to the very last of the last. They lit up of themselves like stars.

Mamma danced best of all.

CHAPTER III

Night arrived in the form of red, green and yellow lanterns. While there were no lanterns, there was no night. And now it lay everywhere. It crawled into the bushes; it covered the entire garden with darkness, as with water, and it covered the sky. Everything looked as beautiful as the very best fairy tale with coloured pictures. At one place the house had disappeared entirely; only the square window made of red light remained. And the chimney of the house was visible and there a certain spark glistened, looked down and seemed to think of its own affairs. What affairs do chimneys have? Various affairs.

Of the people in the garden only their voices remained. As long as some one walked near the lanterns he could be seen; but as soon as he walked away all seemed to melt, melt, melt, and the voice above the ground laughed, talked, floating fearlessly in the darkness. But the officers and the students could be seen even in the dark - a white spot, and above it a small light of a cigarette and a big voice.

And now the most joyous thing commenced for Yura - the fairy tale. The people and the festival and the lanterns remained on earth, while he soared away, transformed into air, melting in the night like a grain of dust. The great mystery of the night became his mystery, and his little heart yearned for still more mystery; in its solitude his heart yearned for the fusion of life and death. That was Yura's second madness that evening - he became invisible. Although he could enter the kitchen as others did, he climbed with difficulty upon the roof of the cellar over which the kitchen window was flooded with light and he looked in; there people were roasting something, busying themselves, and did not know that he was looking at them - and yet he saw everything! Then he went away and looked at papa's and mamma's bedroom; the room was empty; but the beds had already been made for the night and a little image lamp was burning - he saw that. Then he looked into his own room; his own bed was also ready, waiting for him. He passed the room where they were playing cards, also as an invisible being, holding his breath and stepping so lightly, as though he were soaring in the air. Only when he reached the garden, in the dark, he drew a proper breath. Then he resumed his quest. He came over to people who were talking so near him that he could touch them with his hand, and yet they did not know that he was there, and they continued to speak undisturbed. He watched Ninochka for a long time until he learned all her life - he was almost trapped. Ninochka even exclaimed:

"Yurochka, is that you?"

He lay down behind a bush and held his breath. Thus Ninochka was deceived. And she had almost caught him! To make things more mysterious, he started to crawl instead of walk - now the alleys seemed full of danger. Thus a long time went by - according to his own calculations at the time, ten years went by, and he was still hiding and going ever farther away from the people. And thus he went so far that he was seized with dread - between him and the past, when he was walking like everybody else, an abyss was formed over which it seemed to him impossible to cross. Now he would have come out into the light but he was afraid - it was impossible; all was lost. And the music was still playing, and everybody had forgotten him, even mamma. He was alone. There was a breath of cold from the dewy grass; the gooseberry bush scratched him, the darkness could not be pierced with his eyes, and there was no end to it. O Lord!

Without any definite plan, in a state of utter despair, Yura now crawled toward a mysterious, faintly blinking light. Fortunately it turned out to be the same arbour which was covered with wild grapes and in which father and mother had sat that day. He did not recognise it at first! Yes, it was the same arbour. The lights of the lanterns everywhere had gone out, and only two were still burning; a yellow little lantern was still burning brightly, and the other, a yellow one, too, was already beginning to blink. And though there was no wind, that lantern quivered from its own blinking, and everything seemed to quiver slightly. Yura was about to get up to go into the arbour and there begin life anew, with an imperceptible transition from the old, when suddenly he heard voices in the arbour. His mother and the wrong Yura Mikhailovich, the officer, were talking. The right Yura grew petrified in his place; his heart stood still; and his breathing ceased.

Mamma said:

"Stop. You have lost your mind! Somebody may come in here."

Yura Mikhailovich said:

"And you?"

Mamma said:

"I am twenty-six years old to-day. I am old!"

Yura Mikhailovich said:

"He does not know anything. Is it possible that he does not know anything? He does not even suspect? Listen, does he shake everybody's hand so firmly?"

Mamma said:

"What a question! Of course he does! That is - no, not everybody."

Yura Mikhailovich said:

"I feel sorry for him."

Mamma said:

"For him?"

And she laughed strangely. Yurochka understood that they were talking of him, of Yurochka - but what did it all mean, O Lord? And why did she laugh?

Yura Mikhailovich said:

"Where are you going? I will not let you go."

Mamma said:

"You offend me. Let me go! No, you have no right to kiss me. Let me go!"

They became silent. Now Yurochka looked through the leaves and saw that the officer embraced and kissed mamma. Then they spoke of something, but he understood nothing; he heard nothing; he suddenly forgot the meaning of words. And he even forgot the words which he knew and used before. He remembered but one word, "Mamma," and he whispered it uninterruptedly with his dry lips, but that word sounded so terrible, more terrible than anything. And in order not to exclaim it against his will, Yura covered his mouth with both hands, one upon the other, and thus remained until the officer and mamma went out of the arbour.

When Yura came into the room where the people were playing cards, the serious, bald-headed man was scolding papa for something, brandishing the chalk, talking, shouting, saying that father did not act as he should have acted, that what he had done was impossible, that only bad people did such things, that the old man would never again play with father, and so on. And father was smiling, waving his hands, attempting to say something, but the old man would not let him, and he commenced to shout more loudly. And the old man was a little fellow, while father was big, handsome and tall, and his smile was sad, like that of Gulliver pining for his native land of tall and handsome people.

Of course, he must conceal from him - of course, he must conceal from him that which happened in the arbour, and he must love him, and he felt that he loved him so much. And with a wild cry Yura rushed over to the bald-headed old man and began to beat him with his fists with all his strength.

"Don't you dare insult him! Don't you dare insult him!"

O Lord, what has happened! Some one laughed; some one shouted. Father caught Yura in his arms, pressed him closely, causing him pain, and cried:

"Where is mother? Call mother."

Then Yura was seized with a whirlwind of frantic tears, of desperate sobs and mortal anguish. But through his frantic tears he looked at his father to see whether he had guessed it, and when mother came in he started to shout louder in order to divert any suspicion. But he did not go to her arms; he clung more closely to father, so that father had to carry him into his room. But it seemed that he himself did not want to part with Yura. As soon as he carried him out of the room where the guests were he began to kiss him, and he repeated:

"Oh, my dearest! Oh, my dearest!"

And he said to mamma, who walked behind him:

"Just think of the boy!"

Mamma said:

"That is all due to your whist. You were scolding each other so, that the child was frightened."

Father began to laugh, and answered:

"Yes, he does scold harshly. But Yura, oh, what a dear boy!"

In his room Yura demanded that father himself undress him. "Now, you are getting cranky," said father. "I don't know how to do it; let mamma undress you."

"But you stay here."

Mamma had deft fingers and she undressed him quickly, and while she was removing his clothes Yura held father by the hand. He ordered the nurse out of the room; but as father was beginning to grow angry, and he might guess what had happened in the arbour, decided to let him go. But while kissing him he said cunningly:

"He will not scold you any more, will he?"

Papa smiled. Then he laughed, kissed Yura once more and said:

"No, no. And if he does I will throw him across the fence."

"Please, do," said Yura. "You can do it. You are so strong."

"Yes, I am pretty strong. But you had better sleep! Mamma will stay here with you a while."

Mamma said:

"I will send the nurse in. I must attend to the supper."

Father shouted:

"There is plenty of time for that! You can stay a while with the child."

But mamma insisted:

"We have guests! We can't leave them that way."

But father looked at her steadfastly, and shrugged his shoulders. Mamma decided to stay.

"Very well, then, I'll stay here. But see that Maria does not mix up the wines."

Usually it was thus: when mamma sat near Yura as he was falling asleep she held his hand until the last moment - that is what she usually did. But now she sat as though she were all alone, as though Yura, her son, who was falling asleep, was not there at all - she folded her hands in her lap and looked into the distance. To attract her attention Yura stirred, but mamma said briefly:

"Sleep."

And she continued to look. But when Yura's eyes had grown heavy and he was falling asleep with all his sorrow and his tears, mamma suddenly went down on her knees before the little bed and kissed Yura firmly many, many times. But her kisses were wet - hot and wet.

"Why are your kisses wet? Are you crying?" muttered Yura.

"Yes, I am crying."

"You must not cry."

"Very well, I won't," answered mother submissively.

And again she kissed him firmly, firmly, frequently, frequently. Yura lifted both hands with a heavy movement, clasped his mother around the neck and pressed his burning cheek firmly to her wet and cold cheek. She was his mother, after all; there was nothing to be done. But how painful; how bitterly painful!

A STORY WHICH WILL NEVER BE FINISHED

Exhausted with the painful uncertainty of the day, I fell asleep, dressed, on my bed. Suddenly my wife aroused me. In her hand a candle was flickering, which appeared to me in the middle of the night as bright as the sun. And behind the candle her chin, too, was trembling, and enormous, unfamiliar dark eyes stared motionlessly.

"Do you know," she said, "do you know they are building barricades on our street?"

It was quiet. We looked straight into each other's eyes, and I felt my face turning pale. Life vanished somewhere and then returned again with a loud throbbing of the heart. It was quiet and the flame of the candle was quivering, and it was small, dull, but sharp-pointed, like a crooked sword.

"Are you afraid?" I asked.

The pale chin trembled, but her eyes remained motionless and looked at me, without blinking, and only now I noticed what unfamiliar, what terrible eyes they were. For ten years I had looked into them and had known them better than my own eyes, and now there was something new in them which I am unable define. I would have called it pride, but there was something different in them, something new, entirely new. I took her hand; it was cold. She grasped my hand firmly and there was something new, something I had not known before, in her handclasp.

She had never before clasped my hand as she did this time.

"How long?" I asked.

"About an hour already. Your brother has gone away. He was apparently afraid that you would not let him go, so he went away quietly. But I saw it."

It was true then; the time had arrived. I rose, and, for some reason, spent a long time washing myself, as was my wont in the morning before going to work, and my wife held the light. Then we put out the light and walked over to the window overlooking the street. It was spring; it was May, and the air that came in from the open window was such as we had never before felt in that old, large city. For several days the factories and the roads had been idle; and the air, free from smoke, was filled with the fragrance of the fields and the flowering gardens, perhaps with that of the dew. I do not know what it is that smells so wonderfully on spring nights when I go out far beyond the outskirts of the city. Not a lantern, not a carriage, not a single sound of the city over the unconcerned stony surface; if you had closed your eyes you would really have thought that you were in a village. There a dog was barking. I had never before heard a dog barking in the city, and I laughed for happiness.

"Listen, a dog is barking."

My wife embraced me, and said:

"It is there, on the corner."

We bent over the window-sill, and there, in the transparent, dark depth, we saw some movement - not people, but movement. Something was moving about like a shadow. Suddenly the blows of a hatchet or a hammer resounded. They sounded so cheerful, so resonant, as in a forest, as on a river when you are mending a boat or building a dam. And in the presentiment of cheerful, harmonious work, I firmly embraced my wife, while she looked above the houses, above the roofs, looked at the young crescent of the moon, which was already setting. The moon was so young, so strange, even as a young girl who is dreaming and is afraid to tell her dreams; and it was shining only for itself.

"When will we have a full moon?..."

"You must not! You must not!" my wife interrupted. "You must not speak of that which will be. What for? IT is afraid of words. Come here."

It was dark in the room, and we were silent for a long time, without seeing each other, yet thinking of the same thing. And when I started to speak, it seemed to me that some one else was speaking; I was not afraid, yet the voice of the other one was hoarse, as though suffocating for thirst.

"What shall it be?"

"And - they?"

"You will be with them. It will be enough for them to have a mother. I cannot remain."

"And I? Can I?"

I know that she did not stir from her place, but I felt distinctly that she was going away, that she was far - far away. I began to feel so cold, I stretched out my hands - but she pushed them aside.

"People have such a holiday once in a hundred years, and you want to deprive me of it. Why?" she said.

"But they may kill you there. And our children will perish."

"Life will be merciful to me. But even if they should perish - "

And this was said by her, my wife - a woman with whom I had lived for ten years. But yesterday she had known nothing except our children, and had been filled with fear for them; but yesterday she had caught with terror the stern symptoms of the future. What had come over her? Yesterday - but I, too, forgot everything that was yesterday.

"Do you want to go with me?"

"Do not be angry" - she thought that I was afraid, angry - "Don't be angry. To-night, when they began to knock here, and you were still sleeping, I suddenly understood that my husband, my children - all these were simply temporary... I love you, very much" - she found my hand and shook it with the same new, unfamiliar grasp - "but do you hear how they are knocking there? They are knocking, and something seems to be falling, some kind of walls seem to be falling - and it is so spacious, so wide, so free. It is night now, and yet it seems to me that the sun is shining. I am thirty years of age, and I am old already, and yet it seems to me that I am only seventeen, and that I love some one with my first love - a great, boundless love."

"What a night!" I said. "It is as if the city were no more. You are right, I have also forgotten how old I am."

"They are knocking, and it sounds to me like music, like singing of which I have always dreamed - all my life. And I did not know whom it was that I loved with such a boundless love, which made me feel like crying and laughing and singing. There is freedom - do not take my happiness away, let me die with those who are working there, who are calling the future so bravely, and who are rousing the dead past from its grave."

"There is no such thing as time."

"What do you say?"

"There is no such thing as time. Who are you? I did not know you. Are you a human being?"

She burst into such ringing laughter as though she were really only seventeen years old.

"I did not know you, either. Are you, too, a human being? How strange and how beautiful it is - a human being!"

That which I am writing happened long ago, and those who are sleeping now in the sleep of grey life and who die without awakening - those will not believe me: in those days there was no such thing as time. The sun was rising and setting, and the hand was moving around the dial - but time did not exist. And many other great and wonderful things happened in those days.... And those who are sleeping now the sleep of this grey life and who die without awakening, will not believe me.

"I must go," said I.

"Wait, I will give you something to eat. You haven't eaten anything to-day. See how sensible I am: I shall go to-morrow. I shall give the children away and find you."

"Comrade," said I.

"Yes, comrade."

Through the open windows came the breath of the fields, and silence, and from time to time, the cheerful strokes of the axe, and I sat by the table and looked and listened, and everything was so mysteriously new that I felt like laughing. I looked at the walls and they seemed to me to be transparent. As if embracing all eternity with one glance, I saw how all these walls had been built, I saw how they were being destroyed, and I alone always was and always will be. Everything will pass, but I shall remain. And everything seemed to me strange and queer - so unnatural - the table and the food upon it, and everything outside of me. It all seemed to me transparent and light, existing only temporarily.

"Why don't you eat?" asked my wife.

I smiled:

"Bread - it is so strange."

She glanced at the bread, at the stale, dry crust of bread, and for some reason her face became sad. Still continuing to look at it, she silently adjusted her apron with her hands and her head turned slightly, very slightly, in the direction where the children were sleeping.

"Do you feel sorry for them?" I asked.

She shook her head without removing her eyes from the bread.

"No, but I was thinking of what happened in our life before."

How incomprehensible! As one who awakens from a long sleep, she surveyed the room with her eyes and all seemed to her so incomprehensible. Was this the place where we had lived?

"You were my wife."

"And there are our children."

"Here, beyond the wall, your father died."

"Yes. He died. He died without awakening."

The smallest child, frightened at something in her sleep, began to cry. And this simple childish cry, apparently demanding something, sounded so strange amid these phantom walls, while there, below, people were building barricades.

She cried and demanded - caresses, certain queer words and promises to soothe her. And she soon was soothed.

"Well, go!" said my wife in a whisper.

"I should like to kiss them."

"I am afraid you will wake them up."

"No, I will not."

It turned out that the oldest child was awake - he had heard and understood everything. He was but nine years old, but he understood everything - he met me with a deep, stern look.

"Will you take your gun?" he asked thoughtfully and earnestly.

"I will."

"It is behind the stove."

"How do you know? Well, kiss me. Will you remember me?"

He jumped up in his bed, in his short little shirt, hot from sleep, and firmly clasped my neck. His arms were burning - they were so soft and delicate. I lifted his hair on the back of his head and kissed his little neck.

"Will they kill you?" he whispered right into my ear.

"No, I will come back."

But why did he not cry? He had cried sometimes when I had simply left the house for a while: Is it possible that IT had reached him, too? Who knows? So many strange things happened during the great days.

I looked at the walls, at the bread, at the candle, at the flame which had kept flickering, and took my wife by the hand.

"Well - 'till we meet again!"

"Yes - 'till we meet again!"

That was all. I went out. It was dark on the stairway and there was the odour of old filth. Surrounded on all sides by the stones and the darkness, groping down the stairs, I was seized with a tremendous, powerful and all-absorbing feeling of the new, unknown and joyous something to which I was going.

ON THE DAY OF THE CRUCIFIXION

On that terrible day, when the universal injustice was committed and Jesus Christ was crucified in Golgotha among robbers - on that day, from early morning, Ben-Tovit, a tradesman of Jerusalem, suffered from an unendurable toothache. His toothache had commenced on the day before, toward evening; at first his right jaw started to pain him, and one tooth, the one right next the wisdom tooth, seemed to have risen somewhat, and when his tongue touched the tooth, he felt a slightly painful sensation. After supper, however, his toothache had passed, and Ben-Tovit had forgotten all about it - he had made a profitable deal on that day, had bartered an old donkey for a young, strong one, so he was very cheerful and paid no heed to any ominous signs.

And he slept very soundly. But just before daybreak something began to disturb him, as if some one were calling him on a very important matter, and when Ben-Tovit awoke angrily, his teeth were aching, aching openly and maliciously, causing him an acute, drilling pain. And he could no longer understand whether it was only the same tooth that had ached on the previous day, or whether others had joined that tooth; Ben-Tovit's entire mouth and his head were filled with terrible sensations of pain, as though he had been forced to chew thousands of sharp, red-hot nails, he took some water into his mouth from an earthen jug - for a minute the acuteness of the pain subsided, his teeth twitched and swayed like a wave, and this sensation was even pleasant as compared with the other.

Ben-Tovit lay down again, recalled his new donkey, and thought how happy he would have been if not for his toothache, and he wanted to fall asleep. But the water was warm, and five minutes later his toothache began to rage more severely than ever; Ben-Tovit sat up in his bed and swayed back and forth like a pendulum. His face became wrinkled and seemed to have shrunk, and a drop of cold perspiration was hanging on his nose, which had turned pale from his sufferings. Thus, swaying back and forth and groaning for pain, he met the first rays of the sun, which was destined to see Golgotha and the three crosses, and grow dim from horror and sorrow.

Ben-Tovit was a good and kind man, who hated any injustice, but when his wife awoke he said many unpleasant things to her, opening his mouth with difficulty, and he complained that he was left alone, like a jackal, to groan and writhe for pain. His wife met the undeserved reproaches patiently, for she knew that they came not from an angry heart - and she brought him numerous good remedies: rats' litter to be applied to his cheek, some strong liquid in which a scorpion was preserved, and a real chip of the tablets that Moses had broken. He began to feel a little better from the rats' litter, but not for long, also from the liquid and the stone, but the pain returned each time with renewed intensity.

During the moments of rest Ben-Tovit consoled himself with the thought of the little donkey, and he dreamed of him, and when he felt worse he moaned, scolded his wife, and threatened to dash his head against a rock if the pain should not subside. He kept pacing back and forth on the flat roof of his house from one corner to the other, feeling ashamed to come close to the side facing the street, for his head was tied around with a kerchief like that of a woman. Several times children came running to him and told him hastily about Jesus of Nazareth. Ben-Tovit paused, listened to them for a while, his face wrinkled, but then he stamped his foot angrily and chased them away. He was a kind man and he loved children, but now he was angry at them for bothering him with trifles.

It was disagreeable to him that a large crowd had gathered in the street and on the neighbouring roofs, doing nothing and looking curiously at Ben-Tovit, who had his head tied around with a kerchief like a woman. He was about to go down, when his wife said to him:

"Look, they are leading robbers there. Perhaps that will divert you."

"Let me alone. Don't you see how I am suffering?" Ben-Tovit answered angrily.

But there was a vague promise in his wife's words that there might be a relief for his toothache, so he walked over to the parapet unwillingly. Bending his head on one side, closing one eye, and supporting his cheek with his hand, his face assumed a squeamish, weeping expression, and he looked down to the street.

On the narrow street, going uphill, an enormous crowd was moving forward in disorder, covered with dust and shouting uninterruptedly. In the middle of the crowd walked the criminals, bending down under the weight of their crosses, and over them the scourges of the Roman soldiers were wriggling about like black snakes. One of the men, he of the long light hair, in a torn blood-stained cloak, stumbled over a stone which was thrown under his feet, and he fell. The shouting grew louder, and the crowd, like coloured sea water, closed in about the man on the ground. Ben-Tovit suddenly shuddered for pain; he felt as though some one had pierced a red-hot needle into his tooth and turned it there; he groaned and walked away from the parapet, angry and squeamishly indifferent.

"How they are shouting!" he said enviously, picturing to himself their wide-open mouths with strong, healthy teeth, and how he himself would have shouted if he had been well. This intensified his toothache, and he shook his muffled head frequently, and roared: "Moo-Moo...."

"They say that He restored sight to the blind," said his wife, who remained standing at the parapet, and she threw down a little cobblestone near the place where Jesus, lifted by the whips, was moving slowly.

"Of course, of course! He should have cured my toothache," replied Ben-Tovit ironically, and he added bitterly with irritation: "What dust they have kicked up! Like a herd of cattle! They should all be driven away with a stick! Take me down, Sarah!"

The wife proved to be right. The spectacle had diverted Ben-Tovit slightly - perhaps it was the rats' litter that had helped after all - he succeeded in falling asleep. When he awoke, his toothache had passed almost entirely, and only a little inflammation had formed over his right jaw. His wife told him that it was not noticeable at all, but Ben-Tovit smiled cunningly - he knew how kind-hearted his wife was and how fond she was of telling him pleasant things.

Samuel, the tanner, a neighbour of Ben-Tovit's, came in, and Ben-Tovit led him to see the new little donkey and listened proudly to the warm praises for himself and his animal.

Then, at the request of the curious Sarah, the three went to Golgotha to see the people who had been crucified. On the way Ben-Tovit told Samuel in detail how he had felt a pain in his right jaw on the day before, and how he awoke at night with a terrible toothache. To illustrate it he made a martyr's face, closing his eyes, shook his head, and groaned while the grey-bearded Samuel nodded his head compassionately and said:

"Oh, how painful it must have been!"

Ben-Tovit was pleased with Samuel's attitude, and he repeated the story to him, then went back to the past, when his first tooth was spoiled on the left side. Thus, absorbed in a lively conversation, they reached Golgotha. The sun, which was destined to shine upon the world on that terrible day, had already set beyond the distant hills, and in the west a narrow, purple-red strip was burning, like a stain of blood. The crosses stood out darkly but vaguely against this background, and at the foot of the middle cross white kneeling figures were seen indistinctly.

The crowd had long dispersed; it was growing chilly, and after a glance at the crucified men, Ben-Tovit took Samuel by the arm and carefully turned him in the direction toward his house. He felt that he was particularly eloquent just then, and he was eager to finish the story of his toothache. Thus they walked, and Ben-Tovit made a martyr's face, shook his head and groaned skilfully, while Samuel nodded compassionately and uttered exclamations from time to time, and from the deep, narrow defiles, out of the distant, burning plains, rose the black night. It seemed as though it wished to hide from the view of heaven the great crime of the earth.

THE SERPENT'S STORY

Hush! Hush! Hush! Come closer to me. Look into my eyes!

I always was a fascinating creature, tender, sensitive, and grateful. I was wise and I was noble. And I am so flexible in the writhing of my graceful body that it will afford you joy to watch my easy dance. Now I shall coil up into a ring, flash my scales dimly, wind myself around tenderly and clasp my steel body in my gentle, cold embraces. One in many! One in many!

Hush! Hush! Look into my eyes!

You do not like my writhing and my straight, open look? Oh, my head is heavy - therefore I sway about so quietly. Oh, my head is heavy - therefore I look so straight ahead, as I sway about. Come closer to me. Give me a little warmth; stroke my wise forehead with your fingers; in its fine outlines you will find the form of a cup into which flows wisdom, the dew of the evening-flowers. When I draw the air by my writhing, a trace is left in it - the design of the finest of webs, the web of dream-charms, the enchantment of noiseless movements, the inaudible hiss of gliding lines. I am silent and I sway myself. I look ahead and I sway myself. What strange burden am I carrying on my neck?

I love you.

I always was a fascinating creature, and loved tenderly those I loved. Come closer to me. Do you see my white, sharp, enchanting little teeth? Kissing, I used to bite. Not painfully, no - just a trifle. Caressing tenderly, I used to bite a little, until the first bright little drops appeared, until a cry came forth which sounded like the laugh produced by tickling. That was very pleasant - think not it was unpleasant; otherwise they whom I kissed would not come back for more kisses. It is now that I can kiss only once - how sad - only once! One kiss for each - how little for a loving heart, for a sensitive soul, striving for a great union! But it is only I, the sad one, who kiss but once, and must seek love again - he knows no other love any more: to him my one, tender, nuptial kiss is inviolable and eternal. I am speaking to you frankly; and when my story is ended - I will kiss you.

I love you.

Look into my eyes. Is it not true that mine is a magnificent, a powerful look? A firm look and a straight look? And it is steadfast, like steel forced against your heart. I look ahead and sway myself, I look and I enchant; in my green eyes I gather your fear, your loving, fatigued, submissive longing. Come closer to me. Now I am a queen and you dare not fail to see my beauty; but there was a strange time - Ah, what a strange time! Ah, what a strange time! At the mere recollection I am agitated - Ah, what a strange time! No one loved me. No one respected me. I was persecuted with cruel ferocity, trampled in the mud and jeered - Ah, what a strange time it was! One in many! One in many!

I say to you: Come closer to me.

Why did they not love me? At that time I was also a fascinating creature, but without malice; I was gentle and I danced wonderfully. But they tortured me. They burnt me with fire. Heavy and coarse beasts trampled upon me with the dull steps of terribly heavy feet; cold tusks of bloody mouths tore my tender body - and in my powerless sorrow I bit the sand, I swallowed the dust of the ground - I was dying of despair. Crushed, I was dying every day. Every day I was dying of despair. Oh, what a terrible time that was! The stupid forest has forgotten everything - it does not remember that time, but you have pity on me. Come closer to me. Have pity on me, on the offended, on the sad one, on the loving one, on the one who dances so beautifully.

I love you.

How could I defend myself? I had only my white, wonderful, sharp little teeth - they were good only for kisses. How could I defend myself? It is only now that I carry on my neck this terrible burden of a head, and my look is commanding and straight, but then my head was light and my eyes gazed meekly. Then I had no poison yet. Oh, my head is so heavy and it is hard for me to hold it up! Oh, I have grown tired of my look - two stones are in my forehead, and these are my eyes. Perhaps the glittering stones are precious - but it is hard to carry them instead of gentle eyes - they oppress my brain. It is so hard for my head! I look ahead and sway myself; I see you in a green mist - you are so far away. Come closer to me.

You see, even in sorrow I am beautiful, and my look is languid because of my love. Look into my pupil; I will narrow and widen it, and give it a peculiar glitter - the twinkling of a star at night, the playfulness of all precious stones - of diamonds, of green emeralds, of yellowish topaz, of blood-red rubies. Look into my eyes: It is I, the queen - I am crowning myself, and that which is glittering, burning and glowing - that robs you of your reason, your freedom and your life - it is poison. It is a drop of my poison.

How has it happened? I do not know. I did not bear ill-will to the living.

I lived and suffered. I was silent. I languished. I hid myself hurriedly when I could hide myself; I crawled away hastily. But they have never seen me weep - I cannot weep; and my easy dance grew ever faster and ever more beautiful. Alone in the stillness, alone in the thicket, I danced with sorrow in my heart - they despised my swift dance and would have been glad to kill me as I danced. Suddenly my head began to grow heavy - How strange it is! - My head grew heavy. Just as small and beautiful, just as wise and beautiful, it had suddenly grown terribly heavy; it bent my neck to the ground, and caused me pain. Now I am somewhat used to it, but at first it was dreadfully awkward and painful. I thought I was sick.

And suddenly... Come closer to me. Look into my eyes. Hush! Hush! Hush!

And suddenly my look became heavy - it became fixed and strange - I was even frightened! I want to glance and turn away - but cannot. I always look straight ahead, I pierce with my eyes ever more deeply, I am as though petrified. Look into my eyes. It is as though I am petrified, as though everything I look upon is petrified. Look into my eyes.

I love you. Do not laugh at my frank story, or I shall be angry. Every hour I open my sensitive heart, for all my efforts are in vain - I am alone. My one and last kiss is full of ringing sorrow - and the one I love is not here, and I seek love again, and I tell my tale in vain - my heart cannot bare itself, and the poison torments me and my head grows heavier. Am I not beautiful in my despair? Come closer to me.

I love you.

Once I was bathing in a stagnant swamp in the forest - I love to be clean - it is a sign of noble birth, and I bathe frequently. While bathing, dancing in the water, I saw my reflection, and as always, fell in love with myself. I am so fond of the beautiful and the wise! And suddenly I saw - on my forehead, among my other inborn adornments, a new, strange sign - Was it not this sign that has brought the heaviness, the petrified look, and the sweet taste in my mouth? Here a cross is darkly outlined on my forehead - right here - look. Come closer to me. Is this not strange? But I did not understand it at that time, and I liked it. Let there be no more adornment. And on the same day, on that same terrible day, when the cross appeared, my first kiss became also my last - my kiss became fatal. One in many! One in many!

Oh!

You love precious stones, but think, my beloved, how far more precious is a little drop of my poison. It is such a little drop. - Have you ever seen it? Never, never. But you shall find it out. Consider, my beloved, how much suffering, painful humiliation, powerless rage devoured me: I had to experience in order to bring forth this little drop. I am a queen! I am a queen! In one drop, brought forth by myself, I carry death unto the living, and my kingdom is limitless, even as grief is limitless, even as death is limitless. I am queen! My look is inexorable. My dance is terrible! I am beautiful! One in many! One in many!

Oh!

Do not fall. My story is not yet ended. Come closer to me.

And then I crawled into the stupid forest, into my green dominion.

Now it is a new way, a terrible way! I was kind like a queen; and like a queen I bowed graciously to the right and to the left. And they - they ran away! Like a queen I bowed benevolently to the right and to the left - and they, queer people - they ran away. What do you think? Why did they run away? What do you think? Look into my eyes. Do you see in them a certain glimmer and a flash? The rays of my crown blind your eyes, you are petrified, you are lost. I shall soon dance my last dance - do not fall. I shall coil into rings, I shall flash my scales dimly, and I shall clasp my steel body in my gentle, cold embraces. Here I am! Accept my only kiss, my nuptial kiss - in it is the deadly grief of all oppressed lives. One in many! One in many!

Bend down to me. I love you.

Die!

LOVE, FAITH AND HOPE

He loved.

According to his passport, he was called Max Z. But as it was stated in the same passport that he had no special peculiarities about his features, I prefer to call him Mr. N+1. He represented a long line of young men who possess wavy, dishevelled locks, straight, bold, and open looks, well-formed and strong bodies, and very large and powerful hearts.

All these youths have loved and perpetuated their love. Some of them have succeeded in engraving it on the tablets of history, like Henry IV; others, like Petrarch, have made literary preserves of it; some have availed themselves for that purpose of the newspapers, wherein the happenings of the day are recorded, and where they figured among those who had strangled themselves, shot themselves, or who had been shot by others; still others, the happiest and most modest of all, perpetuated their love by entering it in the birth records - by creating posterity.

The love of N+1 was as strong as death, as a certain writer put it; as strong as life, he thought.

Max was firmly convinced that he was the first to have discovered the method of loving so intensely, so unrestrainedly, so passionately, and he regarded with contempt all who had loved before him. Still more, he was convinced that even after him no one would love as he did, and he felt sorry that with his death the secret of true love would be lost to mankind. But, being a modest young man, he attributed part of his achievement to her - to his beloved. Not that she was perfection itself, but she came very close to it, as close as an ideal can come to reality.

There were prettier women than she, there were wiser women, but was there ever a better woman? Did there ever exist a woman on whose face was so clearly and distinctly written that she alone was worthy of love - of infinite, pure, and devoted love? Max knew that there never were, and that there never would be such women. In this respect, he had no special peculiarities, just as Adam did not have them, just as you, my reader, do not have them. Beginning with Grandmother Eve and ending with the woman upon whom your eyes were directed - before you read these lines - the same inscription is to be clearly and distinctly read on the face of every woman at a certain time. The difference is only in the quality of the ink.

A very nasty day set in - it was Monday or Tuesday - when Max noticed with a feeling of great terror that the inscription upon the dear face was fading. Max rubbed his eyes, looked first from a distance, then from all sides; but the fact was undeniable - the inscription was fading. Soon the last letter also disappeared - the face was white like the recently whitewashed wall of a new house. But he was convinced that the inscription had disappeared not of itself, but that some one had wiped it off. Who?

Max went to his friend, John N. He knew and he felt sure that such a true, disinterested, and honest friend there never was and never would be. And in this respect, too, as you see, Max had no special peculiarities. He went to his friend for the purpose of taking his advice concerning the mysterious disappearance of the inscription, and found John N. exactly at the moment when he was wiping away that inscription by his kisses. It was then that the records of the local occurrences were enriched by another unfortunate incident, entitled "An Attempt at Suicide."

. . . .

It is said that death always comes in due time. Evidently, that time had not yet arrived for Max, for he remained alive - that is, he ate, drank, walked, borrowed money and did not return it, and altogether he showed by a series of psycho-physiological acts that he was a living being, possessing a stomach, a will, and a mind - but his soul was dead, or, to be more exact, it was absorbed in lethargic sleep. The sound of human speech reached his ears, his eyes saw tears and laughter, but all that did not stir a single echo, a single emotion in his soul. I do not know what space of time had elapsed. It may have been one year, and it may have been ten years, for the length of such intermissions in life depends on how quickly the actor succeeds in changing his costume.

One beautiful day - it was Wednesday or Thursday - Max awakened completely. A careful and guarded liquidation of his spiritual property made it clear that a fair piece of Max's soul, the part which contained his love for woman and for his friends, was dead, like a paralysis-stricken hand or foot. But what remained was, nevertheless, enough for life. That was love for and faith in mankind. Then Max, having renounced personal happiness, started to work for the happiness of others.

That was a new phase - he believed.

All the evil that is tormenting the world seemed to him to be concentrated in a "red flower," in one red flower. It was but necessary to tear it down, and the incessant, heart-rending cries and moans which rise to the indifferent sky from all points of the earth, like its natural breathing, would be silenced. The evil of the world, he believed, lay in the evil will and in the madness of the people. They themselves were to blame for being unhappy, and they could be happy if they wished. This seemed so clear and simple that Max was dumfounded in his amazement at human stupidity. Humanity reminded him of a crowd huddled together in a spacious temple and panic-stricken at the cry of "Fire!"

Instead of passing calmly through the wide doors and saving

themselves, the maddened people, with the cruelty of frenzied beasts, cry and roar, crush one another and perish - not from the fire (for it is only imaginary), but from their own madness. It is enough sometimes when one sensible, firm word is uttered to this crowd - the crowd calms down and imminent death is thus averted. Let, then, a hundred calm, rational voices be raised to mankind, showing them where to escape and where the danger lies - and heaven will be established on earth, if not immediately, then at least within a very brief time.

Max began to utter his word of wisdom. How he uttered it you will learn later. The name of Max was mentioned in the newspapers, shouted in the market places, blessed and cursed; whole books were written on what Max N+1 had done, what he was doing, and what he intended to do. He appeared here and there and everywhere. He was seen standing at the head of the crowd, commanding it; he was seen in chains and under the knife of the guillotine. In this respect Max did not have any special peculiarities, either. A preacher of humility and peace, a stern bearer of fire and sword, he was the same Max - Max the believer. But while he was doing all this, time kept passing on. His nerves were shattered; his wavy locks became thin and his head began to look like that of Elijah the Prophet; here and there he felt a piercing pain....

The earth continued to turn light-mindedly around the sun, now coming nearer to it, now retreating coquettishly, and giving the impression that it fixed all its attention upon its household friend, the moon; the days were replaced by other days, and the dark nights by other dark nights, with such pedantic German punctuality and correctness that all the artistic natures were compelled to move over to the far north by degrees, where the devil himself would break his head endeavouring to distinguish between day and night - when suddenly something happened to Max.

Somehow it happened that Max became misunderstood. He had calmed the crowd by his words of wisdom many a time before and had saved them from mutual destruction but now he was not understood. They thought that it was he who had shouted "Fire!" With all the eloquence of which he was capable he assured them that he was exerting all his efforts for their sake alone; that he himself needed absolutely nothing, for he was alone, childless; that he was ready to forget the sad misunderstanding and serve them again with faith and truth - but all in vain. They would not trust him. And in this respect Max did not have any special peculiarities, either. The sad incident ended for Max in a new intermission.

· · · · · · · ·

Max was alive, as was positively established by medical experts, who had made a series of simple tests. Thus, when they pricked a needle into his foot, he shook his foot and tried to remove the needle. When they put food before him, he ate it, but he did not walk and did not ask for any loans, which clearly testified to the complete decline of his energy. His soul was dead - as much as the soul can be dead while the body is alive. To Max all that he had loved and believed in was dead. Impenetrable gloom wrapped his soul. There were neither feelings in it, nor desires, nor thoughts. And there was not a more unhappy man in the world than Max, if he was a man at all.

But he was a man.

According to the calendar, it was Friday or Saturday, when Max awakened as from a prolonged sleep. With the pleasant sensation of an owner to whom his property has been restored which had wrongly been taken from him, Max realised that he was once more in possession of all his five senses.

His sight reported to him that he was all alone, in a place which might in justice be called either a room or a chimney. Each wall of the room was about a metre and a half wide and about ten metres high. The walls were straight, white, smooth, with no openings, except one through which food was brought to Max. An electric lamp was burning brightly on the ceiling.

It was burning all the time, so that Max did not know now what darkness was. There was no furniture in the room, and Max had to lie on the stone floor. He lay curled together, as the narrowness of the room did not permit him to stretch himself.

His sense of hearing reported to him that until the day of his death he would not leave this room.... Having reported this, his hearing sank into inactivity, for not the slightest sound came from without, except the sounds which Max himself produced, tossing about, or shouting until he was hoarse, until he lost his voice.

Max looked into himself. In contrast to the outward light which never went out he saw within himself impenetrable, heavy, and motionless darkness. In that darkness his love and faith were buried.

Max did not know whether time was moving or whether it stood motionless. The same even, white light poured down on him - the same silence and quiet. Only by the beating of his heart Max could judge that Chronos had not left his chariot. His body was aching ever more from the unnatural position in which it lay, and the constant light and silence were growing ever more tormenting. How happy are they for whom night exists, near whom people are shouting, making noise, beating drums; who may sit on a chair, with their feet hanging down, or lie with their feet outstretched, placing the head in a corner and covering it with the hands in order to create the illusion of darkness.

Max made an effort to recall and to picture to himself what there is in life; human faces, voices, the stars.... He knew that his eyes would never in life see that again. He knew it, and yet he lived. He could have destroyed himself, for there is no position in which a man can not do that, but instead Max worried about his health, trying to eat, although he had no appetite, solving mathematical problems to occupy his mind so as not to lose his reason. He struggled against death as if it were not his deliverer, but his enemy; and as if life were to him not the worst of infernal tortures - but love, faith, and happiness. Gloom in the Past, the grave in the Future, and infernal tortures in the Present - and yet he lived. Tell me, John N., where did he get the strength for that?

He hoped.

THE OCEAN

CHAPTER I

A misty February twilight is descending over the ocean. The newly fallen snow has melted and the warm air is heavy and damp. The northwestern wind from the sea is driving it silently toward the mainland, bringing in its wake a sharply fragrant mixture of brine, of boundless space, of undisturbed, free and mysterious distances.

In the sky, where the sun is setting, a noiseless destruction of an unknown city, of an unknown land, is taking place; structures, magnificent palaces with towers, are crumbling; mountains are silently splitting asunder and, bending slowly, are tumbling down. But no cry, no moan, no crash of the fall reaches the earth - the monstrous play of shadows is noiseless; and the great surface of the ocean, as though ready for something, as though waiting for something, reflecting it faintly, listens to it in silence.

Silence reigns also in the fishermen's settlement. The fishermen have gone fishing; the children are sleeping and only the restless women, gathered in front of the houses, are talking softly, lingering before going to sleep, beyond which there is always the unknown.

The light of the sea and the sky behind the houses, and the houses and their bark roofs are black and sharp, and there is no perspective: the houses that are far and those that are near seem to stand side by side as if attached to one another, the roofs and the walls embracing one another, pressing close to one another, seized with the same uneasiness before the eternal unknown.

Right here there is also a little church, its side wall formed crudely of rough granite, with a deep window which seems to be concealing itself.

A cautious sound of women's voices is heard, softened by uneasiness and by the approaching night.

"We can sleep peacefully to-night. The sea is calm and the rollers are breaking like the clock in the steeple of old Dan."

"They will come back with the morning tide. My husband told me that they will come back with the morning tide."

"Perhaps they will come back with the evening tide. It is better for us to think they will come back in the evening, so that our waiting will not be in vain."

"But I must build a fire in the stove."

"When the men are away from home, one does not feel like starting a fire. I never build a fire, even when I am awake; it seems to me that fire brings a storm. It is better to be quiet and silent."

"And listen to the wind? No, that is terrible."

"I love the fire. I should like to sleep near the fire, but my husband does not allow it."

"Why doesn't old Dan come here? It is time to strike the hour."

"Old Dan will play in the church to-night; he cannot bear such silence as this. When the sea is roaring, old Dan hides himself and is silent - he is afraid of the sea. But, as soon as the waves calm down, Dan crawls out quietly and sits down to play his organ."

The women laugh softly.

"He reproaches the sea."

"He is complaining to God against it. He knows how to complain well. One feels like crying when he tells God about those who have perished at sea. Mariet, have you seen Dan to-day? Why are you silent, Mariet?"

Mariet is the adopted daughter of the abbot, in whose house old Dan, the organist, lives. Absorbed in thought, she does not hear the question.

"Mariet, do you hear? Anna is asking you whether you have seen Dan to-day."

"Yes, I think I have. I don't remember. He is in his room. He does not like to leave his room when father goes fishing."

"Dan is fond of the city priests. He cannot get used to the idea of a priest who goes fishing, like an ordinary fisherman, and who goes to sea with our husbands."

"He is simply afraid of the sea."

"You may say what you like, but I believe we have the very best priest in the world."

"That's true. I fear him, but I love him as a father."

"May God forgive me, but I would have been proud and always happy, if I were his adopted daughter. Do you hear, Mariet?"

The women laugh softly and tenderly.

"Do you hear, Mariet?"

"I do. But aren't you tired of always laughing at the same thing? Yes, I am his daughter - Is it so funny that you will laugh all your life at it?"

The women commence to justify themselves confusedly.

"But he laughs at it himself."

"The abbot is fond of jesting. He says so comically: 'My adopted daughter,' and then he strikes himself with his fist and shouts: 'She's my real daughter, not my adopted daughter. She's my real daughter.'"

"I have never known my mother, but this laughter would have been unpleasant to her. I feel it," says Mariet.

The women grow silent. The breakers strike against the shore dully with the regularity of a great pendulum. The unknown city, wrapped with fire and smoke, is still being destroyed in the sky; yet it does not fall down completely; and the sea is waiting. Mariet lifts her lowered head.

"What were you going to say, Mariet?"

"Didn't he pass here?" asks Mariet in a low voice.

Another woman answers timidly:

"Hush! Why do you speak of him? I fear him. No, he did not pass this way."

"He did. I saw from the window that he passed by."

"You are mistaken; it was some one else."

"Who else could that be? Is it possible to make a mistake, if you have once seen him walk? No one walks as he does."

"Naval officers, Englishmen, walk like that."

"No. Haven't I seen naval officers in the city? They walk firmly, but openly; even a girl could trust them."

"Oh, look out!"

Frightened and cautious laughter.

"No, don't laugh. He walks without looking at the ground; he puts his feet down as if the ground itself must take them cautiously and place them."

"But if there's a stone on the road? We have many stones here."

"He does not bend down, nor does he hide his head when a strong wind blows."

"Of course not. Of course not. He does not hide his head."

"Is it true that he is handsome? Who has seen him at close range?"

"I," says Mariet.

"No, no, don't speak of him; I shall not be able to sleep all night. Since they settled on that hill, in that accursed castle, I know no rest; I am dying of fear. You are also afraid. Confess it."

"Well, not all of us are afraid."

"What have they come here for? There are two of them. What is there for them to do here in our poor land, where we have nothing but stones and the sea?"

"They drink gin. The sailor comes every morning for gin."

"They are simply drunkards who don't want anybody to disturb their drinking. When the sailor passes along the street he leaves behind him an odour as of an open bottle of rum."

"But is that their business - drinking gin? I fear them. Where is the ship that brought them here? They came from the sea."

"I saw the ship," says Mariet.

The women begin to question her in amazement.

"You? Why, then, didn't you say anything about it? Tell us what you know."

Mariet maintains silence. Suddenly one of the women exclaims:

"Ah, look! They have lit a lamp. There is a light in the castle!"

On the left, about half a mile away from the village, a faint light flares up, a red little coal in the dark blue of the twilight and the distance. There upon a high rock, overhanging the sea, stands an ancient castle, a grim heritage of grey and mysterious antiquity. Long destroyed, long ruined, it blends with the rocks, continuing and delusively ending them by the broken, dented line of its batteries, its shattered roofs, its half-crumbled towers. Now the rocks and the castle are covered with a smoky shroud of twilight. They seem airy, devoid of any weight, and almost as fantastic as those monstrous heaps of structures which are piled up and which are falling so noiselessly in the sky. But while the others are falling this one stands, and a live light reddens against the deep blue - and it is just as strange a sight as if a human hand were to kindle a light in the clouds.

Turning their heads in that direction, the women look on with frightened eyes.

"Do you see," says one of them. "It is even worse than a light on a cemetery. Who needs a light among the tombstones?"

"It is getting cold toward night and the sailor must have

thrown some branches into the fireplace, that's all. At least, I think so," says Mariet.

"And I think that the abbot should have gone there with holy water long ago."

"Or with the gendarmes! If that isn't the devil himself, it is surely one of his assistants."

"It is impossible to live peacefully with such neighbours close by."

"I am afraid for the children."

"And for your soul?"

Two elderly women rise silently and go away. Then a third, an old woman, also rises.

"We must ask the abbot whether it isn't a sin to look at such a light."

She goes off. The smoke in the sky is ever increasing and the fire is subsiding, and the unknown city is already near its dark end. The sea odour is growing ever sharper and stronger. Night is coming from the shore.

Their heads turned, the women watch the departing old woman. Then they turn again toward the light.

Mariet, as though defending some one, says softly:

"There can't be anything bad in light. For there is light in the candles on God's altar."

"But there is also fire for Satan in hell," says another old woman, heavily and angrily, and then goes off. Now four remain, all young girls.

"I am afraid," says one, pressing close to her companion.

The noiseless and cold conflagration in the sky is ended; the city is destroyed; the unknown land is in ruins. There are no longer any walls or falling towers; a heap of pale blue gigantic shapes have fallen silently into the abyss of the ocean and the night. A young little star glances at the earth with frightened eyes; it feels like coming out of the clouds near the castle, and because of its inmost neighbourship the heavy castle grows darker, and the light in its window seems redder and darker.

"Good night, Mariet," says the girl who sat alone, and then she goes off.

"Let us also go; it is getting cold," say the other two, rising. "Good night, Mariet."

"Good night."

"Why are you alone, Mariet? Why are you alone, Mariet, in the daytime and at night, on week days and on merry holidays? Do you love to think of your betrothed?"

"Yes, I do. I love to think of Philipp."

The girl laughs.

"But you don't want to see him. When he goes out to sea, you look at the sea for hours; when he comes back - you are not there. Where are you hiding yourself?"

"I love to think of Philipp."

"Like a blind man he gropes among the houses, forever calling: 'Mariet! Mariet! Have you not seen Mariet?'"

They go off laughing and repeating:

"Good night, Mariet. 'Have you not seen Mariet! Mariet!'"

The girl is left alone. She looks at the light in the castle. She hears soft, irresolute footsteps.

Old Dan, of small stature, slim, a coughing old man with a clean-shaven face, comes out from behind the church. Because of his irresoluteness, or because of the weakness of his eyes, he steps uncertainly, touching the ground cautiously and with a certain degree of fear.

"Oho! Oho!"

"Is that you, Dan?"

"The sea is calm, Dan. Are you going to play to-night?"

"Oho! I shall ring the bell seven times. Seven times I shall ring it and send to God seven of His holy hours."

He takes the rope of the bell and strikes the hour - seven ringing and slow strokes. The wind plays with them, it drops them to the ground, but before they touch it, it catches them tenderly, sways them softly and with a light accompaniment of whistling carries them off to the dark coast.

"Oh, no!" mutters Dan. "Bad hours, they fall to the ground. They are not His holy hours and He will send them back. Oh, a storm is coming! O Lord, have mercy on those who are perishing at sea!"

He mutters and coughs.

"Dan, I have seen the ship again to-day. Do you hear, Dan?"

"Many ships are going out to sea."

"But this one had black sails. It was again going toward the sun."

"Many ships are going out to sea. Listen, Mariet, there was

once a wise king - Oh, how wise he was! - and he commanded that the sea be lashed with chains. Oho!"

"I know, Dan. You told me about it."

"Oho, with chains! But it did not occur to him to christen the sea. Why did it not occur to him to do that, Mariet? Ah, why did he not think of it? We have no such kings now."

"What would have happened, Dan?"

"Oho!"

He whispers softly:

"All the rivers and the streams have already been christened, and the cross of the Lord has touched even many stagnant swamps; only the sea remained - that nasty, salty, deep pool."

"Why do you scold it? It does not like to be scolded," Mariet reproaches him.

"Oho! Let the sea not like it - I am not afraid of it. The sea thinks it is also an organ and music for God. It is a nasty, hissing, furious pool. A salty spit of satan. Fie! Fie! Fie!"

He goes to the doors at the entrance of the church muttering angrily, threatening, as though celebrating some victory:

"Oho! Oho!"

"Dan!"

"Go home."

"Dan! Why don't you light candles when you play? Dan, I don't love my betrothed. Do you hear, Dan?"

Dan turns his head unwillingly.

"I have heard it long ago, Mariet. Tell it to your father."

"Where is my mother, Dan?"

"Oho! You are mad again, Mariet? You are gazing too much at the sea - yes. I am going to tell - I am going to tell your father, yes."

He enters the church. Soon the sounds of the organ are heard. Faint in the first, long-drawn, deeply pensive chords, they rapidly gain strength. And with a passionate sadness, their human melodies now wrestle with the dull and gloomy plaintiveness of the tireless surf. Like seagulls in a storm, the sounds soar amidst the high waves, unable to rise higher on their overburdened wings. The stern ocean holds them captive by its wild and eternal charms. But when they have risen, the lowered ocean roars more dully; now they rise still higher - and the heavy, almost voiceless pile of water is shaking helplessly. Varied voices resound through the expanse of the resplendent distances. Day has one sorrow, night has another sorrow, and the proud, ever rebellious, black ocean suddenly seems to become an eternal slave.

Her cheek pressed against the cold stone of the wall, Mariet is listening, all alone. She is growing reconciled to something; she is grieving ever more quietly.

Suddenly, firm footsteps are heard on the road; the cobble-stones are creaking under the vigorous steps - and a man appears from behind the church. He walks slowly and sternly, like those who do not roam in vain, and who know the earth from end to end. He carries his hat in his hands; he is thinking of something, looking ahead. On his broad shoulders is set a round, strong head, with short hair; his dark profile is stern and commandingly haughty, and, although the man is dressed in a partly military uniform, he does not subject his body to the discipline of his clothes, but masters it as a free man. The folds of his clothes fall submissively.

Mariet greets him:

"Good evening."

He walks on quite a distance, then stops and turns his head slowly. He waits silently, as though regretting to part with his silence.

"Did you say 'Good evening' to me?" he asks at last.

"Yes, to you. Good evening."

He looks at her silently.

"Well, good evening. This is the first time I have been greeted in this land, and I was surprised when I heard your voice. Come nearer to me. Why don't you sleep when all are sleeping? Who are you?"

"I am the daughter of the abbot of this place."

He laughs:

"Have priests children? Or are there special priests in your land?"

"Yes, the priests are different here."

"Now, I recall, Khorre told me something about the priest of this place."

"Who is Khorre?"

"My sailor. The one who buys gin in your settlement."

He suddenly laughs again and continues:

"Yes, he told me something. Was it your father who cursed the Pope and declared his own church independent?"

"Yes."

"And he makes his own prayers? And goes to sea with the fishermen? And punishes with his own hands those who disobey him?"

"Yes. I am his daughter. My name is Mariet. And what is your name?"

"I have many names. Which one shall I tell you?"

"The one by which you were christened."

"What makes you think that I was christened?"

"Then tell me the name by which your mother called you."

"What makes you think that I had a mother? I do not know my mother."

Mariet says softly:

"Neither do I know my mother."

Both are silent. They look at each other kindly.

"Is that so?" he says. "You, too, don't know your mother? Well, then, call me Haggart."

"Haggart?"

"Yes. Do you like the name? I have invented it myself - Haggart. It's a pity that you have been named already. I would have invented a fine name for you."

Suddenly he frowned.

"Tell me, Mariet, why is your land so mournful? I walk along your paths and only the cobblestones creak under my feet. And on both sides are huge rocks."

"That is on the road to the castle - none of us ever go there. Is it true that these stones stop the passersby with the question: 'Where are you going?'"

"No, they are mute. Why is your land so mournful? It is almost a week since I've seen my shadow. It is impossible! I don't see my shadow."

"Our land is very cheerful and full of joy. It is still winter now, but soon spring will come, and sunshine will come back with it. You shall see it, Haggart."

He speaks with contempt:

"And you are sitting and waiting calmly for its return? You must be a fine set of people! Ah, if I only had a ship!"

"What would you have done?"

He looks at her morosely and shakes his head suspiciously.

"You are too inquisitive, little girl. Has any one sent you over to me?"

"No. What do you need a ship for?"

Haggart laughs good-naturedly and ironically:

"She asks what a man needs a ship for. You must be a fine set of people. You don't know what a man needs a ship for! And you speak seriously? If I had a ship I would have rushed toward the sun. And it would not matter how it sets its golden sails, I would overtake it with my black sails. And I would force it to outline my shadow on the deck of my ship. And I would put my foot upon it this way!"

He stamps his foot firmly. Then Mariet asks, cautiously:

"Did you say with black sails?"

"That's what I said. Why do you always ask questions? I have no ship, you know. Good-bye."

He puts on his hat, but does not move. Mariet maintains silence. Then he says, very angrily:

"Perhaps you, too, like the music of your old Dan, that old fool?"

"You know his name?"

"Khorre told me it. I don't like his music, no, no. Bring me a good, honest dog, or beast, and he will howl. You will say that he knows no music - he does, but he can't bear falsehood. Here is music. Listen!"

He takes Mariet by the hand and turns her roughly, her face toward the ocean.

"Do you hear? This is music. Your Dan has robbed the sea and the wind. No, he is worse than a thief, he is a deceiver! He should be hanged on a sailyard - your Dan! Good-bye!"

He goes, but after taking two steps he turns around.

"I said good-bye to you. Go home. Let this fool play alone. Well, go."

Mariet is silent, motionless. Haggart laughs:

"Are you afraid perhaps that I have forgotten your name? I remember it. Your name is Mariet. Go, Mariet."

She says softly:

"I have seen your ship."

Haggart advances to her quickly and bends down. His face is terrible.

"It is not true. When?"

"Last evening."

"It is not true! Which way was it going?"

"Toward the sun."

"Last evening I was drunk and I slept. But this is not true. I have never seen it. You are testing me. Beware!"

"Shall I tell you if I see it again?"

"How can you tell me?"

"I shall come up your hill."

Haggart looks at her attentively.

"If you are only telling me the truth. What sort of people are there in your land - false or not? In the lands I know, all the people are false. Has any one else seen that ship?"

"I don't know. I was alone on the shore. Now I see that it was not your ship. You are not glad to hear of it."

Haggart is silent, as though he has forgotten her presence.

"You have a pretty uniform. You are silent? I shall come up to you."

Haggart is silent. His dark profile is stern and wildly gloomy; every motion of his powerful body, every fold of his clothes, is full of the dull silence of the taciturnity of long hours, or days, or perhaps of a lifetime.

"Your sailor will not kill me? You are silent. I have a betrothed. His name is Philipp, but I don't love him. You are now like that rock which lies on the road leading to the castle."

Haggart turns around silently and starts.

"I also remember your name. Your name is Haggart."

He goes away.

"Haggart!" calls Mariet, but he has already disappeared behind the house. Only the creaking of the scattered cobblestones is heard, dying away in the misty air. Dan, who has taken a rest, is playing again; he is telling God about those who have perished at sea.

The night is growing darker. Neither the rock nor the castle is visible now; only the light in the window is redder and brighter.

The dull thuds of the tireless breakers are telling the story of different lives.

CHAPTER II

A strong wind is tossing the fragment of a sail which is hanging over the large, open window. The sail is too small to cover the entire window, and, through the gaping hole, the dark night is breathing inclement weather. There is no rain, but the warm wind, saturated with the sea, is heavy and damp.

Here in the tower live Haggart and his sailor, Khorre. Both are sleeping now a heavy, drunken sleep. On the table and in the corners of the room there are empty bottles, and the remains of food; the only taburet is overturned, lying on one side. Toward evening the sailor got up, lit a large illumination lamp, and was about to do more, but he was overcome by intoxication again and fell asleep upon his thin mattress of straw and seagrass. Tossed by the wind, the flame of the illumination-lamp is quivering in yellow, restless spots over the uneven, mutilated walls, losing itself in the dark opening of the door, which leads to the other rooms of the castle.

Haggart lies on his back, and the same quivering yellow shades run noiselessly over his strong forehead, approach his closed eyes, his straight, sharply outlined nose, and, tossing about in confusion, rush back to the wall. The breathing of the sleeping man is deep and uneven; from time to time his heavy, strange hand lifts itself, makes several weak, unfinished movements, and falls down on his breast helplessly.

Outside the window the breakers are roaring and raging, beating against the rocks - this is the second day a storm is raging in the ocean. The ancient tower is quivering from the violent blows of the waves. It responds to the storm with the

LEONID ANDREYEV

rustling of the falling plaster, with the rattling of the little cobblestones as they are torn down, with the whisper and moans of the wind which has lost its way in the passages. It whispers and mutters like an old woman.

The sailor begins to feel cold on the stone floor, on which the wind spreads itself like water; he tosses about, folds his legs under himself, draws his head into his shoulders, gropes for his imaginary clothes, but is unable to wake up - his intoxication produced by a two days' spree is heavy and severe. But now the wind whines more powerfully than before; something heaves a deep groan. Perhaps a part of a destroyed wall has sunk into the sea. The quivering yellow spots commence to toss about upon the crooked wall more desperately, and Khorre awakes.

He sits up on his mattress, looks around, but is unable to understand anything.

The wind is hissing like a robber summoning other robbers, and filling the night with disquieting phantoms. It seems as if the sea were full of sinking vessels, of people who are drowning and desperately struggling with death. Voices are heard. Somewhere near by people are shouting, scolding each other, laughing and singing, like madmen, or talking sensibly and rapidly - it seems that soon one will see a strange human face distorted by horror or laughter, or fingers bent convulsively. But there is a strong smell of the sea, and that, together with the cold, brings Khorre to his senses.

"Noni!" he calls hoarsely, but Haggart does not hear him. After a moment's thought, he calls once more:

"Captain. Noni! Get up."

But Haggart does not answer and the sailor mutters:

"Noni is drunk and he sleeps. Let him sleep. Oh, what a cold night it is. There isn't enough warmth in it even to warm your nose. I am cold. I feel cold and lonesome, Noni. I can't drink like that, although everybody knows I am a drunkard. But it is one thing to drink, and another to drown in gin - that's an entirely different matter. Noni - you are like a drowned man, simply like a corpse. I feel ashamed for your sake, Noni. I shall drink now and - "

He rises, and staggering, finds an unopened bottle and drinks.

"A fine wind. They call this a storm - do you hear, Noni? They call this a storm. What will they call a real storm?"

He drinks again.

"A fine wind!"

He goes over to the window and, pushing aside the corner of the sail, looks out.

"Not a single light on the sea, or in the village. They have hidden themselves and are sleeping - they are waiting for the storm to pass. B-r-r, how cold! I would have driven them all out to sea; it is mean to go to sea only when the weather is calm. That is cheating the sea. I am a pirate, that's true; my name is Khorre, and I should have been hanged long ago on a yard, that's true, too - but I shall never allow myself such meanness as to cheat the sea. Why did you bring me to this hole, Noni?"

He picks up some brushwood, and throws it into the fireplace.

"I love you, Noni. I am now going to start a fire to warm your feet. I used to be your nurse, Noni; but you have lost your reason - that's true. I am a wise man, but I don't understand your conduct at all. Why did you drop your ship? You will be hanged, Noni, you will be hanged, and I will dangle by your side. You have lost your reason, that's true!"

He starts a fire, then prepares food and drink.

"What will you say when you wake up? 'Fire.' And I will answer, 'Here it is.' Then you will say, 'Something to drink.' And I will answer, 'Here it is.' And then you will drink your fill again, and I will drink with you, and you will prate nonsense. How long is this going to last? We have lived this way two months now, or perhaps two years, or twenty years - I am drowning in gin - I don't understand your conduct at all, Noni."

He drinks.

"Either I have lost my mind from this gin, or a ship is being wrecked near by. How they are crying!"

He looks out of the window.

"No, no one is here. It is the wind. The wind feels weary, and it plays all by itself. It has seen many shipwrecks, and now it is inventing. The wind itself is crying; the wind itself is scolding and sobbing; and the wind itself is laughing - the rogue! But if you think that this rag with which I have covered the window is a sail, and that this ruin of a castle is a three-masted brig, you are a fool! We are not going anywhere! We are standing securely at our moorings, do you hear?"

He pushes the sleeping man cautiously.

"Get up, Noni. I feel lonesome. If we must drink, let's drink together - I feel lonesome. Noni!"

Haggart awakens, stretches himself and says, without opening his eyes:

"Fire."

"Here it is."

"Something to drink."

"Here it is! A fine wind, Noni. I looked out of the window, and the sea splashed into my eyes. It is high tide now and the water-dust flies up to the tower. I feel lonesome, Noni. I want to speak to you. Don't be angry!"

"It's cold."

"Soon the fire will burn better. I don't understand your actions. Don't be angry, Noni, but I don't understand your actions! I am afraid that you have lost your mind."

"Did you drink again?"

"I did."

"Give me some."

He drinks from the mouth of the bottle lying on the floor, his eyes wandering over the crooked mutilated walls, whose every projection and crack is now lighted by the bright flame in the fireplace. He is not quite sure yet whether he is awake, or whether it is all a dream. With each strong gust of wind the flame is hurled from the fireplace, and then the entire tower seems to dance - the last shadows melt and rush off into the open door.

"Don't drink it all at once, Noni! Not all at once!" says the sailor and gently takes the bottle away from him. Haggart seats himself and clasps his head with both hands.

"I have a headache. What is that cry? Was there a shipwreck?"

"No, Noni. It is the wind playing roguishly."

"Khorre!"

"Captain."

"Give me the bottle."

He drinks a little more and sets the bottle on the table. Then he paces the room, straightening his shoulders and his chest, and looks out of the window. Khorre looks over his shoulder and whispers:

"Not a single light. It is dark and deserted. Those who had to die have died already, and the cautious cowards are sitting on the solid earth."

Haggart turns around and says, wiping his face:

"When I am intoxicated, I hear voices and singing. Does that happen to you, too, Khorre? Who is that singing now?"

"The wind is singing, Noni - only the wind."

"No, but who else? It seems to me a human being is singing, a woman is singing, and others are laughing and shouting something. Is that all nothing but the wind?"

"Only the wind."

"Why does the wind deceive me?" says Haggart haughtily.

"It feels lonesome, Noni, just as I do, and it laughs at the human beings. Have you heard the wind lying like this and mocking in the open sea? There it tells the truth, but here - it frightens the people on shore and mocks them. The wind does not like cowards. You know it."

Haggart says morosely:

"I heard their organist playing not long ago in church. He lies."

"They are all liars."

"No!" exclaims Haggart angrily. "Not all. There are some who tell the truth there, too. I shall cut your ears off if you will slander honest people. Do you hear?"

"Yes."

They are silent; they listen to the wild music of the sea. The wind has evidently grown mad. Having taken into its embrace a multitude of instruments with which human beings produce their music - harps, reed-pipes, priceless violins, heavy drums and brass trumpets - it breaks them all, together with a wave, against the sharp rocks. It dashes them and bursts into laughter - only thus does the wind understand music - each time in the death of an instrument, each time in the breaking of strings, in the snapping of the clanging brass. Thus does the mad musician understand music. Haggart heaves a deep sigh and with some amazement, like a man just awakened from sleep, looks around on all sides. Then he commands shortly:

"Give me my pipe."

"Here it is."

Both commence to smoke.

"Don't be angry, Noni," says the sailor. "You have become so angry that one can't come near you at all. May I chat with you?"

"There are some who do tell the truth there, too," says Haggart sternly, emitting rings of smoke.

"How shall I say it you, Noni?" answers the sailor cautiously but stubbornly. "There are no truthful people there. It has been so ever since the deluge. At that time all the honest people went out to sea, and only the cowards and liars remained upon the solid earth."

Haggart is silent for a minute; then he takes the pipe from his mouth and laughs gaily.

"Have you invented it yourself?"

"I think so," says Khorre modestly.

"Clever! And it was worth teaching you sacred history for that! Were you taught by a priest?"

"Yes. In prison. At that time I was as innocent as a dove. That's also from sacred scriptures, Noni. That's what they always say there."

"He was a fool! It was not necessary to teach you, but to hang you," says Haggart, adding morosely: "Don't talk nonsense, sailor. Hand me a bottle."

They drink. Khorre stamps his foot against the stone floor and asks:

"Do you like this motionless floor?"

"I should have liked to have the deck of a ship dancing under my feet."

"Noni!" exclaims the sailor enthusiastically. "Noni! Now I hear real words! Let us go away from here. I cannot live like this. I am drowning in gin. I don't understand your actions at all, Noni! You have lost your mind. Reveal yourself to me, my boy. I was your nurse. I nursed you, Noni, when your father brought you on board ship. I remember how the city was burning then and we were putting out to sea, and I didn't know what to do with you; you whined like a little pig in the cook's room. I even wanted to throw you overboard - you annoyed me so much. Ah, Noni, it is all so touching that I can't bear to recall it. I must have a drink. Take a drink, too, my boy, but not all at once, not all at once!"

They drink. Haggart paces the room heavily and slowly, like a man who is imprisoned in a dungeon but does not want to escape.

"I feel sad," he says, without looking at Khorre. Khorre, as though understanding, shakes his head in assent.

"Sad? I understand. Since then?"

"Ever since then."

"Ever since we drowned those people? They cried so loudly."

"I did not hear their cry. But this I heard - something snapped in my heart, Khorre. Always sadness, everywhere sadness! Let me drink!"

He drinks.

"He who cried - am I perhaps afraid of him, Khorre? That would be fine! Tears were trickling from his eyes; he wept like one who is unfortunate. Why did he do that? Perhaps he came from a land where the people had never heard of death - what do you think, sailor?"

"I don't remember him, Noni. You speak so much about him, while I don't remember him."

"He was a fool," says Haggart. "He spoilt his death for himself, and spoilt me my life. I curse him, Khorre. May he be cursed. But that doesn't matter, Khorre - no!"

Silence.

"They have good gin on this coast," says Khorre. "He'll pass easily, Noni. If you have cursed him there will be no delay; he'll slip into hell like an oyster."

Haggart shakes his head:

"No, Khorre, no! I am sad. Ah, sailor, why have I stopped here, where I hear the sea? I should go away, far away on land, where the people don't know the sea at all, where the people have never heard about the sea - a thousand miles away, five thousand miles away!"

"There is no such land."

"There is, Khorre. Let us drink and laugh, Khorre. That organist lies. Sing something for me, Khorre - you sing well. In your hoarse voice I hear the creaking of ropes. Your refrain is like a sail that is torn by the storm. Sing, sailor!"

Khorre nods his head gloomily.

"No, I will not sing."

"Then I shall force you to pray as they prayed!"

"You will not force me to pray, either. You are the Captain, and you may kill me, and here is your revolver. It is loaded, Noni. And now I am going to speak the truth, Captain! Khorre, the boatswain, speaks to you in the name of the entire crew."

Haggart says:

"Drop this performance, Khorre. There is no crew here. You'd better drink something."

He drinks.

"But the crew is waiting for you, you know it. Captain, is it your intention to return to the ship and assume command again?"

"No."

"Captain, is it perhaps your intention to go to the people on the coast and live with them?"

"No."

"I can't understand your actions, Noni. What do you intend to do, Captain?"

Haggart drinks silently.

"Not all at once, Noni, not at once. Captain, do you intend to stay in this hole and wait until the police dogs come from the city? Then they will hang us, and not upon a mast, but simply on one of their foolish trees."

"Yes. The wind is getting stronger. Do you hear, Khorre? The wind is getting stronger!"

"And the gold which we have buried here?" He points below, with his finger.

"The gold? Take it and go with it wherever you like."

The sailor says angrily:

"You are a bad man, Noni. You have only set foot on earth a little while ago, and you already have the thoughts of a traitor. That's what the earth is doing!"

"Be silent, Khorre. I am listening. Our sailors are singing. Do you hear? No, that's the wine rushing to my head. I'll be drunk soon. Give me another bottle."

"Perhaps you will go to the priest? He would absolve your sins."

"Silence!" roars Haggart, clutching at his revolver.

Silence. The storm is increasing. Haggart paces the room in agitation, striking against the walls. He mutters something abruptly. Suddenly he seizes the sail and tears it down furiously, admitting the salty wind. The illumination lamp is extinguished and the flame in the fireplace tosses about wildly - like Haggart.

"Why did you lock out the wind? It's better now. Come here."

"You were the terror of the seas!" says the sailor.

"Yes, I was the terror of the seas."

"You were the terror of the coasts! Your famous name resounded like the surf over all the coasts, wherever people live. They saw you in their dreams. When they thought of the ocean, they thought of you. When they heard the storm, they heard you, Noni!"

"I burnt their cities. The deck of my ship is shaking under my feet, Khorre. The deck is shaking under me!"

He laughs wildly, as if losing his senses.

"You sank their ships. You sent to the bottom the Englishman who was chasing you."

"He had ten guns more than I."

"And you burnt and drowned him. Do you remember, Noni, how the wind laughed then? The night was as black as this night, but you made day of it, Noni. We were rocked by a sea of fire."

Haggart stands pale-faced, his eyes closed. Suddenly he shouts commandingly:

"Boatswain!"

"Yes," Khorre jumps up.

"Whistle for everybody to go up on deck."

"Yes."

The boatswain's shrill whistle pierces sharply into the open body of the storm. Everything comes to life, and it looks as though they were upon the deck of a ship. The waves are crying with human voices. In semi-oblivion, Haggart is commanding passionately and angrily:

"To the shrouds! - The studding sails! Be ready, forepart! Aim at the ropes; I don't want to sink them all at once. Starboard the helm, sail by the wind. Be ready now. Ah, fire! Ah, you are already burning! Board it now! Get the hooks ready."

And Khorre tosses about violently, performing the mad instructions.

"Yes, yes."

"Be braver, boys. Don't be afraid of tears! Eh, who is crying there? Don't dare cry when you are dying. I'll dry your mean eyes upon the fire. Fire! Fire everywhere! Khorre - sailor! I am dying. They have poured molten tar into my chest. Oh, how it burns!"

"Don't give way, Noni. Don't give way. Recall your father. Strike them on the head, Noni!"

"I can't, Khorre. My strength is failing. Where is my power?"

"Strike them on the head, Noni. Strike them on the head!"

"Take a knife, Khorre, and cut out my heart. There is no ship, Khorre - there is nothing. Cut out my heart, comrade - throw out the traitor from my breast."

"I want to play some more, Noni. Strike them on the head!"

"There is no ship, Khorre, there is nothing - it is all a lie. I want to drink."

He takes a bottle and laughs:

"Look, sailor - here the wind and the storm and you and I are locked. It is all a deception, Khorre!"

"I want to play."

"Here my sorrow is locked. Look! In the green glass it seems like water, but it isn't water. Let us drink, Khorre - there on the bottom I see my laughter and your song. There is no ship - there is nothing! Who is coming?"

He seizes his revolver. The fire in the fire-place is burning faintly; the shadows are tossing about - but two of these shadows are darker than the others and they are walking. Khorre shouts:

"Halt!"

A man's voice, heavy and deep, answers:

"Hush! Put down your weapons. I am the abbot of this place."

"Fire, Noni, fire! They have come for you."

"I have come to help you. Put down your knife, fool, or I will break every bone in your body without a knife. Coward, are you frightened by a woman and a priest?"

Haggart puts down his revolver and says ironically:

"A woman and a priest! Is there anything still more terrible? Pardon my sailor, Mr. abbot, he is drunk, and when he is drunk he is very reckless and he may kill you. Khorre, don't turn your knife."

"He has come after you, Noni."

"I have come to warn you; the tower may fall. Go away from here!" says the abbot.

"Why are you hiding yourself, girl? I remember your name; your name is Mariet," says Haggart.

"I am not hiding. I also remember your name - it is Haggart," replies Mariet.

"Was it you who brought him here?"

"I."

"I have told you that they are all traitors, Noni," says Khorre.

"Silence!"

"It is very cold here. I will throw some wood into the fireplace. May I do it?" asks Mariet.

"Do it," answers Haggart.

"The tower will fall down before long," says the abbot. "Part of the wall has caved in already; it is all hollow underneath. Do you hear?"

He stamps his foot on the stone floor.

"Where will the tower fall?"

"Into the sea, I suppose! The castle is splitting the rocks."

Haggart laughs:

"Do you hear, Khorre? This place is not as motionless as it seemed to you - while it cannot move, it can fall. How many people have you brought along with you, priest, and where have you hidden them?"

"Only two of us came, my father and I," says Mariet.

"You are rude to a priest. I don't like that," says the abbot.

"You have come here uninvited. I don't like that either," says Haggart.

"Why did you lead me here, Mariet? Come," says the abbot.

Haggart speaks ironically:

"And you leave us here to die? That is unChristian, Christian."

"Although I am a priest, I am a poor Christian, and the Lord knows it," says the abbot angrily. "I have no desire to save such a rude scamp. Let us go, Mariet."

"Captain?" asks Khorre.

"Be silent, Khorre," says Haggart. "So that's the way you speak, abbot; so you are not a liar?"

"Come with me and you shall see."

"Where shall I go with you?"

"To my house."

"To your house? Do you hear, Khorre? To the priest! But do you know whom you are calling to your house?"

"No, I don't know. But I see that you are young and strong. I see that although your face is gloomy, it is handsome, and I think that you could be as good a workman as others."

"A workman? Khorre, do you hear what the priest says?"

Both laugh. The abbot says angrily:

"You are both drunk."

"Yes, a little! But if I were sober I would have laughed still more," answers Haggart.

"Don't laugh, Haggart," says Mariet.

Haggart replies angrily:

"I don't like the tongues of false priests, Mariet - they are coated with truth on top, like a lure for flies. Take him away, and you, girl, go away, too! I have forgotten your name!"

He sits down and stares ahead sternly. His eyebrows move close together, and his hand is pressed down heavily by his lowered head, by his strong chin.

"He does not know you, father! Tell him about yourself. You speak so well. If you wish it, he will believe you, father. Haggart!"

Haggart maintains silence.

"Noni! Captain!"

Silence. Khorre whispers mysteriously:

"He feels sad. Girl, tell the priest that he feels sad."

"Khorre," begins Mariet. Haggart looks around quickly.

"What about Khorre? Why don't you like him, Mariet? We are so much like each other."

"He is like you?" says the woman with contempt. "No, Haggart! But here is what he did: He gave gin to little Noni again to-day. He moistened his finger and gave it to him. He will kill him, father."

Haggart laughs:

"Is that so bad? He did the same to me."

"And he dipped him in cold water. The boy is very weak," says

Mariet morosely.

"I don't like to hear you speak of weakness. Our boy must be strong. Khorre! Three days without gin."

He shows him three fingers.

"Who should be without gin? The boy or I?" asks Khorre gloomily.

"You!" replies Haggart furiously. "Begone!"

The sailor sullenly gathers his belongings - the pouch, the pipe, and the flask - and wabbling, goes off. But he does not go far - he sits down upon a neighbouring rock. Haggart and his wife look at him.

CHAPTER III

The work is ended. Having lost its gloss, the last neglected fish lies on the ground; even the children are too lazy to pick it up; and an indifferent, satiated foot treads it into the mud. A quiet, fatigued conversation goes on, mingled with gay and peaceful laughter.

"What kind of a prayer is our abbot going to say to-day? It is already time for him to come."

"And do you think it is so easy to compose a good prayer? He is thinking."

"Selly's basket broke and the fish were falling out. We laughed so much! It seems so funny to me even now!"

Laughter. Two fishermen look at the sail in the distance.

"All my life I have seen large ships sailing past us. Where are they going? They disappear beyond the horizon, and I go off to sleep; and I sleep, while they are forever going, going. Where are they going? Do you know?"

"To America."

"I should like to go with them. When they speak of America my heart begins to ring. Did you say America on purpose, or is that the truth?"

Several old women are whispering:

"Wild Gart is angry again at his sailor. Have you noticed it?"

"The sailor is displeased. Look, how wan his face is."

"Yes, he looks like the evil one when he is compelled to listen to a psalm. But I don't like Wild Gart, either. No. Where did he come from?"

They resume their whispers. Haggart complains softly:

"Why have you the same name, Mariet, for everybody? It should not be so in a truthful land."

Mariet speaks with restrained force, pressing both hands to her breast:

"I love you so dearly, Gart; when you go out to sea, I set my teeth together and do not open them until you come back. When you are away, I eat nothing and drink nothing; when you are away, I am silent, and the women laugh: 'Mute Mariet!' But I would be insane if I spoke when I am alone."

HAGGART - Here you are again compelling me to smile. You must not, Mariet - I am forever smiling.

MARIET - I love you so dearly, Gart. Every hour of the day and the night I am thinking only of what I could still give to you, Gart. Have I not given you everything? But that is so little - everything! There is but one thing I want to do - to keep on giving to you, giving! When the sun sets, I present you the sunset; when the sun rises, I present you the sunrise - take it, Gart! And are not all the storms yours? Ah, Haggart, how I love you!

HAGGART - I am going to toss little Noni so high to-day that I will toss him up to the clouds. Do you want me to do it? Let us laugh, dear little sister Mariet. You are exactly like myself. When you stand that way, it seems to me that I am standing there - I have to rub my eyes. Let us laugh! Some day

I may suddenly mix things up - I may wake up and say to you: "Good morning, Haggart!"

MARIET - Good morning, Mariet.

HAGGART - I will call you Haggart. Isn't that a good idea?

MARIET - And I will call you Mariet.

HAGGART - Yes - no. You had better call me Haggart, too.

"You don't want me to call you Mariet?" asks Mariet sadly.

The abbot and old Dan appear. The abbot says in a loud, deep voice:

"Here I am. Here I am bringing you a prayer, children. I have just composed it; it has even made me feel hot. Dan, why doesn't the boy ring the bell? Oh, yes, he is ringing. The fool - he isn't swinging the right rope, but that doesn't matter; that's good enough, too. Isn't it, Mariet?"

Two thin but merry bells are ringing.

Mariet is silent and Haggart answers for her:

"That's good enough. But what are the bells saying, abbot?"

The fishermen who have gathered about them are already prepared to laugh - the same undying jest is always repeated.

"Will you tell no one about it?" says the abbot, in a deep voice, slily winking his eye. "Pope's a rogue! Pope's a rogue!"

The fishermen laugh merrily.

"This man," roars the abbot, pointing at Haggart, "is my favourite man! He has given me a grandson, and I wrote the Pope about it in Latin. But that wasn't so hard; isn't that true,

Mariet? But he knows how to look at the water. He foretells a storm as if he himself caused it. Gart, do you produce the storm yourself? Where does the wind come from? You are the wind yourself."

All laugh approval. An old fisherman says:

"That's true, father. Ever since he has been here, we have never been caught in a storm."

"Of course it is true, if I say it. 'Pope's a rogue! Pope's a rogue!'"

Old Dan walks over to Khorre and says something to him. Khorre nods his head negatively. The abbot, singing "Pope's a rogue," goes around the crowd, throws out brief remarks, and claps some people on the shoulder in a friendly manner.

"Hello, Katerina, you are getting stout. Oho! Are you all ready? And Thomas is missing again - this is the second time he has stayed away from prayer. Anna, you are rather sad - that isn't good. One must live merrily, one must live merrily! I think that it is jolly even in hell, but in a different way. It is two years since you have stopped growing, Philipp. That isn't good."

Philipp answers gruffly:

"Grass also stops growing if a stone falls upon it."

"What is still worse than that - worms begin to breed under the rock."

Mariet says softly, sadly and entreatingly:

"Don't you want me to call you Mariet?"

Haggart answers obstinately and sternly:

"I don't. If my name will be Mariet, I shall never kill that man. He disturbs my life. Make me a present of his life, Mariet. He kissed you."

"How can I present you that which is not mine? His life belongs to God and to himself."

"That is not true. He kissed you; do I not see the burns upon your lips? Let me kill him, and you will feel as joyful and carefree as a seagull. Say 'yes,' Mariet."

"No; you shouldn't do it, Gart. It will be painful to you."

Haggart looks at her and speaks with deep irony.

"Is that it? Well, then, it is not true that you give me anything. You don't know how to give, woman."

"I am your wife."

"No! A man has no wife when another man, and not his wife, grinds his knife. My knife is dull, Mariet!"

Mariet looks at him with horror and sorrow.

"What did you say, Haggart? Wake up; it is a terrible dream, Haggart! It is I - look at me. Open your eyes wider, wider, until you see me well. Do you see me, Gart?"

Haggart slowly rubs his brow.

"I don't know. It is true I love you, Mariet. But how incomprehensible your land is - in your land a man sees dreams even when he is not asleep. Perhaps I am smiling already. Look, Mariet."

The abbot stops in front of Khorre.

"Ah, old friend, how do you do? You are smiling already.

Look, Mariet."

"I don't want to work," ejaculates the sailor sternly.

"You want your own way? This man," roars the abbot, pointing at Khorre, "thinks that he is an atheist. But he is simply a fool; he does not understand that he is also praying to God - but he is doing it the wrong way, like a crab. Even a fish prays to God, my children; I have seen it myself. When you will be in hell, old man,give my regards to the Pope. Well, children, come closer, and don't gnash your teeth. I am going to start at once. Eh, you, Mathias - you needn't put out the fire in your pipe; isn't it the same to God what smoke it is, incense or tobacco, if it is only well meant. Why do you shake your head, woman?"

WOMAN - His tobacco is contraband.

YOUNG FISHERMAN - God wouldn't bother with such trifles. The abbot thinks a while:

"No; hold on. I think contraband tobacco is not quite so good. That's an inferior grade. Look here; you better drop your pipe meanwhile, Mathias; I'll think the matter over later. Now, silence, perfect silence. Let God take a look at us first."

All stand silent and serious. Only a few have lowered their heads. Most of the people are looking ahead with wide-open, motionless eyes, as though they really saw God in the blue of the sky, in the boundless, radiant, distant surface of the sea. The sea is approaching with a caressing murmur; high tide has set in.

"My God and the God of all these people! Don't judge us for praying, not in Latin but in our own language, which our mothers have taught us. Our God! Save us from all kinds of terrors, from unknown sea monsters; protect us against storms and hurricanes, against tempests and gales. Give us calm weather and a kind wind, a clear sun and peaceful waves. And another thing, O Lord! we ask You; don't allow the devil, to come close to our bedside when we are asleep. In our sleep we are defenceless, O Lord! and the devil terrifies us, tortures us to convulsions, torments us to the very blood of our heart. And there is another thing, O Lord! Old Rikke, whom You know, is beginning to extinguish Your light in his eyes and he can make nets no longer - "

Rikke frequently shakes his head in assent.

"I can't, I can't!"

"Prolong, then, O Lord! Your bright day and bid the night wait. Am I right, Rikke?"

"Yes."

"And here is still another, the last request, O Lord. I shall not ask any more: The tears do not dry up in the eyes of our old women crying for those who have perished. Take their memory away, O Lord, and give them strong forgetfulness. There are still other trifles, O Lord, but let the others pray whose turn has come before You. Amen."

Silence. Old Dan tugs the abbot by the sleeve, and whispers something in his ear.

ABBOT - Dan is asking me to pray for those who perished at sea.

The women exclaim in plaintive chorus:

"For those who perished at sea! For those who died at sea!"

Some of them kneel. The abbot looks tenderly at their bowed heads, exhausted with waiting and fear, and says:

"No priest should pray for those who died at sea - these women should pray. Make it so, O Lord, that they should not weep so much!"

Silence. The incoming tide roars more loudly - the ocean is carrying to the earth its noise, its secrets, its bitter, briny taste of unexplored depths.

Soft voices say:

"The sea is coming."

"High tide has started."

"The sea is coming."

Mariet kisses her father's hand.

"Woman!" says the priest tenderly. "Listen, Gart, isn't it strange that this - a woman" - he strokes his daughter tenderly with his finger on her pure forehead - "should be born of me, a man?"

Haggart smiles.

"And is it not strange that this should have become a wife to me, a man?" He embraces Mariet, bending her frail shoulders.

"Let us go to eat, Gart, my son. Whoever she may be, I know one thing well. She has prepared for you and me an excellent dinner."

The people disperse quickly. Mariet says confusedly and cheerfully:

"I'll run first."

"Run, run," answers the abbot. "Gart, my son, call the atheist to dinner. I'll hit him with a spoon on the forehead; an atheist understands a sermon best of all if you hit him with a spoon."

He waits and mutters:

"The boy has commenced to ring the bells again. He does it for himself, the rogue. If we did not lock the steeple, they would pray there from morning until night."

Haggart goes over to Khorre, near whom Dan is sitting.

"Khorre! Let us go to eat - the priest called you."

"I don't want to go, Noni."

"So? What are you going to do here on shore?"

"I will think, Noni, think. I have so much to think to be able to understand at least something."

Haggart turns around silently. The abbot calls from the distance:

"He is not coming? Well, then, let him stay there. And Dan - never call Dan, my son" - says the priest in his deep whisper, "he eats at night like a rat. Mariet purposely puts something away for him in the closet for the night; when she looks for it in the morning, it is gone. Just think of it, no one ever hears when he takes it. Does he fly?"

Both go off. Only the two old men, seated in a friendly manner on two neighbouring rocks, remain on the deserted shore. And the old men resemble each other so closely, and whatever they may say to each other, the whiteness of their hair, the deep lines of their wrinkles, make them kin.

The tide is coming.

"They have all gone away," mutters Khorre. "Thus will they cook hot soup on the wrecks of our ship, too. Eh, Dan! Do you know he ordered me to drink no gin for three days. Let the old dog croak! Isn't that so, Noni?"

"Of those who died at sea... Those who died at sea," mutters Dan. "A son taken from his father, a son from his father. The father said go, and the son perished in the sea. Oi, oi, oi!"

"What are you prating there, old man? I say, he ordered me to drink no gin. Soon he will order, like that King of yours, that the sea be lashed with chains."

"Oho! With chains."

"Your king was a fool. Was he married, your king?"

"The sea is coming, coming!" mutters Dan. "It brings along its noise, its secret, its deception. Oh, how the sea deceives man. Those who died at sea - yes, yes, yes. Those who died at sea."

"Yes, the sea is coming. And you don't like it?" asks Khorre, rejoicing maliciously. "Well, don't you like it? I don't like your music. Do you hear, Dan? I hate your music!"

"Oho! And why do you come to hear it? I know that you and Gart stood by the wall and listened."

Khorre says sternly:

"It was he who got me out of bed."

"He will get you out of bed again."

"No!" roars Khorre furiously. "I will get up myself at night. Do you hear, Dan? I will get up at night and break your music."

"And I will spit into your sea."

"Try," says the sailor distrustfully. "How will you spit?"

"This way," and Dan, exasperated, spits in the direction of the sea. The frightened Khorre, in confusion, says hoarsely:

"Oh, what sort of man are you? You spat! Eh, Dan, look out; it will be bad for you - you yourself are talking about those who died at sea."

Dan shouts, frightened:

"Who speaks of those that perished at sea? You, you dog!"

He goes away, grumbling and coughing, swinging his hand and stooping. Khorre is left alone before the entire vastness of the sea and the sky.

"He is gone. Then I am going to look at you, O sea, until my eyes will burst of thirst!"

The ocean, approaching, is roaring.

CHAPTER IV

At the very edge of the water, upon a narrow landing on the rocky shore, stands a man - a small, dark, motionless dot. Behind him is the cold, almost vertical slope of granite, and before his eyes the ocean is rocking heavily and dully in the impenetrable darkness. Its mighty approach is felt in the open voice of the waves which are rising from the depths. Even sniffing sounds are heard - it is as though a drove of monsters, playing, were splashing, snorting, lying down on their backs, and panting contentedly, deriving their monstrous pleasures.

The ocean smells of the strong odour of the depths, of decaying seaweeds, of its grass. The sea is calm to-day and, as always, alone.

And there is but one little light in the black space of water and night - the distant lighthouse of the Holy Cross.

The rattle of cobblestones is heard from under a cautious step: Haggart is coming down to the sea along a steep path. He pauses, silent with restraint, breathing deeply after the strain of passing the dangerous slope, and goes forward. He is now at the edge - he straightens himself and looks for a long time at him who had long before taken his strange but customary place at the very edge of the deep. He makes a few steps forward and greets him irresolutely and gently - Haggart greets him even timidly:

"Good evening, stranger. Have you been here long?"

A sad, soft, and grave voice answers:

"Good evening, Haggart. Yes, I have been here long."

"You are watching?"

"I am watching and listening."

"Will you allow me to stand near you and look in the same direction you are looking? I am afraid that I am disturbing you by my uninvited presence - for when I came you were already here - but I am so fond of this spot. This place is isolated, and the sea is near, and the earth behind is silent; and here my eyes open. Like a night-owl, I see better in the dark; the light of day dazzles me. You know, I have grown up on the sea, sir."

"No, you are not disturbing me, Haggart. But am I not disturbing you? Then I shall go away."

"You are so polite, sir," mutters Haggart.

"But I also love this spot," continues the sad, grave voice. "I, too, like to feel that the cold and peaceful granite is behind me. You have grown up on the sea, Haggart - tell me, what is that faint light on the right?"

"That is the lighthouse of the Holy Cross."

"Aha! The lighthouse of the Holy Cross. I didn't know that. But can such a faint light help in time of a storm? I look and it always seems to me that the light is going out. I suppose it isn't so."

Haggart, agitated but restrained, says:

"You frighten me, sir. Why do you ask me what you know better than I do? You want to tempt me - you know everything."

There is not a trace of a smile in the mournful voice - nothing but sadness.

"No, I know little. I know even less than you do, for I know more. Pardon my rather complicated phrase, Haggart, but the tongue responds with so much difficulty not only to our feeling, but also to our thought."

"You are polite," mutters Haggart agitated. "You are polite and always calm. You are always sad and you have a thin hand with rings upon it, and you speak like a very important personage. Who are you, sir?"

"I am he whom you called - the one who is always sad."

"When I come, you are already here; when I go away, you remain. Why do you never want to go with me, sir?"

"There is one way for you, Haggart, and another for me."

"I see you only at night. I know all the people around this settlement, and there is no one who looks like you. Sometimes I think that you are the owner of that old castle where I lived. If that is so I must tell you the castle was destroyed by the storm."

"I don't know of whom you speak."

"I don't understand how you know my name, Haggart. But I don't want to deceive you. Although my wife Mariet calls me so, I invented that name myself. I have another name - my real name - of which no one has ever heard here."

"I know your other name also, Haggart. I know your third name, too, which even you do not know. But it is hardly worth speaking of this. You had better look into this dark sea and tell me about your life. Is it true that it is so joyous? They say that you are forever smiling. They say that you are the bravest and most handsome fisherman on the coast. And they also say that you love your wife Mariet very dearly."

"O sir!" exclaims Haggart with restraint, "my life is so sad that you could not find an image like it in this dark deep. O sir! My sufferings are so deep that you could not find a more terrible place in this dark abyss."

"What is the cause of your sorrow and your sufferings, Haggart?"

"Life, sir. Here your noble and sad eyes look in the same direction my eyes look - into this terrible, dark distance. Tell me, then, what is stirring there? What is resting and waiting there, what is silent there, what is screaming and singing and complaining there in its own voices? What are the voices that agitate me and fill my soul with phantoms of sorrow, and yet say nothing? And whence comes this night? And whence comes my sorrow? Are you sighing, sir, or is it the sigh of the ocean blending with your voice? My hearing is beginning to fail me, my master, my dear master."

The sad voice replies:

"It is my sigh, Haggart. My great sorrow is responding to your sorrow. You see at night like an owl, Haggart; then look at my thin hands and at my rings. Are they not pale? And look at my face - is it not pale? Is it not pale - is it not pale? Oh, Haggart, my dear Haggart."

They grieve silently. The heavy ocean is splashing, tossing about, spitting and snorting and sniffing peacefully. The sea is calm to-night and alone, as always.

"Tell Haggart - " says the sad voice.

"Very well. I will tell Haggart."

"Tell Haggart that I love him."

Silence - and then a faint, plaintive reproach resounds softly:

"If your voice were not so grave, sir, I would have thought that you were laughing at me. Am I not Haggart that I should tell something to Haggart? But no - I sense a different meaning in your words, and you frighten me again. And when Haggart is afraid, it is real terror. Very well, I will tell Haggart everything you have said."

"Adjust my cloak; my shoulder is cold. But it always seems to me that the light over there is going out. You called it the lighthouse of the Holy Cross, if I am not mistaken?"

"Yes, it is called so here."

"Aha! It is called so here."

Silence.

"Must I go now?" asks Haggart.

"Yes, go."

"And you will remain here?"

"I will remain here."

Haggart retreats several steps.

"Good-bye, sir."

"Good-bye, Haggart."

Again the cobblestones rattle under his cautious steps; without looking back, Haggart climbs the steep rocks.

Of what great sorrow speaks this night?

CHAPTER V

"Your hands are in blood, Haggart. Whom have you killed, Haggart?"

"Silence, Khorre, I killed that man. Be silent and listen - he will commence to play soon. I stood here and listened, but suddenly my heart sank, and I cannot stay here alone."

"Don't confuse my mind, Noni; don't tempt me. I will run away from here. At night, when I am already fast asleep, you swoop down on me like a demon, grab me by the neck, and drag me over here - I can't understand anything. Tell me, my boy, is it necessary to hide the body?"

"Yes, yes."

"Why didn't you throw it into the sea?"

"Silence! What are you prating about? I have nothing to throw into the sea."

"But your hands are in blood."

"Silence, Khorre! He will commence soon. Be silent and listen - I say to you - Are you a friend to me or not, Khorre?"

He drags him closer to the dark window of the church. Khorre mutters:

"How dark it is. If you raised me out of bed for this accursed music - "

"Yes, yes; for this accursed music."

"Then you have disturbed my honest sleep in vain; I want no music, Noni."

"So! Was I perhaps to run through the street, knock at the windows and shout: 'Eh, who is there; where's a living soul? Come and help Haggart, stand up with him against the cannons.'"

"You are confusing things, Noni. Drink some gin, my boy. What cannons?"

"Silence, sailor."

He drags him away from the window.

"Oh, you shake me like a squall!"

"Silence! I think he looked at us from the window; something white flashed behind the window pane. You may laugh. Khorre - if he came out now I would scream like a woman."

He laughs softly.

"Are you speaking of Dan? I don't understand anything, Noni."

"But is that Dan? Of course it is not Dan - it is some one else. Give me your hand, sailor."

"I think that you simply drank too much, like that time - remember, in the castle? And your hand is quivering. But then the game was different - "

"Tss!"

Khorre lowers his voice:

"But your hand is really in blood. Oh, you are breaking my fingers!"

Haggart threatens:

"If you don't keep still, dog, I'll break every bone of your body! I'll pull every vein out of your body, if you don't keep still, you dog!"

Silence. The distant breakers are softly groaning, as if complaining - the sea has gone far away from the black earth. And the night is silent. It came no one knows whence and spread over the earth; it spread over the earth and is silent; it is silent, waiting for something. And ferocious mists have swung themselves to meet it - the sea breathed phantoms, driving to the earth a herd of headless submissive giants. A heavy fog is coming.

"Why doesn't he light a lamp?" asks Khorre sternly but submissively.

"He needs no light."

"Perhaps there is no one there any longer."

"Yes, he's there."

"A fog is coming. How quiet it is! There's something wrong in the air - what do you think, Noni?"

"Tss!"

The first soft sounds of the organ resound. Some one is sitting alone in the dark and is speaking to God in an incomprehensible language about the most important things. And however faint the sounds - suddenly the silence vanishes, the night trembles and stares into the dark church with all its myriads of phantom eyes. An agitated voice whispers:

"Listen! He always begins that way. He gets a hold of your soul at once! Where does he get the power? He gets a hold of your heart!"

"I don't like it."

"Listen! Now he makes believe he is Haggart, Khorre! Little Haggart in his mother's lap. Look, all hands are filled with golden rays; little Haggart is playing with golden rays. Look!"

"I don't see it, Noni. Leave my hand alone, it hurts."

"Now he makes believe he is Haggart! Listen!"

The oppressive chords resound faintly. Haggart moans softly.

"What is it, Noni? Do you feel any pain?"

"Yes. Do you understand of what he speaks?"

"No."

"He speaks of the most important - of the most vital, Khorre - if we could only understand it - I want to understand it. Listen, Khorre, listen! Why does he make believe that he is Haggart? It is not my soul. My soul does not know this."

"What, Noni?"

"I don't know. What terrible dreams there are in this land! Listen. There! Now he will cry and he will say: 'It is Haggart crying.' He will call God and will say: 'Haggart is calling.' He lies - Haggart did not call, Haggart does not know God."

He moans again, trying to restrain himself.

"Do you feel any pain?"

"Yes - Be silent."

Haggart exclaims in a muffled voice:

"Oh, Khorre!"

"What is it, Noni?"

"Why don't you tell him that it isn't Haggart? It is a lie!" whispers Haggart rapidly. "He thinks that he knows, but he does not know anything. He is a small, wretched old man with red eyes, like those of a rabbit, and to-morrow death will mow him down. Ha! He is dealing in diamonds, he throws them from one hand to the other like an old miser, and he himself is dying of hunger. It is a fraud, Khorre, a fraud. Let us shout loudly, Khorre, we are alone here."

He shouts, turning to the thundering organ:

"Eh, musician! Even a fly cannot rise on your wings, even the smallest fly cannot rise on your wings. Eh, musician! Let me have your torn hat and I will throw a penny into it; your lie is worth no more. What are you prating there about God, you rabbit's eyes? Be silent, I am shamed to listen to you. I swear, I am ashamed to listen to you! Don't you believe me? You are still calling? Whither?"

"Strike them on the head, Noni."

"Be silent, you dog! But what a terrible land! What are they doing here with the human heart? What terrible dreams there are in this land?"

He stops speaking. The organ sings solemnly.

"Why did you stop speaking, Noni?" asks the sailor with alarm.

"I am listening. It is good music, Khorre. Have I said anything?"

"You even shouted, Noni, and you forced me to shout with you."

"That is not true. I have been silent all the time. Do you know, I haven't even opened my mouth once! You must have been dreaming, Khorre. Perhaps you are thinking that you are near the church? You are simply sleeping in your bed, sailor. It is a dream."

Khorre is terrified.

"Drink some gin, Noni."

"I don't need it. I drank something else already."

"Your hands?"

"Be silent, Khorre. Don't you see that everything is silent and is listening, and you alone are talking? The musician may feel offended!"

He laughs quietly. Brass trumpets are roaring harmoniously about the triumphant conciliation between man and God. The fog is growing thicker.

A loud stamping of feet - some one runs through the deserted street in agitation.

"Noni!" whispers the sailor. "Who ran by?"

"I hear."

"Noni! Another one is running. Something is wrong."

Frightened people are running about in the middle of the night - the echo of the night doubles the sound of their footsteps, increasing their terror tenfold, and it seems as if the entire village, terror-stricken, is running away somewhere. Rocking, dancing silently, as upon waves, a lantern floats by.

"They have found him, Khorre. They have found the man I killed, sailor! I did not throw him into the sea; I brought him and set his head up against the door of his house. They have found him."

Another lantern floats by, swinging from side to side. As if hearing the alarm, the organ breaks off at a high chord. An instant of silence, emptiness of dread waiting, and then a woman's sob of despair fills it up to the brim.

The mist is growing thicker.

CHAPTER VI

The flame in the oil-lamp is dying out, having a smell of burning. It is near sunrise. A large, clean, fisherman's hut. A skilfully made little ship is fastened to the ceiling, and even the sails are set. Involuntarily this little ship has somehow become the centre of attraction and all those who speak, who are silent and who listen, look at it, study each familiar sail. Behind the dark curtain lies the body of Philipp - this hut belonged to him.

The people are waiting for Haggart - some have gone out to search for him. On the benches along the walls, the old fishermen have seated themselves, their hands folded on their knees; some of them seem to be slumbering; others are smoking their pipes. They speak meditatively and cautiously, as though eager to utter no unnecessary words. Whenever a belated fisherman comes in, he looks first at the curtain, then he silently squeezes himself into the crowd, and those who have no place on the bench apparently feel embarrassed.

The abbot paces the room heavily, his hands folded on his back, his head lowered; when any one is in his way, he quietly pushes him aside with his hand. He is silent and knits his brows convulsively. Occasionally he glances at the door or at the window and listens.

The only woman present there is Mariet. She is sitting by the table and constantly watching her father with her burning eyes. She shudders slightly at each loud word, at the sound of the door as it opens, at the noise of distant footsteps.

At night a fog came from the sea and covered the earth. And such perfect quiet reigns now that long-drawn tolling is heard in the distant lighthouse of the Holy Cross. Warning is thus given to the ships that have lost their way in the fog.

Some one in the corner says:

"Judging from the blow, it was not one of our people that killed him. Our people can't strike like that. He stuck the knife here, then slashed over there, and almost cut his head off."

"You can't do that with a dull knife!"

"No. You can't do it with a weak hand. I saw a murdered sailor on the wharf one day - he was cut up just like this."

Silence.

"And where is his mother?" asks some one, nodding at the curtain.

"Selly is taking care of her. Selly took her to her house."

An old fisherman quietly asks his neighbour:

"Who told you?"

"Francina woke me. Who told you, Marle?"

"Some one knocked on my window."

"Who knocked on your window?"

"I don't know."

Silence.

"How is it you don't know? Who was the first to see?"

"Some one passed by and noticed him."

"None of us passed by. There was nobody among us who passed by."

A fisherman seated at the other end, says:

"There was nobody among us who passed by. Tell us, Thomas."

Thomas takes out his pipe:

"I am a neighbour of Philipp's, of that man there - " he points at the curtain. "Yes, yes, you all know that I am his neighbour. And if anybody does not know it - I'll say it again, as in a court of justice: I am his neighbour - I live right next to him - " he turns to the window.

An elderly fisherman enters and forces himself silently into the line.

"Well, Tibo?" asks the abbot, stopping.

"Nothing."

"Haven't you found Haggart?"

"No. It is so foggy that they are afraid of losing themselves. They walk and call each other; some of them hold each other by the hand. Even a lantern can't be seen ten feet away."

The abbot lowers his head and resumes his pacing. The old fisherman speaks, without addressing any one in particular.

"There are many ships now staring helplessly in the sea."

"I walked like a blind man," says Tibo. "I heard the Holy Cross ringing. But it seems as if it changed its place. The sound comes from the left side."

"The fog is deceitful."

Old Desfoso says:

"This never happened here. Since Dugamel broke Jack's head with a shaft. That was thirty - forty years ago."

"What did you say, Desfoso?" the abbot stops.

"I say, since Dugamel broke Jack's head - "

"Yes, yes!" says the abbot, and resumes pacing the room.

"Then Dugamel threw himself into the sea from a rock and was dashed to death - that's how it happened. He threw himself down."

Mariet shudders and looks at the speaker with hatred. Silence.

"What did you say, Thomas?"

Thomas takes his pipe out of his mouth.

"Nothing. I only said that some one knocked at my window."

"You don't know who?"

"No. And you will never know. I came out, I looked - and there Philipp was sitting at his door. I wasn't surprised - Philipp often roamed about at night ever since - "

He stops irresolutely. Mariet asks harshly:

"Since when? You said 'since.'"

Silence. Desfoso replies frankly and heavily:

"Since your Haggart came. Go ahead, Thomas, tell us about it."

"So I said to him: 'Why did you knock, Philipp? Do you want anything?' But he was silent."

"And he was silent?"

"He was silent. 'If you don't want anything, you had better go to sleep, my friend,' said I. But he was silent. Then I looked at him - his throat was cut open."

Mariet shudders and looks at the speaker with aversion. Silence. Another fisherman enters, looks at the curtain and silently forces his way into the crowd. Women's voices are heard behind the door; the abbot stops.

"Eh, Lebon! Chase the women away," he says. "Tell them, there is nothing for them to do here."

Lebon goes out.

"Wait," the abbot stops. "Ask how the mother is feeling; Selly is taking care of her."

Desfoso says:

"You say, chase away the women, abbot? And your daughter? She is here."

The abbot looks at Mariet. She says:

"I am not going away from here."

Silence. The abbot paces the room again; he looks at the little ship fastened to the ceiling and asks:

"Who made it?"

All look at the little ship.

"He," answers Desfoso. "He made it when he wanted to go to

America as a sailor. He was always asking me how a three-masted brig is fitted out."

They look at the ship again, at its perfect little sails - at the little rags. Lebon returns.

"I don't know how to tell you about it, abbot. The women say that Haggart and his sailor are being led over here. The women are afraid."

Mariet shudders and looks at the door; the abbot pauses.

"Oho, it is daybreak already, the fog is turning blue!" says one fisherman to another, but his voice breaks off.

"Yes. Low tide has started," replies the other dully.

Silence. Then uneven footsteps resound. Several young fishermen with excited faces bring in Haggart, who is bound, and push Khorre in after him, also bound. Haggart is calm; as soon as the sailor was bound, something wildly free appeared in his movements, in his manners, in the sharpness of his swift glances.

One of the men who brought Haggart says to the abbot in a low voice:

"He was near the church. Ten times we passed by and saw no one, until he called: 'Aren't you looking for me?' It is so foggy, father."

The abbot shakes his head silently and sits down. Mariet smiles to her husband with her pale lips, but he does not look at her. Like all the others, he has fixed his eyes in amazement on the toy ship.

"Hello, Haggart," says the abbot.

"Hello, father."

"You call me father?"

"Yes, you."

"You are mistaken, Haggart. I am not your father."

The fishermen exchanged glances contentedly.

"Well, then. Hello, abbot," says Haggart with indifference, and resumes examining the little ship. Khorre mutters:

"That's the way, be firm, Noni."

"Who made this toy?" asks Haggart, but no one replies.

"Hello, Gart!" says Mariet, smiling. "It is I, your wife, Mariet. Let me untie your hands."

With a smile, pretending that she does not notice the stains of blood, she unfastens the ropes. All look at her in silence. Haggart also looks at her bent, alarmed head.

"Thank you," he says, straightening his hands.

"It would be a good thing to untie my hands, too," said Khorre, but there is no answer.

ABBOT - Haggart, did you kill Philipp?

HAGGART - I.

ABBOT - Do you mean to say - eh, you, Haggart - that you yourself killed him with your own hands? Perhaps you said to the sailor: "Sailor, go and kill Philipp," and he did it, for he loves you and respects you as his superior? Perhaps it happened that way! Tell me, Haggart. I called you my son, Haggart.

HAGGART - No, I did not order the sailor to do it. I killed Philipp with my own hand.

Silence.

KHORRE - Noni! Tell them to unfasten my hands and give me back my pipe.

"Don't be in a hurry," roars the priest. "Be bound awhile, drunkard! You had better be afraid of an untied rope - it may be formed into a noose."

But obeying a certain swift movement or glance of Haggart, Mariet walks over to the sailor and opens the knots of the rope. And again all look in silence upon her bent, alarmed head. Then they turn their eyes upon Haggart. Just as they looked at the little ship before, so they now look at him. And he, too, has forgotten about the toy. As if aroused from sleep, he surveys the fishermen, and stares long at the dark curtain.

ABBOT - Haggart, I am asking you. Who carried Philipp's body?

HAGGART - I. I brought it and put it near the door, his head against the door, his face against the sea. It was hard to set him that way, he was always falling down. But I did it.

ABBOT - Why did you do it?

HAGGART - I don't know exactly. I heard that Philipp has a mother, an old woman, and I thought this might please them better - both him and his mother.

ABBOT - (With restraint.) You are laughing at us?

HAGGART - No. What makes you think I am laughing? I am just as serious as you are. Did he - did Philipp make this little ship?

No one answers. Mariet, rising and bending over to Haggart across the table, says:

"Didn't you say this, Haggart: 'My poor boy, I killed you because I had to kill you, and now I am going to take you to your mother, my dear boy'?"

"These are very sad words. Who told them to you, Mariet?" asks Haggart, surprised.

"I heard them. And didn't you say further: 'Mother, I have brought you your son, and put him down at your door - take your boy, mother'?"

Haggart maintains silence.

"I don't know," roars the abbot bitterly. "I don't know; people don't kill here, and we don't know how it is done. Perhaps that is as it should be - to kill and then bring the murdered man to his mother's threshold. What are you gaping at, you scarecrow?"

Khorre replies rudely:

"According to my opinion, he should have thrown him into the sea. Your Haggart is out of his mind; I have said it long ago."

Suddenly old Desfoso shouts amid the loud approval of the others:

"Hold your tongue! We will send him to the city, but we will hang you like a cat ourselves, even if you did not kill him."

"Silence, old man, silence!" the abbot stops him, while Khorre looks over their heads with silent contempt. "Haggart, I am asking you, why did you take Philipp's life? He needed his life just as you need yours."

"He was Mariet's betrothed - and - "

"Well?"

"And - I don't want to speak. Why didn't you ask me before, when he was alive? Now I have killed him."

"But" - says the abbot, and there is a note of entreaty in his heavy voice. "But it may be that you are already repenting, Haggart? You are a splendid man, Gart. I know you; when you are sober you cannot hurt even a fly. Perhaps you were intoxicated - that happens with young people - and Philipp may have said something to you, and you - "

"No."

"No? Well, then, let it be no. Am I not right, children? But perhaps something strange came over you - it happens with people - suddenly a red mist will get into a man's head, the beast will begin to howl in his breast, and - In such cases one word is enough - "

"No, Philipp did not say anything to me. He passed along the road, when I jumped out from behind a large rock and stuck a knife into his throat. He had no time even to be scared. But if you like - " Haggart surveys the fishermen with his eyes irresolutely - "I feel a little sorry for him. That is, just a little. Did he make this toy?"

The abbot lowers his head sternly. And Desfoso shouts again, amidst sobs of approval from the others:

"No! Abbot, you better ask him what he was doing at the church. Dan saw them from the window. Wouldn't you tell us what you and your accursed sailor were doing at the church? What were you doing there? Speak."

Haggart looks at the speaker steadfastly and says slowly:

"I talked with the devil."

A muffled rumbling follows. The abbot jumps from his place and roars furiously:

"Then let him sit on your neck! Eh, Pierre, Jules, tie him down as fast as you can until morning. And the other one, too. And in the morning - in the morning, take him away to the city, to the Judges. I don't know their accursed city laws" - cries the abbot in despair - "but they will hang you, Haggart! You will dangle on a rope, Haggart!"

Khorre rudely pushes aside the young fisherman who comes over to him with a rope, and says to Desfoso in a low voice:

"It's an important matter, old man. Go away for a minute - he oughtn't to hear it," he nods at Haggart.

"I don't trust you."

"You needn't. That's nothing. Noni, there is a little matter here. Come, come, and don't be afraid. I have no knife."

The people step aside and whisper. Haggart is silently waiting to be bound, but no one comes over to him. All shudder when Mariet suddenly commences to speak:

"Perhaps you think that all this is just, father? Why, then, don't you ask me about it? I am his wife. Don't you believe that I am his wife? Then I will bring little Noni here. Do you want me to bring little Noni? He is sleeping, but I will wake him up. Once in his life he may wake up at night in order to say that this man whom you want to hang in the city is his father."

"Don't!" says Haggart.

"Very well," replies Mariet obediently. "He commands and I must obey - he is my husband. Let little Noni sleep. But I am not sleeping, I am here. Why, then, didn't you ask me: 'Mariet, how was it possible that your husband, Haggart, should kill Philipp'?"

Silence. Desfoso, who has returned and who is

agitated, decides:

"Let her speak. She is his wife."

"You will not believe, Desfoso," says Mariet, turning to the old fisherman with a tender and mournful smile. "Desfoso, you will not believe what strange and peculiar creatures we women are!"

Turning to all the people with the same smile, she continues:

"You will not believe what queer desires, what cunning, malicious little thoughts we women have. It was I who persuaded my husband to kill Philipp. Yes, yes - he did not want to do it, but I urged him; I cried so much and threatened him, so he consented. Men always give in - isn't that true, Desfoso?"

Haggart looks at his wife in a state of great perplexity, his eyebrows brought close to each other. Mariet continues, without looking at him, still smiling as before:

"You will ask me, why I wanted Philipp's death? Yes, yes, you will ask this question, I know it. He never did me any harm, that poor Philipp, isn't that true? Then I will tell you: He was my betrothed. I don't know whether you will be able to understand me. You, old Desfoso - you would not kill the girl you kissed one day? Of course not. But we women are such strange creatures - you can't even imagine what strange, suspicious, peculiar creatures we are. Philipp was my betrothed, and he kissed me - "

She wipes her mouth and continues, laughing:

"Here I am wiping my mouth even now. You have all seen how I wiped my mouth. I am wiping away Philipp's kisses. You are laughing. But ask your wife, Desfoso - does she want the life of the man who kissed her before you? Ask all women who love - even the old women! We never grow old in love.

We are born so, we women."

Haggart almost believes her. Advancing a step forward, he asks:

"You urged me? Perhaps it is true, Mariet - I don't remember."

Mariet laughs.

"Do you hear? He has forgotten. Go on, Gart. You may say that it was your own idea? That's the way you men are - you forget everything. Will you say perhaps that I - "

"Mariet!" Haggart interrupts her threateningly.

Mariet, turning pale, looking sorrowfully at his terrible eyes which are now steadfastly fixed upon her, continues, still smiling:

"Go on, Gart! Will you say perhaps that I - Will you say perhaps that I dissuaded you? That would be funny - "

HAGGART - No, I will not say that. You lie, Mariet! Even I, Haggart - just think of it, people - even I believed her, so cleverly does this woman lie.

MARIET - Go - on - Haggart.

HAGGART - You are laughing? Abbot, I don't want to be the husband of your daughter - she lies.

ABBOT - You are worse than the devil, Gart! That's what I say - You are worse than the devil, Gart!

HAGGART - You are all foolish people! I don't understand you; I don't know now what to do with you. Shall I laugh? Shall I be angry? Shall I cry? You want to let me go - why, then, don't you let me go? You are sorry for Philipp. Well, then, kill me - I have told you that it was I who killed the boy. Am I disputing? But you are making grimaces like monkeys that have found bananas - or have you such a game in your land? Then I don't want to play it. And you, abbot, you are like a juggler in the marketplace. In one hand you have truth and in the other hand you have truth, and you are forever performing tricks. And now she is lying - she lies so well that my heart contracts with belief. Oh, she is doing it well!

And he laughs bitterly.

MARIET - Forgive me, Gart.

HAGGART - When I wanted to kill him, she hung on my hand like a rock, and now she says that she killed him. She steals from me this murder; she does not know that one has to earn that, too! Oh, there are queer people in your land!

"I wanted to deceive them, not you, Gart. I wanted to save you," says Mariet.

Haggart replies:

"My father taught me: 'Eh, Noni, beware! There is one truth and one law for all - for the sun, for the wind, for the waves, for the beasts - and only for man there is another truth. Beware of this truth of man, Noni!' so said my father. Perhaps this is your truth? Then I am not afraid of it, but I feel very sad and very embittered. Mariet, if you sharpened my knife and said: 'Go and kill that man' - it may be that I would not have cared to kill him. 'What is the use of cutting down a withered tree?' - I would have said. But now - farewell, Mariet! Well, bind me and take me to the city."

He waits haughtily, but no one approaches him. Mariet has lowered her head upon her hands, her shoulders are twitching. The abbot is also absorbed in thought, his large head lowered. Desfoso is carrying on a heated conversation in whispers with the fishermen. Khorre steps forward and speaks, glancing at Haggart askance:

"I had a little talk with them, Noni - they are all right, they are good fellows, Noni. Only the priest - but he is a good man, too - am I right, Noni? Don't look so crossly at me, or I'll mix up the whole thing! You see, kind people, it's this way: this man, Haggart, and I have saved up a little sum of money, a little barrel of gold. We don't need it, Noni, do we? Perhaps you will take it for yourselves? What do you think? Shall we give them the gold, Noni? You see, here I've entangled myself already."

He winks slyly at Mariet, who has now lifted her head.

"What are you prating there, you scarecrow?" asks the abbot.

Khorre continues:

"Here it goes, Noni; I am straightening it out little by little! But where have we buried it, the barrel? Do you remember, Noni? I have forgotten. They say it's from the gin, kind people; they say that one's memory fails from too much gin. I am a drunkard, that's true."

"If you are not inventing - then you had better choke yourself with your gold, you dog!" says the abbot.

HAGGART - Khorre!

KHORRE - Yes.

HAGGART - To-morrow you will get a hundred lashes. Abbot, order a hundred lashes for him!

ABBOT - With pleasure, my son. With pleasure.

The movements of the fishermen are just as slow and languid, but there is something new in their increased puffing and pulling at their pipes, in the light quiver of their tanned hands. Some of them arise and look out of the window with feigned indifference.

"The fog is rising!" says one, looking out of the window. "Do you hear what I said about the fog?"

"It's time to go to sleep. I say, it's time to go to sleep!"

Desfoso comes forward and speaks cautiously:

"That isn't quite so, abbot. It seems you didn't say exactly what you ought to say, abbot. They seem to think differently. I don't say anything for myself - I am simply talking about them. What do you say, Thomas?"

THOMAS - We ought to go to sleep, I say. Isn't it true that it is time to go to sleep?

MARIET (softly) - Sit down, Gart. You are tired to-night. You don't answer?

An old fisherman says:

"There used to be a custom in our land, I heard, that a murderer was to pay a fine for the man he killed. Have you heard about it, Desfoso?"

Another voice is heard:

"Philipp is dead. Philipp is dead already, do you hear, neighbour? Who is going to support his mother?"

"I haven't enough even for my own! And the fog is rising, neighbour."

"Abbot, did you hear us say: 'Gart is a bad man; Gart is a good-for-nothing, a city trickster?' No, we said: 'This thing has never happened here before,'" says Desfoso.

Then a determined voice remarks:

"Gart is a good man! Wild Gart is a good man!"

DESFOSO - If you looked around, abbot, you couldn't find a single, strong boat here. I haven't enough tar for mine. And the church - is that the way a good church ought to look? I am not saying it myself, but it comes out that way - it can't be helped, abbot.

Haggart turns to Mariet and says:

"Do you hear, woman?"

"I do."

"Why don't you spit into their faces?"

"I can't. I love you, Haggart. Are there only ten Commandments of God? No, there is still another: 'I love you, Haggart.'"

"What sad dreams there are in your land."

The abbot rises and walks over to the fishermen.

"Well, what did you say about the church, old man? You said something interesting about the church, or was I mistaken?"

He casts a swift glance at Mariet and Haggart.

"It isn't the church alone, abbot. There are four of us old men: Legran, Stoffle, Puasar, Kornu, and seven old women. Do I say that we are not going to feed them? Of course, we will, but don't be angry, father - it is hard! You know it yourself, abbot - old age is no fun."

"I am an old man, too!" begins old Rikke, lisping, but suddenly he flings his hat angrily to the ground. "Yes, I am an old man. I don't want any more, that's all! I worked, and now I don't want to work. That's all! I don't want to work."

He goes out, swinging his hand. All look sympathetically at his stooping back, at his white tufts of hair. And then they look again at Desfoso, at his mouth, from which their words come out. A voice says:

"There, Rikke doesn't want to work any more."

All laugh softly and forcedly.

"Suppose we send Gart to the city - what then?" Desfoso goes on, without looking at Haggart. "Well, the city people will hang him - and then what? The result will be that a man will be gone, a fisherman will be gone - you will lose a son, and Mariet will lose her husband, and the little boy his father. Is there any joy in that?"

"That's right, that's right!" nods the abbot, approvingly. "But what a mind you have, Desfoso!"

"Do you pay attention to them, Abbot?" asked Haggart.

"Yes, I do, Haggart. And it wouldn't do you any harm to pay attention to them. The devil is prouder than you, and yet he is only the devil, and nothing more."

Desfoso affirms:

"What's the use of pride? Pride isn't necessary."

He turns to Haggart, his eyes still lowered; then he lifts his eyes and asks:

"Gart! But you don't need to kill anybody else. Excepting Philipp, you don't feel like killing anybody else, do you?"

"No."

"Only Philipp, and no more? Do you hear? Only Philipp, and no more. And another question - Gart, don't you want to send away this man, Khorre? We would like you to do it. Who knows him? People say that all this trouble comes through him."

Several voices are heard:

"Through him. Send him away, Gart! It will be better for him!"

The abbot upholds them.

"True!"

"You, too, priest!" says Khorre, gruffly. Haggart looks with a faint smile at his angry, bristled face, and says:

"I rather feel like sending him away. Let him go."

"Well, then, Abbot," says Desfoso, turning around, "we have decided, in accordance with our conscience - to take the money. Do I speak properly?"

One voice answers for all:

"Yes."

DESFOSO - Well, sailor, where is the money?

KHORRE - Captain?

HAGGART - Give it to them.

KHORRE (rudely) - Then give me back my knife and my pipe first! Who is the eldest among you - you? Listen, then: Take crowbars and shovels and go to the castle. Do you know the tower, the accursed tower that fell? Go over there - "

He bends down and draws a map on the floor with his crooked finger. All bend down and look attentively; only the abbot gazes sternly out of the window, behind which the heavy fog is still grey. Haggart whispers in a fit of rage:

"Mariet, it would have been better if you had killed me as I killed Philipp. And now my father is calling me. Where will be the end of my sorrow, Mariet? Where the end of the world is. And where is the end of the world? Do you want to take my sorrow, Mariet?"

"I do, Haggart."

"No, you are a woman."

"Why do you torture me, Gart? What have I done that you should torture me so? I love you."

"You lied."

"My tongue lied. I love you."

"A serpent has a double tongue, but ask the serpent what it wants - and it will tell you the truth. It is your heart that lied. Was it not you, girl, that I met that time on the road? And you said: 'Good evening.' How you have deceived me!"

Desfoso asks loudly:

"Well, abbot? You are coming along with us, aren't you, father. Otherwise something wrong might come out of it. Do I speak properly?"

The abbot replies merrily:

"Of course, of course, children. I am going with you. Without me, you will think of the church. I have just been thinking of the church - of the kind of church you need. Oh, it's hard to get along with you, people!"

The fishermen go out very slowly - they are purposely lingering.

"The sea is coming," says one. "I can hear it."

"Yes, yes, the sea is coming! Did you understand what he said?"

The few who remained are more hasty in their movements. Some of them politely bid Haggart farewell.

"Good-bye, Gart."

"I am thinking, Haggart, what kind of a church we need. This one will not do, it seems. They prayed here a hundred years; now it is no good, they say. Well, then, it is necessary to have a new one, a better one. But what shall it be?"

"'Pope's a rogue, Pope's a rogue.' But, then, I am a rogue, too. Don't you think, Gart, that I am also something of a rogue? One moment, children, I am with you."

There is some crowding in the doorway. The abbot follows the last man with his eyes and roars angrily:

"Eh, you, Haggart, murderer! What are you smiling at? You have no right to despise them like that. They are my children. They have worked - have you seen their hands, their backs? If you haven't noticed that, you are a fool! They are tired. They want to rest. Let them rest, even at the cost of the blood of the one you killed. I'll give them each a little, and the rest I will throw out into the sea. Do you hear, Haggart?"

"I hear, priest."

The abbot exclaims, raising his arms:

"O Lord! Why have you made a heart that can have pity on both the murdered and the murderer! Gart, go home. Take him home, Mariet, and wash his hands!"

"To whom do you lie, priest?" asks Haggart, slowly. "To God

or to the devil? To yourself or to the people? Or to everybody?"

He laughs bitterly.

"Eh, Gart! You are drunk with blood."

"And with what are you drunk?"

They face each other. Mariet cries angrily, placing herself between them:

"May a thunder strike you down, both of you, that's what I am praying to God. May a thunder strike you down! What are you doing with my heart? You are tearing it with your teeth like greedy dogs. You didn't drink enough blood, Gart, drink mine, then! You will never have enough, Gart, isn't that true?"

"Now, now," says the abbot, calming them. "Take him home, Mariet. Go home, Gart, and sleep more."

Mariet comes forward, goes to the door and pauses there.

"Gart! I am going to little Noni."

"Go."

"Are you coming along with me?"

"Yes - no - later."

"I am going to little Noni. What shall I tell him about his father when he wakes up?"

Haggart is silent. Khorre comes back and stops irresolutely at the threshold. Mariet casts at him a glance full of contempt and then goes out. Silence.

"Khorre!"

"Yes."

"Gin!"

"Here it is, Noni. Drink it, my boy, but not all at once, not all at once, Noni."

Haggart drinks; he examines the room with a smile.

"Nobody. Did you see him, Khorre? He is there, behind the curtain. Just think of it, sailor - here we are again with him alone."

"Go home, Noni!"

"Right away. Give me some gin."

He drinks.

"And they? They have gone?"

"They ran, Noni. Go home, my boy! They ran off like goats. I was laughing so much, Noni."

Both laugh.

"Take down that toy, Khorre. Yes, yes, a little ship. He made it, Khorre."

They examine the toy.

"Look how skilfully the jib was made, Khorre. Good boy, Philipp! But the halyards are bad, look. No, Philipp! You never saw how real ships are fitted out - real ships which rove over the ocean, tearing its grey waves. Was it with this toy that you wanted to quench your little thirst - fool?"

He throws down the little ship and rises:

"Khorre! Boatswain!"

"Yes."

"Call them! I assume command again, Khorre!"

The sailor turns pale and shouts enthusiastically:

"Noni! Captain! My knees are trembling. I will not be able to reach them and I will fall on the way."

"You will reach them! We must also take our money away from these people - what do you think, Khorre? We have played a little, and now it is enough - what do you think, Khorre?"

He laughs. The sailor looks at him, his hands folded as in prayer, and he weeps.

CHAPTER VII

"These are your comrades, Haggart? I am so glad to see them. You said, Gart, yes - you said that their faces were entirely different from the faces of our people, and that is true. Oh, how true it is! Our people have handsome faces, too - don't think our fishermen are ugly, but they haven't these deep, terrible sears. I like them very much, I assure you, Gart. I suppose you are a friend of Haggart's - you have such stern, fine eyes? But you are silent? Why are they silent, Haggart; did you forbid them to speak? And why are you silent yourself, Haggart? Haggart!"

Illuminated by the light of torches, Haggart stands and listens to the rapid, agitated speech. The metal of the guns and the uniforms vibrates and flashes; the light is also playing on the faces of those who have surrounded Haggart in a close circle - these are his nearest, his friends. And in the distance there is a different game - there a large ship is dancing silently, casting its light upon the black waves, and the black water plays with them, pleating them like a braid, extinguishing them and kindling them again.

A noisy conversation and the splashing of the waters - and the dreadful silence of kindred human lips that are sealed.

"I am listening to you, Mariet," says Haggart at last. "What do you want, Mariet? It is impossible that some one should have offended you. I ordered them not to touch your house."

"Oh, no, Haggart, no! No one has offended me!" exclaimed Mariet cheerfully. "But don't you like me to hold little Noni in my arms? Then I will put him down here among the rocks. Here he will be warm and comfortable as in his cradle. That's the way! Don't be afraid of waking him, Gart; he sleeps soundly and will not hear anything. You may shout, sing, fire a pistol - the boy sleeps soundly."

"What do you want, Mariet? I did not call you here, and I am not pleased that you have come."

"Of course, you did not call me here, Haggart; of course, you didn't. But when the fire was started, I thought: 'Now it will light the way for me to walk. Now I will not stumble.' And I went. Your friends will not be offended, Haggart, if I will ask them to step aside for awhile? I have something to tell you, Gart. Of course, I should have done that before, I understand, Gart; but I only just recalled it now. It was so light to walk!"

Haggart says sternly:

"Step aside, Flerio, and you all - step aside with him."

They all step aside.

"What is it that you have recalled, Mariet? Speak! I am going away forever from your mournful land, where one dreams such painful dreams, where even the rocks dream of sorrow. And I have forgotten everything."

Gently and submissively, seeking protection and kindness, the woman presses close to his hand.

"O, Haggart! O, my dear Haggart! They are not offended because I asked them so rudely to step aside, are they? O, my dear Haggart! The galloons of your uniform scratched my cheek, but it is so pleasant. Do you know, I never liked it when you wore the clothes of our fishermen - it was not becoming to you, Haggart. But I am talking nonsense, and you are getting angry, Gart. Forgive me!"

"Don't kneel. Get up."

"It was only for a moment. Here, I got up. You ask me what I want? This is what I want: Take me with you, Haggart! Me and little Noni, Haggart!"

Haggart retreats.

"You say that, Mariet? You say that I should take you along? Perhaps you are laughing, woman? Or am I dreaming again?"

"Yes, I say that: Take me with you. Is this your ship? How large and beautiful it is, and it has black sails, I know it. Take me on your ship, Haggart. I know, you will say: 'We have no women on the ship,' but I will be the woman: I will be your soul. Haggart, I will be your song, your thoughts, Haggart! And if it must be so, let Khorre give gin to little Noni - he is a strong boy."

"Eh, Mariet?" says Haggart sternly. "Do you perhaps want me to believe you again? Eh, Mariet? Don't talk of that which you do not know, woman. Are the rocks perhaps casting a spell over me and turning my head? Do you hear the noise, and something like voices? That is the sea, waiting for me. Don't hold my soul. Let it go, Mariet."

"Don't speak, Haggart! I know everything. It was not as though I came along a fiery road, it was not as though I saw blood to-day. Be silent, Haggart! I have seen something more terrible, Haggart! Oh, if you could only understand me! I have seen cowardly people who ran without defending themselves. I have seen clutching, greedy fingers, crooked like those of birds, like those of birds, Haggart! And out of these fingers, which were forced open, gold was taken. And suddenly I saw a man sobbing. Think of it, Haggart! They were taking gold from him, and he was sobbing."

She laughs bitterly. Haggart advances a step toward her and puts his heavy hand upon her shoulder:

"Yes, yes, Mariet. Speak on, girl, let the sea wait."

Mariet removes his hand and continues:

"'No,' I thought. 'These are not my brethren at all!' I thought and laughed. And father shouted to the cowards: 'Take shafts and strike them.' But they were running. Father is such a splendid man."

"Father is a splendid man," Haggart affirms cheerfully.

"Such a splendid man! And then one sailor bent down close to Noni - perhaps he did not want to do any harm to him, but he bent down to him too closely, so, I fired at him from your pistol. Is it nothing that I fired at our sailor?"

Haggart laughs:

"He had a comical face! You killed him, Mariet."

"No. I don't know how to shoot. And it was he who told me where you were. O Haggart, O brother!"

She sobs, and then she speaks angrily with a shade of a serpentine hiss in her voice:

"I hate them! They were not tortured enough; I would have tortured them still more, still more. Oh, what cowardly rascals they are! Listen, Haggart, I was always afraid of your power - to me there was always something terrible and incomprehensible in your power. 'Where is his God?' I wondered, and I was terrified. Even this morning I was afraid, but now that this night came, this terror has fled, and I came running to you over the fiery road: I am going with you, Haggart. Take me, Haggart, I will be the soul of your ship!"

"I am the soul of my ship, Mariet. But you will be the song of my liberated soul, Mariet. You shall be the song of my ship, Mariet! Do you know where we are going? We are going to look for the end of the world, for unknown lands, for unknown monsters. And at night Father Ocean will sing to us, Mariet!"

"Embrace me, Haggart. Ah, Haggart, he is not a God who makes cowards of human beings. We shall go to look for a new God."

Haggart whispers stormily:

"I lied when I said that I have forgotten everything - I learned this in your land. I love you, Mariet, as I love fire. Eh, Flerio, comrade!" He shouts cheerfully: "Eh, Flerio, comrade! Have you prepared a salute?"

"I have, Captain. The shores will tremble when our cannons speak."

"Eh, Flerio, comrade! Don't gnash your teeth, without biting - no one will believe you. Did you put in cannon balls - round, east-iron, good cannon balls? Give them wings, comrade - let them fly like blackbirds on land and sea."

"Yes, Captain."

Haggart laughs:

"I love to think how the cannon ball flies, Mariet. I love to watch its invisible flight. If some one comes in its way - let him! Fate itself strikes down like that. What is an aim? Only fools need an aim, while the devil, closing his eyes, throws stones - the wise game is merrier this way. But you are silent! What are you thinking of, Mariet?"

"I am thinking of them. I am forever thinking of them."

"Are you sorry for them?" Haggart frowns.

"Yes, I am sorry for them. But my pity is my hatred, Haggart. I hate them, and I would kill them, more and more!"

"I feel like flying faster - my soul is so free. Let us jest, Mariet! Here is a riddle, guess it: For whom will the cannons roar soon? You think, for me? No. For you? no, no, not for you, Mariet! For little Noni, for him - for little Noni who is boarding the ship to-night. Let him wake up from this thunder. How our little Noni will be surprised! And now be quiet, quiet - don't disturb his sleep - don't spoil little Noni's awakening."

The sound of voices is heard - a crowd is approaching.

"Where is the captain?"

"Here. Halt, the captain is here!"

"It's all done. They can be crammed into a basket like herrings."

"Our boatswain is a brave fellow! A jolly man."

Khorre, intoxicated and jolly, shouts:

"Not so loud, devils! Don't you see that the captain is here? They scream like seagulls over a dead dolphin."

Mariet steps aside a little distance, where little Noni is sleeping.

KHORRE - Here we are, Captain. No losses, Captain. And how we laughed, Noni.

HAGGART - You got drunk rather early. Come to the point.

KHORRE - Very well. The thing is done, Captain. We've picked up all our money - not worse than the imperial tax collectors. I could not tell which was ours, so I picked up all the money. But if they have buried some of the gold, forgive us, Captain - we are not peasants to plough the ground.

Laughter. Haggart also laughs.

"Let them sow, we shall reap."

"Golden words, Noni. Eh, Tommy, listen to what the Captain is saying. And another thing: Whether you will be angry or not - I have broken the music. I have scattered it in small pieces. Show your pipe, Tetyu! Do you see, Noni, I didn't do it at once, no. I told him to play a jig, and he said that he couldn't do it. Then he lost his mind and ran away. They all lost their minds there, Captain. Eh, Tommy, show your beard. An old woman tore half of his beard out, Captain - now he is a disgrace to look upon. Eh, Tommy! He has hidden himself, he's ashamed to show his face, Captain. And there's another thing: The priest is coming here."

Mariet exclaims:

"Father!"

Khorre, astonished, asks:

"Are you here? If she came to complain, I must report to you, Captain - the priest almost killed one of our sailors. And she, too. I ordered the men to bind the priest - "

"Silence."

"I don't understand your actions, Noni - "

Haggart, restraining his rage, exclaims:

"I shall have you put in irons! Silence!"

With ever-growing rage:

"You dare talk back to me, riff-raff! You - "

Mariet cautions him:

"Gart! They have brought father here."

Several sailors bring in the abbot, bound. His clothes are in disorder, his face is agitated and pale. He looks at Mariet with some amazement, and lowers his eyes. Then he heaves a sigh.

"Untie him!" says Mariet. Haggart corrects her restrainedly:

"Only I command here, Mariet. Khorre, untie him."

Khorre unfastens the knots. Silence.

ABBOT - Hello, Haggart.

"Hello, abbot."

"You have arranged a fine night, Haggart!"

Haggart speaks with restraint:

"It is unpleasant for me to see you. Why did you come here? Go home, priest, no one will touch you. Keep on fishing - and what else were you doing? Oh, yes - make your own prayers. We are going out to the ocean; your daughter, you know, is also going with me. Do you see the ship? That is mine. It's a pity that you don't know about ships - you would have laughed for joy at the sight of such a beautiful ship! Why is he silent, Mariet? You had better tell him."

ABBOT - Prayers? In what language? Have you, perhaps, discovered a new language in which prayers reach God? Oh, Haggart, Haggart!

He weeps, covering his face with his hands. Haggart, alarmed, asks:

"You are crying, abbot?"

"Look, Gart, he is crying. Father never cried. I am afraid, Gart."

The abbot stops crying. Heaving a deep sigh, he says:

"I don't know what they call you: Haggart or devil or something else - I have come to you with a request. Do you hear, robber, with a request? Tell your crew not to gnash their teeth like that - I don't like it."

Haggart replies morosely:

"Go home, priest! Mariet will stay with me."

"Let her stay with you. I don't need her, and if you need her, take her. Take her, Haggart. But - "

He kneels before him. A murmur of astonishment. Mariet, frightened, advances a step to her father.

"Father! You are kneeling?"

ABBOT - Robber! Give us back the money. You will rob more for yourself, but give this money to us. You are young yet, you will rob some more yet -

HAGGART - You are insane! There's a man - he will drive the devil himself to despair! Listen, priest, I am shouting to you: You have simply lost your mind!

The abbot, still kneeling, continues:

"Perhaps, I have - by God, I don't know. Robber, dearest, what is this to you? Give us this money. I feel sorry for them, for the scoundrels! They rejoiced so much, the scoundrels. They blossomed forth like an old blackthorn which has nothing but thorns and a ragged bark. They are sinners. But am I imploring God for their sake? I am imploring you. Robber, dearest - "

Mariet looks now at Haggart, now at the priest. Haggart is hesitating. The abbot keeps muttering:

"Robber, do you want me to call you son? Well, then - son - it makes no difference now - I will never see you again. It's all the same! Like an old blackthorn, they bloomed - oh, Lord, those scoundrels, those old scoundrels!"

"No," Haggart replied sternly.

"Then you are the devil, that's who you are. You are the devil," mutters the abbot, rising heavily from the ground. Haggart shows his teeth, enraged.

"Do you wish to sell your soul to the devil? Yes? Eh, abbot - don't you know yet that the devil always pays with spurious money? Let me have a torch, sailor!"

He seizes a torch and lifts it high over his head - he covers his terrible face with fire and smoke.

"Look, here I am! Do you see? Now ask me, if you dare!"

He flings the torch away. What does the abbot dream in this land full of monstrous dreams? Terrified, his heavy frame trembling, helplessly pushing the people aside with his hands, he retreats. He turns around. Now he sees the glitter of the metal, the dark and terrible faces; he hears the angry splashing of the waters - and he covers his head with his hands and walks off quickly. Then Khorre jumps up and strikes him with a knife in his back.

"Why have you done it?" - the abbot clutches the hand that struck him down.

"Just so - for nothing!"

The abbot falls to the ground and dies.

"Why have you done it?" cries Mariet.

"Why have you done it?" roars Haggart.

And a strange voice, coming from some unknown depths, answers with Khorre's lips:

"You commanded me to do it."

Haggart looks around and sees the stern, dark faces, the quivering glitter of the metal, the motionless body; he hears the mysterious, merry dashing of the waves. And he clasps his head in a fit of terror.

"Who commanded? It was the roaring of the sea. I did not want to kill him - no, no!"

Sombre voices answer:

"You commanded. We heard it. You commanded."

Haggart listens, his head thrown back. Suddenly he bursts into loud laughter:

"Oh, devils, devils! Do you think that I have two ears in order that you may lie in each one? Go down on your knees, rascal!"

He hurls Khorre to the ground.

"String him up with a rope! I would have crushed your venomous head myself - but let them do it. Oh, devils, devils! String him up with a rope."

Khorre whines harshly:

"Me, Captain! I was your nurse, Noni."

"Silence! Rascal!"

"I? Noni! Your nurse? You squealed like a little pig in the cook's room. Have you forgotten it, Noni?" mutters the sailor plaintively.

"Eh," shouts Haggart to the stern crowd. "Take him!"

Several men advance to him. Khorre rises.

"If you do it to me, to your own nurse - then you have recovered, Noni! Eh, obey the captain! Take me! I'll make you cry enough, Tommy! You are always the mischief-maker!"

Grim laughter. Several sailors surround Khorre as Haggart watches them sternly. A dissatisfied voice says:

"There is no place where to hang him here. There isn't a single tree around."

"Let us wait till we get aboard ship! Let him die honestly on the mast."

"I know of a tree around here, but I won't tell you," roars Khorre hoarsely. "Look for it yourself! Well, you have astonished me, Noni. How you shouted, 'String him up with a rope!' Exactly like your father - he almost hanged me, too. Good-bye, Noni, now I understand your actions. Eh, gin! and then - on the rope!"

Khorre goes off. No one dares approach Haggart; still enraged, he paces back and forth with long strides. He pauses, glances at the body and paces again. Then he calls:

"Flerio! Did you hear me give orders to kill this man?"

"No, Captain."

"You may go."

He paces back and forth again, and then calls:

"Flerio! Have you ever heard the sea lying?"

"No."

"If they can't find a tree, order them to choke him with their hands."

He paces back and forth again. Mariet is laughing quietly.

"Who is laughing?" asks Haggart in fury.

"I," answers Mariet. "I am thinking of how they are hanging him and I am laughing. O, Haggart, O, my noble Haggart! Your wrath is the wrath of God, do you know it? No. You are strange, you are dear, you are terrible, Haggart, but I am not afraid of you. Give me your hand, Haggart, press it firmly, firmly. Here is a powerful hand!"

"Flerio, my friend, did you hear what he said? He says the sea never lies."

"You are powerful and you are just - I was insane when I feared your power, Gart. May I shout to the sea: 'Haggart, the Just'?"

"That is not true. Be silent, Mariet, you are intoxicated with blood. I don't know what justice is."

"Who, then, knows it? You, you, Haggart! You are God's justice, Haggart. Is it true that he was your nurse? Oh, I know what it means to be a nurse; a nurse feeds you, teaches you to walk - you love a nurse as your mother. Isn't that true, Gart - you love a nurse as a mother? And yet - 'string him up with a rope, Khorre'!"

She laughs quietly.

A loud, ringing laughter resounds from the side where Khorre was led away. Haggart stops, perplexed.

"What is it?"

"The devil is meeting his soul there," says Mariet.

"No. Let go of my hand! Eh, who's there?"

A crowd is coming. They are laughing and grinning, showing their teeth. But noticing the captain, they become serious. The people are repeating one and the same name:

"Khorre! Khorre! Khorre!"

And then Khorre himself appears, dishevelled, crushed, but happy - the rope has broken. Knitting his brow, Haggart is waiting in silence.

"The rope broke, Noni," mutters Khorre hoarsely, modestly, yet with dignity. "There are the ends! Eh, you there, keep quiet! There is nothing to laugh at - they started to hang me, and the rope broke, Noni."

Haggart looks at his old, drunken, frightened, and happy face, and he laughs like a madman. And the sailors respond with roaring laughter. The reflected lights are dancing more merrily upon the waves - as if they are also laughing with the people.

"Just look at him, Mariet, what a face he has," Haggart is almost choking with laughter. "Are you happy? Speak - are you happy? Look, Mariet, what a happy face he has! The rope broke - that's very strong - it is stronger even than what I said: 'String him up with a rope.' Who said it? Don't you know, Khorre? You are out of your wits, and you don't know anything - well, never mind, you needn't know. Eh, give him gin! I am glad, very glad that you are not altogether through with your gin. Drink, Khorre!"

Voices shout:

"Gin!"

"Eh, the boatswain wants a drink! Gin!"

Khorre drinks it with dignity, amid laughter and shouts of approval. Suddenly all the noise dies down and a sombre silence reigns - a woman's strange voice drowns the noise - so strange and unfamiliar, as if it were not Mariet's voice at all, but another voice speaking with her lips:

"Haggart! You have pardoned him, Haggart?"

Some of the people look at the body; those standing near it step aside. Haggart asks, surprised:

"Whose voice is that? Is that yours, Mariet? How strange! I did not recognise your voice."

"You have pardoned him, Haggart?"

"You have heard - the rope broke - "

"Tell me, did you pardon the murderer? I want to hear your voice, Haggart."

A threatening voice is heard from among the crowd:

"The rope broke. Who is talking there? The rope broke."

"Silence!" exclaims Haggart, but there is no longer the same commanding tone in his voice. "Take them all away! Boatswain! Whistle for everybody to go aboard. The time is up! Flerio! Get the boats ready."

"Yes, yes."

Khorre whistles. The sailors disperse unwillingly, and the same threatening voice sounds somewhere from the darkness:

"I thought at first it was the dead man who started to speak. But I would have answered him too: 'Lie there! The rope broke.'"

Another voice replies:

"Don't grumble. Khorre has stronger defenders than you are."

"What are you prating about, devils?" says Khorre. "Silence! Is that you, Tommy? I know you, you are always the mischief-maker - "

"Come on, Mariet!" says Haggart. "Give me little Noni, I want to carry him to the boat myself. Come on, Mariet."

"Where, Haggart?"

"Eh, Mariet! The dreams are ended. I don't like your voice, woman - when did you find time to change it? What a land of jugglers! I have never seen such a land before!"

"Eh, Haggart! The dreams are ended. I don't like your voice, either - little Haggart! But it may be that I am still sleeping - then wake me. Haggart, swear that it was you who said it: 'The rope broke.' Swear that my eyes have not grown blind and that they see Khorre alive. Swear that this is your hand, Haggart!"

Silence. The voice of the sea is growing louder - there is the splash and the call and the promise of a stern caress.

"I swear."

Silence. Khorre and Flerio come up to Haggart.

"All's ready, Captain," says Flerio.

"They are waiting, Noni. Go quicker! They want to feast to-night, Noni! But I must tell you, Noni, that they - "

HAGGART - Did you say something, Flerio? Yes, yes, everything is ready. I am coming. I think I am not quite through yet with land. This is such a remarkable land, Flerio; the dreams here drive their claws into a man like thorns, and they hold him. One has to tear his clothing, and perhaps his body as well. What did you say, Mariet?

MARIET - Don't you want to kiss little Noni? You shall never kiss him again.

"No, I don't want to."

Silence.

"You will go alone."

"Yes, I will go alone."

"Did you ever cry, Haggart?"

"No."

"Who is crying now? I hear some one crying bitterly."

"That is not true - it is the roaring of the sea."

"Oh, Haggart! Of what great sorrow does that voice speak?"

"Be silent, Mariet. It is the roaring of the sea."

Silence.

"Is everything ended now, Haggart?"

"Everything is ended, Mariet."

Mariet, imploring, says:

"Gart! Only one motion of the hand! Right here - against the heart - Gart!"

"No. Leave me alone."

"Only one motion of the hand! Here is your knife. Have pity on me, kill me with your hand. Only one motion of your hand, Gart!"

"Let go. Give me my knife."

"Gart, I bless you! One motion of your hand, Gart!"

Haggart tears himself away, pushing the woman aside:

"No! Don't you know that it is just as hard to make one motion of the hand as it is for the sun to come down from the sky? Good-bye, Mariet!"

"You are going away?"

"Yes, I am going away. I am going away, Mariet. That's how it sounds."

"I shall curse you, Haggart. Do you know! I shall curse you, Haggart. And little Noni will curse you, Haggart - Haggart!"

Haggart exclaims cheerfully and harshly:

"Eh, Khorre. You, Flerio, my old friend. Come here, give me your hand - Oh, what a powerful hand it is! Why do you pull me by the sleeve, Khorre? You have such a funny face. I can almost see how the rope snapped, and you came down like a sack. Flerio, old friend, I feel like saying something funny, but I have forgotten how to say it. How do they say it? Remind me, Flerio. What do you want, sailor?"

Khorre whispers to him hoarsely:

"Noni, be on your guard. The rope broke because they used a rotten rope intentionally. They are betraying you! Be on your guard, Noni. Strike them on the head, Noni."

Haggart bursts out laughing.

"Now you have said something funny. And I? Listen, Flerio, old friend. This woman who stands and looks - No, that will not be funny!"

He advances a step.

"Khorre, do you remember how well this man prayed? Why was he killed? He prayed so well. But there is one prayer he did not know - this one - 'To you I bring my great eternal sorrow; I am going to you, Father Ocean!'"

And a distant voice, sad and grave, replies:

"Oh, Haggart, my dear Haggart."

But who knows - perhaps it was the roaring of the waves. Many sad and strange dreams come to man on earth.

"All aboard!" exclaims Haggart cheerily, and goes off without looking around. Below, a gay noise of voices and laughter resounds. The cobblestones are rattling under the firm footsteps - Haggart is going away.

"Haggart!"

He goes, without turning around.

"Haggart!"

He has gone away.

Loud shouting is heard - the sailors are greeting Haggart. They drink and go off into the darkness. On the shore, the torches which were cast aside are burning low, illumining the body, and a woman is rushing about. She runs swiftly from one spot to another, bending down over the steep rocks. Insane Dan comes crawling out.

"Is that you, Dan? Do you hear, they are singing, Dan? Haggart has gone away."

"I was waiting for them to go. Here is another one. I am gathering the pipes of my organ. Here is another one."

"Be accursed, Dan!"

"Oho? And you, too, Mariet, be accursed!"

Mariet clasps the child in her arms and lifts him high. Then she calls wildly:

"Haggart, turn around! Turn around, Haggart! Noni is calling you. He wants to curse you, Haggart. Turn around! Look, Noni, look - that is your father. Remember him, Noni. And when you grow up, go out on every sea and find him, Noni. And when you find him - hang your father high on a mast, my little one."

The thundering salute drowns her cry. Haggart has boarded his ship. The night grows darker and the dashing of the waves fainter - the ocean is moving away with the tide. The great desert of the sky is mute and the night grows darker and the dashing of the waves ever fainter.

JUDAS ISCARIOT AND OTHERS

CHAPTER I

Jesus Christ had often been warned that Judas Iscariot was a man of very evil repute, and that He ought to beware of him. Some of the disciples, who had been in Judaea, knew him well, while others had heard much about him from various sources, and there was none who had a good word for him. If good people in speaking of him blamed him, as covetous, cunning, and inclined to hypocrisy and lying, the bad, when asked concerning him, inveighed against him in the severest terms.

"He is always making mischief among us," they would say, and spit in contempt. "He always has some thought which he keeps to himself. He creeps into a house quietly, like a scorpion, but goes out again with an ostentatious noise. There are friends among thieves, and comrades among robbers, and even liars have wives, to whom they speak the truth; but Judas laughs at thieves and honest folk alike, although he is himself a clever thief. Moreover, he is in appearance the ugliest person in Judaea. No! he is no friend of ours, this foxy-haired Judas Iscariot," the bad would say, thereby surprising the good people, in whose opinion there was not much difference between him and all other vicious people in Judaea. They would recount further that he had long ago deserted his wife, who was living in poverty and misery, striving to eke out a living from the unfruitful patch of land which constituted his estate. He had wandered for many years aimlessly among the people, and had even gone from one sea to the other, - no mean distance, - and everywhere he lied and grimaced, and would make some discovery with his thievish eye, and then suddenly disappear, leaving behind him animosity and strife. Yes, he was as inquisitive, artful and hateful as a one-eyed demon. Children he had none, and this was an additional proof that Judas was a wicked man, that God would not have from him any posterity.

None of the disciples had noticed when it was that this ugly, foxy-haired Jew first appeared in the company of Christ: but he had for a long time haunted their path, joined in their conversations, performed little acts of service, bowing and smiling and currying favour. Sometimes they became quite used to him, so that he escaped their weary eyes; then again he would suddenly obtrude himself on eye and ear, irritating them as something abnormally ugly, treacherous and disgusting. They would drive him away with harsh words, and for a short time he would disappear, only to reappear suddenly, officious, flattering and crafty as a one-eyed demon.

There was no doubt in the minds of some of the disciples that under his desire to draw near to Jesus was hidden some secret intention - some malign and cunning scheme.

But Jesus did not listen to their advice; their prophetic voice did not reach His ears. In that spirit of serene contradiction, which ever irresistibly inclined Him to the reprobate and unlovable, He deliberately accepted Judas, and included him in the circle of the chosen. The disciples were disturbed and murmured under their breath, but He would sit still, with His face towards the setting sun, and listen abstractedly, perhaps to them, perhaps to something else. For ten days there had been no wind, and the transparent atmosphere, wary and sensitive, continued ever the same, motionless and unchanged. It seemed as though it preserved in its transparent depths every cry and song made during those days by men and beasts and birds - tears, laments and cheerful song, prayers and curses - and that on account of these crystallised sounds the air was so heavy, threatening, and saturated with invisible life. Once more the sun was sinking. It rolled heavily downwards in a flaming ball, setting the sky on fire. Everything upon the earth which was turned towards it: the swarthy face of Jesus, the walls of the houses, and the leaves of the trees - everything obediently reflected that distant, fearfully pensive light. Now the white walls were no longer white, and the white city upon the white hill was turned to red.

And lo! Judas arrived. He arrived bowing low, bending his back, cautiously and timidly protruding his ugly, bumpy head - just exactly as his acquaintances had described. He was spare and of good height, almost the same as that of Jesus, who stooped a little through the habit of thinking as He walked, and so appeared shorter than He was. Judas was to all appearances fairly strong and well knit, though for some reason or other he pretended to be weak and somewhat sickly. He had an uncertain voice. Sometimes it was strong and manly, then again shrill as that of an old woman scolding her husband, provokingly thin, and disagreeable to the ear, so that ofttimes one felt inclined to tear out his words from the ear, like rough, decaying splinters. His short red locks failed to hide the curious form of his skull. It looked as if it had been split at the nape of the neck by a double sword-cut, and then joined together again, so that it was apparently divided into four parts, and inspired distrust, nay, even alarm: for behind such a cranium there could be no quiet or concord, but there must ever be heard the noise of sanguinary and merciless strife. The face of Judas was similarly doubled. One side of it, with a black, sharply watchful eye, was vivid and mobile, readily gathering into innumerable tortuous wrinkles. On the other side were no wrinkles. It was deadly flat, smooth, and set, and though of the same size as the other, it seemed enormous on account of its wide-open blind eye. Covered with a whitish film, closing neither night nor day, this eye met light and darkness with the same indifference, but perhaps on account of the proximity of its lively and crafty companion it never got full credit for blindness.

When in a paroxysm of joy or excitement, Judas would close his sound eye and shake his head. The other eye would always shake in unison and gaze in silence. Even people quite devoid of penetration could clearly perceive, when looking at Judas, that such a man could bring no good....

And yet Jesus brought him near to Himself, and once even made him sit next to Him. John, the beloved disciple, fastidiously moved away, and all the others who loved their Teacher cast down their eyes in disapprobation. But Judas sat on, and turning his head from side to side, began in a somewhat thin voice to complain of ill-health, and said that his chest gave him pain in the night, and that when ascending a hill he got out of breath, and when he stood still on the edge of a precipice he would be seized with a dizziness, and could scarcely restrain a foolish desire to throw himself down. And many other impious things he invented, as though not understanding that sicknesses do not come to a man by chance, but as a consequence of conduct not corresponding with the laws of the Eternal. Thus Judas Iscariot kept on rubbing his chest with his broad palm, and even pretended to cough, midst a general silence and downcast eyes.

John, without looking at the Teacher, whispered to his friend Simon Peter -

"Aren't you tired of that lie? I can't stand it any longer. I am going away."

Peter glanced at Jesus, and meeting his eye, quickly arose.

"Wait a moment," said he to his friend.

Once more he looked at Jesus; sharply as a stone torn from a mountain, he moved towards Judas, and said to him in a loud voice, with expansive, serene courtesy -

"You will come with us, Judas."

He gave him a kindly slap on his bent back, and without looking at the Teacher, though he felt His eye upon him, resolutely added in his loud voice, which excluded all objection, just as water excludes air -

"It does not matter that you have such a nasty face. There fall into our nets even worse monstrosities, and they sometimes turn out very tasty food. It is not for us, our Lord's fishermen, to throw away a catch, merely because the fish have spines, or only one eye. I saw once at Tyre an octopus, which had been caught by the local fishermen, and I was so frightened that I wanted to run away. But they laughed at me. A fisherman from Tiberias gave me some of it to eat, and I asked for more, it was so tasty. You remember, Master, that I told you the story, and you laughed, too. And you, Judas, are like an octopus - but only on one side."

And he laughed loudly, content with his joke. When Peter spoke, his words resounded so forcibly, that it seemed as though he were driving them in with nails. When Peter moved, or did anything, he made a noise that could be heard afar, and which called forth a response from the deafest of things: the stone floor rumbled under his feet, the doors shook and rattled, and the very air was convulsed with fear, and roared. In the clefts of the mountains his voice awoke the inmost echo, and in the morning-time, when they were fishing on the lake, he would roll about on the sleepy, glittering water, and force the first shy sunbeams into smiles.

For this apparently he was loved: when on all other faces there still lay the shadow of night, his powerful head, and bare breast, and freely extended arms were already aglow with the light of dawn.

The words of Peter, evidently approved as they were by the Master, dispersed the oppressive atmosphere. But some of the disciples, who had been to the seaside and had seen an octopus, were disturbed by the monstrous image so lightly applied to the new disciple. They recalled the immense eyes, the dozens of greedy tentacles, the feigned repose - and how all at once: it embraced, clung, crushed and sucked, all without one wink of its monstrous eyes. What did it mean? But Jesus remained silent, He smiled with a frown of kindly raillery on Peter, who was still telling glowing tales about the octopus. Then one by one the disciples shame-facedly approached Judas, and began a friendly conversation, with him, but - beat a hasty and awkward retreat.

Only John, the son of Zebedee, maintained an obstinate silence; and Thomas had evidently not made up his mind to say anything, but was still weighing the matter. He kept his gaze attentively fixed on Christ and Judas as they sat together. And that strange proximity of divine beauty and monstrous ugliness, of a man with a benign look, and of an octopus with immense, motionless, dully greedy eyes, oppressed his mind like an insoluble enigma.

He tensely wrinkled his smooth, upright forehead, and screwed up his eyes, thinking that he would see better so, but only succeeded in imagining that Judas really had eight incessantly moving feet. But that was not true. Thomas understood that, and again gazed obstinately.

Judas gathered courage: he straightened out his arms, which had been bent at the elbows, relaxed the muscles which held his jaws in tension, and began cautiously to protrude his bumpy head into the light. It had been the whole time in view of all, but Judas imagined that it had been impenetrably hidden from sight by some invisible, but thick and cunning veil. But lo! now, as though creeping out from a ditch, he felt his strange skull, and then his eyes, in the light: he stopped and then deliberately exposed his whole face. Nothing happened; Peter had gone away somewhere or other. Jesus sat pensive, with His head leaning on His hand, and gently swayed His sunburnt foot. The disciples were conversing together, and only Thomas gazed at him attentively and seriously, like a conscientious tailor taking measurement. Judas smiled; Thomas did not reply to the smile; but evidently took it into account, as he did everything else, and continued to gaze. But something unpleasant alarmed the left side of Judas' countenance as he looked round. John, handsome, pure, without a single fleck upon his snow-white conscience, was looking at him out of a dark corner, with cold but beautiful eyes. And though he walked as others walk, yet Judas felt as if he were dragging himself along the ground like a whipped cur, as he went up to John and said: "Why are you silent, John? Your words are like golden apples in vessels of silver filigree; bestow one of them on Judas, who is so poor."

John looked steadfastly into his wide-open motionless eye, and said nothing. And he looked on, while Judas crept out, hesitated a moment, and then disappeared in the deep darkness of the open door.

Since the full moon was up, there were many people out walking. Jesus went out too, and from the low roof on which Judas had spread his couch he saw Him going out. In the light of the moon each white figure looked bright and deliberate in its movements; and seemed not so much to walk as to glide in front of its dark shadow. Then suddenly a man would be lost in something black, and his voice became audible. And when people reappeared in the moonlight, they seemed silent - like white walls, or black shadows - as everything did in the transparent mist of night. Almost every one was asleep when Judas heard the soft voice of Jesus returning. All in and around about the house was still. A cock crew; somewhere an ass, disturbed in his sleep, brayed aloud and insolently as in daytime, then reluctantly and gradually relapsed into silence. Judas did not sleep at all, but listened surreptitiously. The moon illumined one half of his face, and was reflected strangely in his enormous open eye, as on the frozen surface of a lake.

Suddenly he remembered something, and hastily coughed, rubbing his perfectly healthy chest with his hairy hand: maybe some one was not yet asleep, and was listening to what Judas was thinking!

CHAPTER II

They gradually became used to Judas, and ceased to notice his ugliness. Jesus entrusted the common purse to him, and with it there fell on him all household cares: he purchased the necessary food and clothing, distributed alms, and when they were on the road, it was his duty to choose the place where they were to stop, or to find a night's lodging.

All this he did very cleverly, so that in a short time he had earned the goodwill of some of the disciples, who had noticed his efforts. Judas was an habitual liar, but they became used to this, when they found that his lies were not followed by any evil conduct; nay, they added a special piquancy to his conversation and tales, and made life seem like a comic, and sometimes a tragic, tale.

According to his stories, he seemed to know every one, and each person that he knew had some time in his life been guilty of evil conduct, or even crime. Those, according to him, were called good, who knew how to conceal their thoughts and acts; but if one only embraced, flattered, and questioned such a man sufficiently, there would ooze out from him every untruth, nastiness, and lie, like matter from a pricked wound. He freely confessed that he sometimes lied himself; but affirmed with an oath that others were still greater liars, and that if any one in this world was ever deceived, it was Judas.

Indeed, according to his own account, he had been deceived, time upon time, in one way or another. Thus, a certain guardian of the treasures of a rich grandee once confessed to him, that he had for ten years been continually on the point of stealing the property committed to him, but that he was debarred by fear of the grandee, and of his own conscience. And Judas believed him - and he suddenly committed the theft, and deceived Judas. But even then Judas still trusted him - and then he suddenly restored the stolen treasure to the grandee, and again deceived Judas. Yes, everything deceived him, even animals. Whenever he pets a dog it bites his fingers; but when he beats it with a stick it licks his feet, and looks into his eyes like a daughter. He killed one such dog, and buried it deep, laying a great stone on the top of it - but who knows? Perhaps just because he killed it, it has come to life again, and instead of lying in the trench, is running about cheerfully with other dogs.

All laughed merrily at Judas' tale, and he smiled pleasantly himself, winking his one lively, mocking eye - and by that very smile confessed that he had lied somewhat; that he had not really killed the dog. But he meant to find it and kill it, because he did not wish to be deceived. And at these words of Judas they laughed all the more.

But sometimes in his tales he transgressed the bounds of probability, and ascribed to people such proclivities as even the beasts do not possess, accusing them of such crimes as are not, and never have been. And since he named in this connection the most honoured people, some were indignant at the calumny, while others jokingly asked:

"How about your own father and mother, Judas - were they not good people?"

Judas winked his eye, and smiled with a gesture of his hands. And the fixed, wide-open eye shook in unison with the shaking of his head, and looked out in silence.

"But who was my father? Perhaps it was the man who used to beat me with a rod, or may be - a devil, a goat or a cock.... How can Judas tell? How can Judas tell with whom his mother shared her couch. Judas had many fathers: to which of them do you refer?"

But at this they were all indignant, for they had a profound reverence for parents; and Matthew, who was very learned in the scriptures, said severely in the words of Solomon:

"'Whoso slandereth his father and his mother, his lamp shall be extinguished in deep darkness.'"

But John the son of Zebedee haughtily jerked out: "And what of us? What evil have you to say of us, Judas Iscariot?"

But he waved his hands in simulated terror, whined, and bowed like a beggar, who has in vain asked an alms of a passer-by: "Ah! they are tempting poor Judas! They are laughing at him, they wish to take in the poor, trusting Judas!" And while one side of his face was crinkled up in buffooning grimaces, the other side wagged sternly and severely, and the never-closing eye looked out in a broad stare.

More and louder than any laughed Simon Peter at the jokes of Judas Iscariot. But once it happened that he suddenly frowned, and became silent and sad, and hastily dragging Judas aside by the sleeve, he bent down, and asked in a hoarse whisper -

"But Jesus? What do you think of Jesus? Speak seriously, I entreat you."

Judas cast on him a malign glance.

"And what do you think?"

Peter whispered with awe and gladness -

"I think that He is the son of the living God."

"Then why do you ask? What can Judas tell you, whose father was a goat?"

"But do you love Him? You do not seem to love any one, Judas."

And with the same strange malignity, Iscariot blurted out abruptly and sharply: "I do."

Some two days after this conversation, Peter openly dubbed Judas "my friend the octopus"; but Judas awkwardly, and ever with the same malignity, endeavoured to creep away from him into some dark corner, and would sit there morosely glaring with his white, never-closing eye.

Thomas alone took him quite seriously. He understood nothing of jokes, hypocrisy or lies, nor of the play upon words and thoughts, but investigated everything positively to the very bottom. He would often interrupt Judas' stories about wicked people and their conduct with short practical remarks:

"You must prove that. Did you hear it yourself? Was there any one present besides yourself? What was his name?"

At this Judas would get angry, and shrilly cry out, that he had seen and heard everything himself; but the obstinate Thomas would go on cross-examining quietly and persistently, until Judas confessed that he had lied, or until he invented some new and more probable lie, which provided the others for some time with food for thought. But when Thomas discovered a discrepancy, he would immediately come and calmly expose the liar.

Usually Judas excited in him a strong curiosity, which brought about between them a sort of friendship, full of wrangling, jeering, and invective on the one side, and of quiet insistence on the other. Sometimes Judas felt an unbearable aversion to his strange friend, and, transfixing him with a sharp glance, would say irritably, and almost with entreaty -

"What more do you want? I have told you all."

"I want you to prove how it is possible that a he-goat should be your father," Thomas would reply with calm insistency, and wait for an answer.

It chanced once, that after such a question, Judas suddenly stopped speaking and gazed at him with surprise from head to foot. What he saw was a tall, upright figure, a grey face, honest eyes of transparent blue, two fat folds beginning at the nose and losing themselves in a stiff, evenly-trimmed beard. He said with conviction:

"What a stupid you are, Thomas! What do you dream about - a tree, a wall, or a donkey?"

Thomas was in some way strangely perturbed, and made no reply. But at night, when Judas was already closing his vivid, restless eye for sleep, he suddenly said aloud from where he lay - the two now slept together on the roof -

"You are wrong, Judas. I have very bad dreams. What think you? Are people responsible for their dreams?"

"Does, then, any one but the dreamer see a dream?" Judas replied.

Thomas sighed gently, and became thoughtful. But Judas smiled contemptuously, and firmly closed his roguish eye, and quickly gave himself up to his mutinous dreams, monstrous ravings, mad phantoms, which rent his bumpy skull to pieces.

When, during Jesus' travels about Judaea, the disciples approached a village, Iscariot would speak evil of the inhabitants and foretell misfortune. But almost always it happened that the people, of whom he had spoken evil, met Christ and His friends with gladness, and surrounded them with attentions and love, and became believers, and Judas' money-box became so full that it was difficult to carry. And when they laughed at his mistake, he would make a humble gesture with his hands, and say:

"Well, well! Judas thought that they were bad, and they turned out to be good. They quickly believed, and gave money. That only means that Judas has been deceived once more, the poor, confiding Judas Iscariot!"

But on one occasion, when they had already gone far from a village, which had welcomed them kindly, Thomas and Judas began a hot dispute, to settle which they turned back, and did not overtake Jesus and His disciples until the next day. Thomas wore a perturbed and sorrowful appearance, while Judas had such a proud look, that you would have thought that he expected them to offer him their congratulations and thanks upon the spot. Approaching the Master, Thomas declared with decision: "Judas was right, Lord. They were ill-disposed, stupid people. And the seeds of your words has fallen upon the rock." And he related what had happened in the village.

After Jesus and His disciples left it, an old woman had begun to cry out that her little white kid had been stolen, and she laid the theft at the door of the visitors who had just departed. At first the people had disputed with her, but when she obstinately insisted that there was no one else who could have done it except Jesus, many agreed with her, and even were about to start in pursuit. And although they soon found the kid straying in the underwood, they still decided that Jesus was a deceiver, and possibly a thief.

"So that's what they think of us, is it?" cried Peter, with a snort. "Lord, wilt Thou that I return to those fools, and - "

But Jesus, saying not a word, gazed severely at him, and Peter in silence retired behind the others. And no one ever referred to the incident again, as though it had never occurred, and as though Judas had been proved wrong. In vain did he show himself on all sides, endeavouring to give to his double, crafty, hooknosed face an expression of modesty. They would not look at him, and if by chance any one did glance at him, it was in a very unfriendly, not to say contemptuous, manner.

From that day on Jesus' treatment of him underwent a strange change. Formerly, for some reason or other, Judas never used to speak directly with Jesus, who never addressed Himself directly to him, but nevertheless would often glance at him with kindly eyes, smile at his rallies, and if He had not seen him for some time, would inquire: "Where is Judas?"

But now He looked at him as if He did not see him, although as before, and indeed more determinedly than formerly, He sought him out with His eyes every time that He began to speak to the disciples or to the people; but He was either sitting with His back to him, so that He was obliged, as it were, to cast His words over His head so as to reach Judas, or else He made as though He did not notice him at all. And whatever He said, though it was one thing one day, and then next day quite another, although it might be the very thing that Judas was thinking, it always seemed as though He were speaking against him. To all He was the tender, beautiful flower, the sweet-smelling rose of Lebanon, but for Judas He left only sharp thorns, as though Judas had neither heart, nor sight, nor smell, and did not understand, even better than any, the beauty of tender, immaculate petals.

"Thomas! Do you like the yellow rose of Lebanon, which has a swarthy countenance and eyes like the roe?" he inquired once of his friend, who replied indifferently -

"Rose? Yes, I like the smell. But I have never heard of a rose with a swarthy countenance and eyes like a roe!"

"What? Do you not know that the polydactylous cactus, which tore your new garment yesterday, has only one beautiful flower, and only one eye?"

But Thomas did not know this, although only yesterday a cactus had actually caught in his garment and torn it into wretched rags. But then Thomas never did know anything, though he asked questions about everything, and looked so straight with his bright, transparent eyes, through which, as through a pane of Phoenician glass, was visible a wall, with a dismal ass tied to it.

Some time later another occurrence took place, in which Judas again proved to be in the right.

At a certain village in Judaea, of which Judas had so bad an opinion, that he had advised them to avoid it, the people received Christ with hostility, and after His sermon and exposition of hypocrites they burst into fury, and threatened to stone Jesus and His disciples. Enemies He had many, and most likely they would have carried out their sinister intention, but for Judas Iscariot. Seized with a mad fear for Jesus, as though he already saw the drops of ruby blood upon His white garment, Judas threw himself in blind fury upon the crowd, scolding, screeching, beseeching, and lying, and thus gave time and opportunity to Jesus and His disciples to escape.

Amazingly active, as though running upon a dozen feet, laughable and terrible in his fury and entreaties, he threw himself madly in front of the crowd and charmed it with a certain strange power. He shouted that the Nazarene was not possessed of a devil, that He was simply an impostor, a thief who loved money as did all His disciples, and even Judas himself: and he rattled the money-box, grimaced, and beseeched, throwing himself on the ground. And by degrees the anger of the crowd changed into laughter and disgust, and they let fall the stones which they had picked up to throw at them.

"They are not fit to die by the hands of an honest person," said they, while others thoughtfully followed the rapidly disappearing Judas with their eyes.

Again Judas expected to receive congratulations, praise, and thanks, and made a show of his torn garments, and pretended that he had been beaten; but this time, too, he was greatly mistaken. The angry Jesus strode on in silence, and even Peter and John did not venture to approach Him: and all whose eyes fell on Judas in his torn garments, his face glowing with happiness, but still somewhat frightened, repelled him with curt, angry exclamations.

It was just as though he had not saved them all, just as though he had not saved their Teacher, whom they loved so dearly.

"Do you want to see some fools?" said he to Thomas, who was thoughtfully walking in the rear. "Look! There they go along the road in a crowd, like a flock of sheep, kicking up the dust. But you are wise, Thomas, you creep on behind, and I, the noble, magnificent Judas, creep on behind like a dirty slave, who has no place by the side of his masters."

"Why do you call yourself magnificent?" asked Thomas in surprise.

"Because I am so," Judas replied with conviction, and he went on talking, giving more details of how he had deceived the enemies of Jesus, and laughed at them and their stupid stones.

"But you told lies," said Thomas.

"Of course I did," quickly assented Iscariot. "I gave them what they asked for, and they gave me in return what I wanted. And what is a lie, my clever Thomas? Would not the death of Jesus be the greatest lie of all?"

"You did not act rightly. Now I believe that a devil is your father. It was he that taught you, Judas."

The face of Judas grew pale, and something suddenly came over Thomas, and as if it were a white cloud, passed over and concealed the road and Jesus. With a gentle movement Judas just as suddenly drew Thomas to himself, pressed him closely with a paralysing movement, and whispered in his ear -

"You mean, then, that a devil has instructed me, don't you, Thomas? Well, I saved Jesus. Therefore a devil loves Jesus and has need of Him, and of the truth. Is it not so, Thomas? But then my father was not a devil, but a he-goat. Can a he-goat want Jesus? Eh? And don't you want Him yourselves, and the truth also?"

Angry and slightly frightened, Thomas freed himself with difficulty from the clinging embrace of Judas, and began to stride forward quickly. But he soon slackened his pace as he endeavoured to understand what had taken place.

But Judas crept on gently behind, and gradually came to a standstill. And lo! in the distance the pedestrians became blended into a parti-coloured mass, so that it was impossible any longer to distinguish which among those little figures was Jesus. And lo! The little Thomas, too, changed into a grey spot, and suddenly - all disappeared round a turn in the road.

Looking round, Judas went down from the road and with immense leaps descended into the depths of a rocky ravine. His clothes blew out with the speed and abruptness of his course, and his hands were extended upwards as though he would fly. Lo! now he crept along an abrupt declivity, and suddenly rolled down in a grey ball, rubbing off his skin against the stones; then he jumped up and angrily threatened the mountain with his fist -

"You too, damn you!"

Suddenly he changed his quick movements into a comfortable, concentrated dawdling, chose a place by a big stone, and sat down without hurry. He turned himself, as if seeking a comfortable position, laid his hands side by side on the grey stone, and heavily sank his head upon them. And so for an hour or two he sat on, as motionless and grey as the grey stone itself, so still that he deceived even the birds. The walls of the ravine rose before him, and behind, and on every side, cutting a sharp line all round on the blue sky; while everywhere immense grey stones obtruded from the ground, as though there had been at some time or other, a shower here, and as though its heavy drops had become petrified in endless split, upturned skull, and every stone in it was like a petrified thought; and there were many of them, and they all kept thinking heavily, boundlessly, stubbornly.

A scorpion, deceived by his quietness, hobbled past, on its tottering legs, close to Judas. He threw a glance at it, and, without lifting his head from the stone, again let both his eyes rest fixedly on something - both motionless, both veiled in a strange whitish turbidness, both as though blind and yet terribly alert. And lo! from out of the ground, the stones, and the clefts, the quiet darkness of night began to rise, enveloped the motionless Judas, and crept swiftly up towards the pallid light of the sky. Night was coming on with its thoughts and dreams.

That night Judas did not return to the halting-place. And the disciples, forgetting their thoughts, busied themselves with preparations for their meal, and grumbled at his negligence.

CHAPTER III

Once, about mid-day, Jesus and His disciples were walking along a stony and hilly road devoid of shade, and, since they had been more than five hours afoot, Jesus began to complain of weariness. The disciples stopped, and Peter and his friend John spread their cloaks and those of the other disciples, on the ground, and fastened them above between two high rocks, and so made a sort of tent for Jesus. He lay down in the tent, resting from the heat of the sun, while they amused Him with pleasant conversation and jokes. But seeing that even talking fatigued Him, and being themselves but little affected by weariness and the heat, they went some distance off and occupied themselves in various ways. One sought edible roots among the stones on the slope of the mountain, and when he had found them brought them to Jesus; another, climbing up higher and higher, searched musingly for the limits of the blue distance, and failing, climbed up higher on to new, sharp-pointed rocks. John found a beautiful little blue lizard among the stones, and smiling brought it quickly with tender hands to Jesus. The lizard looked with its protuberant, mysterious eyes into His, and then crawled quickly with its cold body over His warm hand, and soon swiftly disappeared with tender, quivering tail.

But Peter and Philip, not caring about such amusements, occupied themselves in tearing up great stones from the mountain, and hurling them down below, as a test of their strength. The others, attracted by their loud laughter, by degrees gathered round them, and joined in their sport. Exerting their strength, they would tear up from the ground an ancient rock all overgrown, and lifting it high with both hands, hurl it down the slope. Heavily it would strike with a dull thud, and hesitate for a moment; then resolutely it would make a first leap, and each time it touched the ground, gathering from it speed and strength, it would become light, furious, all-subversive. Now it no longer leapt, but flew with grinning teeth, and the whistling wind let its dull round mass pass by. Lo! it is on the edge - with a last, floating motion the stone would sweep high, and then quietly, with ponderous deliberation, fly downwards in a curve to the invisible bottom of the precipice.

"Now then, another!" cried Peter. His white teeth shone between his black beard and moustache, his mighty chest and arms were bare, and the sullen, ancient rocks, dully wondering at the strength which lifted them, obediently, one after another, precipitated themselves into the abyss. Even the frail John threw some moderate-sized stones, and Jesus smiled quietly as He looked at their sport.

"But what are you doing, Judas? Why do you not take part in the game? It seems amusing enough?" asked Thomas, when he found his strange friend motionless behind a great grey stone.

"I have a pain in my chest. Moreover, they have not invited me."

"What need of invitation! At all events, I invite you; come! Look what stones Peter throws!"

Judas somehow or other happened to glance sideward at him, and Thomas became, for the first time, indistinctly aware that he had two faces. But before he could thoroughly grasp the fact, Judas said in his ordinary tone, at once fawning and mocking -

"There is surely none stronger than Peter? When he shouts, all the asses in Jerusalem think that their Messiah has arrived, and lift up their voices too. You have heard them before now, have you not, Thomas?"

Smiling politely; and modestly wrapping his garment round his chest, which was overgrown with red curly hairs, Judas stepped into the circle of players.

And since they were all in high good humour, they met him with mirth and loud jokes, and even John condescended to vouchsafe a smile, when Judas, pretending to groan with the exertion, laid hold of an immense stone. But lo! he lifted it with ease, and threw it, and his blind, wide-open eye gave a jerk, and then fixed itself immovably on Peter; while the other eye, cunning and merry, was overflowing with quiet laughter.

"No! you throw again!" said Peter in an offended tone.

And lo! one after the other they kept lifting and throwing gigantic stones, while the disciples looked on in amazement. Peter threw a great stone, and then Judas a still bigger one. Peter, frowning and concentrated, angrily wielded a fragment of rock, and struggling as he lifted it, hurled it down; then Judas, without ceasing to smile, searched for a still larger fragment, and digging his long fingers into it, grasped it, and swinging himself together with it, and paling, sent it into the gulf. When he had thrown his stone, Peter would recoil and so watch its fall; but Judas always bent himself forward, stretched out his long vibrant arms, as though he were going to fly after the stone. Eventually both of them, first Peter, then Judas, seized hold of an old grey stone, but neither one nor the other could move it. All red with his exertion, Peter resolutely approached Jesus, and said aloud -

"Lord! I do not wish to be beaten by Judas. Help me to throw this stone."

Jesus made answer in a low voice, and Peter, shrugging his broad shoulders in dissatisfaction, but not daring to make any rejoinder, came back with the words -

"He says: 'But who will help Iscariot?'"

Then glancing at Judas, who, panting with clenched teeth, was still embracing the stubborn stone, he laughed cheerfully -

"Look what an invalid he is! See what our poor sick Judas is doing!"

And even Judas laughed at being so unexpectedly exposed in his deception, and all the others laughed too, and even Thomas allowed his pointed, grey, overhanging moustache to relax into a smile.

And so in friendly chat and laughter, they all set out again on the way, and Peter, quite reconciled to his victor, kept from time to time digging him in the ribs, and loudly guffawed -

"There's an invalid for you!"

All of them praised Judas, and acknowledged him victor, and all chatted with him in a friendly manner; but Jesus once again had no word of praise for Judas. He walked silently in front, nibbling the grasses, which He plucked. And gradually, one by one, the disciples craved laughing, and went over to Jesus. So that in a short time it came about, that they were all walking ahead in a compact body, while Judas - the victor, the strong man - crept on behind, choking with dust.

And lo! they stood still, and Jesus laid His hand on Peter's shoulder, while with His other He pointed into the distance, where Jerusalem had just become visible in the smoke. And the broad, strong back of Peter gently accepted that slight sunburnt hand.

For the night they stayed in Bethany, at the house of Lazarus. And when all were gathered together for conversation, Judas thought that they would now recall his victory over Peter, and sat down nearer. But the disciples were silent and unusually pensive. Images of the road they had traversed, of the sun, the rocks and the grass, of Christ lying down under the shelter, quietly floated through their heads, breathing a soft pensiveness, begetting confused but sweet reveries of an eternal movement under the sun. The wearied body reposed sweetly, and thought was merged in something mystically great and beautiful - and no one recalled Judas!

Judas went out, and then returned. Jesus was discoursing, and His disciples were listening to Him in silence.

Mary sat at His feet, motionless as a statue, and gazed into His face with upturned eyes. John had come quite close, and endeavoured to sit so that his hand touched the garment of the Master, but without disturbing Him. He touched Him and was still. Peter breathed loud and deeply, repeating under his breath the words of Jesus.

Iscariot had stopped short on the threshold, and contemptuously letting his gaze pass by the company, he concentrated all its fire on Jesus. And the more he looked the more everything around Him seemed to fade, and to become clothed with darkness and silence, while Jesus alone shone forth with uplifted hand. And then, lo! He was, as it were, raised up into the air, and melted away, as though He consisted of mist floating over a lake, and penetrated by the light of the setting moon, and His soft speech began to sound tenderly, somewhere far, far away. And gazing at the wavering phantom, and drinking in the tender melody of the distant dream-like words, Judas gathered his whole soul into his iron fingers, and in its vast darkness silently began building up some colossal scheme. Slowly, in the profound darkness, he kept lifting up masses, like mountains, and quite easily heaping them one on another: and again he would lift up and again heap them up; and something grew in the darkness, spread noiselessly and burst its bounds. His head felt like a dome, in the impenetrable darkness of which the colossal thing continued to grow, and some one, working on in silence, kept lifting up masses like mountains, and piling them one on another and again lifting up, and so on and on... whilst somewhere in the distance the phantom-like words tenderly sounded.

Thus he stood blocking the doorway, huge and black, while Jesus went on talking, and the strong, intermittent breathing of Peter repeated His words aloud. But on a sudden Jesus broke off an unfinished sentence, and Peter, as though waking from sleep, cried out exultingly -

"Lord! to Thee are known the words of eternal life!"

But Jesus held His peace, and kept gazing fixedly in one direction. And when they followed His gaze they perceived in the doorway the petrified Judas with gaping mouth and fixed eyes. And, not understanding what was the matter, they laughed. But Matthew, who was learned in the Scriptures, touched Judas on the shoulder, and said in the words of Solomon -

"'He that looketh kindly shall be forgiven; but he that is met within the gates will impede others.'"

Judas was silent for a while, and then fretfully and everything about him, his eyes, hands and feet, seemed to start in different directions, as those of an animal which suddenly perceives the eye of man upon him. Jesus went straight to Judas, as though words trembled on His lips, but passed by him through the open, and now unoccupied, door.

In the middle of the night the restless Thomas came to Judas' bed, and sitting down on his heels, asked -

"Are you weeping, Judas?"

"No! Go away, Thomas."

"Why do you groan, and grind your teeth? Are you ill?"

Judas was silent for a while, and then fretfully there fell from his lips distressful words, fraught with grief and anger -

"Why does not He love me? Why does He love the others? Am

I not handsomer, better and stronger than they? Did not I save His life while they ran away like cowardly dogs?"

"My poor friend, you are not quite right. You are not good-looking at all, and your tongue is as disagreeable as your face. You lie and slander continually; how then can you expect Jesus to love you?"

But Judas, stirring heavily in the darkness, continued as though he heard him not -

"Why is He not on the side of Judas, instead of on the side of those who do not love Him? John brought Him a lizard; I would bring him a poisonous snake. Peter threw stones; I would overthrow a mountain for His sake. But what is a poisonous snake? One has but to draw its fangs, and it will coil round one's neck like a necklace. What is a mountain, which it is possible to dig down with the hands, and to trample with the feet? I would give to Him Judas, the bold, magnificent Judas. But now He will perish, and together with him will perish Judas."

"You are speaking strangely, Judas!"

"A withered fig-tree, which must needs be cut down with the axe, such am I: He said it of me. Why then does He not do it? He dare not, Thomas! I know him. He fears Judas. He hides from the bold, strong, magnificent Judas. He loves fools, traitors, liars. You are a liar, Thomas; have you never been told so before?"

Thomas was much surprised, and wished to object, but he thought that Judas was simply railing, and so only shook his head in the darkness. And Judas lamented still more grievously, and groaned and ground his teeth, and his whole huge body could be heard heaving under the coverlet.

"What is the matter with Judas? Who has applied fire to his body? He will give his son to the dogs. He will give his daughter to be betrayed by robbers, his bride to harlotry. And yet has not Judas a tender heart? Go away, Thomas; go away, stupid! Leave the strong, bold, magnificent Judas alone!"

CHAPTER IV

Judas had concealed some denarii, and the deception was discovered, thanks to Thomas, who had seen by chance how much money had been given to them. It was only too probable that this was not the first time that Judas had committed a theft, and they all were enraged. The angry Peter seized Judas by his collar and almost dragged him to Jesus, and the terrified Judas paled but did not resist.

"Master, see! Here he is, the trickster! Here's the thief. You trusted him, and he steals our money. Thief! Scoundrel! If Thou wilt permit, I'll - "

But Jesus held His peace. And attentively regarding him, Peter suddenly turned red, and loosed the hand which held the collar, while Judas shyly rearranged his garment, casting a sidelong glance on Peter, and assuming the downcast look of a repentant criminal.

"So that's how it's to be," angrily said Peter, as he went out, loudly slamming the door. They were all dissatisfied, and declared that on no account would they consort with Judas any longer; but John, after some consideration, passed through the door, behind which might be heard the quiet, almost caressing, voice of Jesus. And when in the course of time he returned, he was pale, and his downcast eyes were red as though with recent tears.

"The Master says that Judas may take as much money as he pleases." Peter laughed angrily. John gave him a quick reproachful glance, and suddenly flushing, and mingling tears with anger, and delight with tears, loudly exclaimed:

"And no one must reckon how much money Judas receives. He is our brother, and all the money is as much his as ours: if he wants much let him take much, without telling any one, or taking counsel with any. Judas is our brother, and you have grievously insulted him - so says the Master. Shame on you, brother!"

In the doorway stood Judas, pale and with a distorted smile on his face. With a light movement John went up to him and kissed him three times. After him, glancing round at one another, James, Philip and the others came up shamefacedly; and after each kiss Judas wiped his mouth, but gave a loud smack as though the sound afforded him pleasure. Peter came up last.

"We were all stupid, all blind, Judas. He alone sees, He alone is wise. May I kiss you?"

"Why not? Kiss away!" said Judas as in consent.

Peter kissed him vigorously, and said aloud in his ear -

"But I almost choked you. The others kissed you in the usual way, but I kissed you on the throat. Did it hurt you?"

"A little."

"I will go and tell Him all. I was angry even with Him," said Peter sadly, trying noiselessly to open the door.

"And what are you going to do, Thomas?" asked John severely. He it was who looked after the conduct and the conversation of the disciples.

"I don't know yet. I must consider."

And Thomas thought long, almost the whole day. The

disciples had dispersed to their occupations, and somewhere on the other side of the wall, Peter was shouting joyfully - but Thomas was still considering. He would have come to a decision more quickly had not Judas hindered him somewhat by continually following him about with a mocking glance, and now and again asking him in a serious tone -

"Well, Thomas, and how does the matter progress?"

Then Judas brought his money-box, and shaking the money and pretending not to look at Thomas, began to count it -

"Twenty-one, two, three.... Look, Thomas, a bad coin again. Oh! what rascals people are; they even give bad money as offerings. Twenty-four... and then they will say again that Judas has stolen it... twenty-five, twenty-six...."

Thomas approached him resolutely... for it was already towards evening, and said -

"He is right, Judas. Let me kiss you."

"Will you? Twenty-nine, thirty. It's no good. I shall steal again. Thirty-one...."

"But how can you steal, when it is neither yours nor another's? You will simply take as much as you want, brother."

"It has taken you a long time to repeat His words! Don't you value time, you clever Thomas?"

"You seem to be laughing at me, brother."

"And consider, are you doing well, my virtuous Thomas, in repeating His words? He said something of His own, but you do not. He really kissed me - you only defiled my mouth. I can still feel your moist lips upon mine. It was so disgusting, my good Thomas. Thirty-eight, thirty-nine, forty. Forty denarii. Thomas, won't you check the sum?"

"Certainly He is our Master. Why then should we not repeat the words of our Master?"

"Is Judas' collar torn away? Is there now nothing to seize him by? The Master will go out of the house, and Judas will unexpectedly steal three more denarii. Won't you seize him by the collar?"

"We know now, Judas. We understand."

"Have not all pupils a bad memory? Have not all masters been deceived by their pupils? But the master has only to lift the rod, and the pupils cry out, 'We know, Master!' But the master goes to bed, and the pupils say: 'Did the Master teach us this?' And so, in this case, this morning you called me a thief, this evening you call me brother. What will you call me to-morrow?"

Judas laughed, and lifting up the heavy rattling money-box with ease, went on:

"When a strong wind blows it raises the dust, and foolish people look at the dust and say: 'Look at the wind!' But it is only dust, my good Thomas, ass's dung trodden underfoot. The dust meets a wall and lies down gently at its foot, but the wind flies farther and farther, my good Thomas."

Judas obligingly pointed over the wall in illustration of his meaning, and laughed again.

"I am glad that you are merry," said Thomas, "but it is a great pity that there is so much malice in your merriment."

"Why should not a man be cheerful, who has been kissed so much, and who is so useful? If I had not stolen the three denarii would John have known the meaning of delight? Is it not pleasant to be a hook, on which John may hang his damp virtue out to dry, and Thomas his moth-eaten mind?"

"I think that I had better be going."

"But I am only joking, my good Thomas. I merely wanted to know whether you really wished to kiss the old obnoxious Judas - the thief who stole the three denarii and gave them to a harlot."

"To a harlot!" exclaimed Thomas in surprise. "And did you tell the Master of it?"

"Again you doubt, Thomas. Yes, to a harlot. But if you only knew, Thomas, what an unfortunate woman she was. For two days she had had nothing to eat."

"Are you sure of that?" said Thomas in confusion.

"Yes! Of course I am. I myself spent two days with her, and saw that she ate and drank nothing except red wine. She tottered from exhaustion, and I was always falling down with her."

Thereupon Thomas got up quickly, and, when he had gone a few steps away, he flung out at Judas:

"You seem to be possessed of Satan, Judas."

And as he went away, he heard in the approaching twilight how dolefully the heavy money-box rattled in Judas' hands. And Judas seemed to laugh.

But the very next day Thomas was obliged to acknowledge that he had misjudged Judas, so simple, so gentle, and at the same time so serious was Iscariot. He neither grimaced nor made ill-natured jokes; he was neither obsequious nor scurrilous, but quietly and unobtrusively went about his work of catering. He was as active as formerly, as though he did not have two feet like other people, but a whole dozen of them, and ran noiselessly without that squeaking, sobbing, and laughter of a hyena, with which he formerly accompanied his actions. And when Jesus began to speak, he would seat himself quickly in a corner, fold his hands and feet, and look so kindly with his great eyes, that many observed it. He ceased speaking evil of people, but rather remained silent, so that even the severe Matthew deemed it possible to praise him, saying in the words of Solomon:

"'He that is devoid of wisdom despiseth his neighbour: but a man of understanding holdeth his peace.'"

And he lifted up his hand, hinting thereby at Judas' former evil-speaking. In a short time all remarked this change in him, and rejoiced at it: only Jesus looked on him still with the same detached look, although he gave no direct indication of His dislike. And even John, for whom Judas now showed a profound reverence, as the beloved disciple of Jesus, and as his own champion in the matter of the three denarii, began to treat him somewhat more kindly, and even sometimes entered into conversation with him.

"What do you think, Judas," said he one day in a condescending manner, "which of us, Peter or I, will be nearest to Christ in His heavenly kingdom?"

Judas meditated, and then answered -

"I suppose that you will."

"But Peter thinks that he will," laughed John.

"No! Peter would scatter all the angels with his shout; you have heard him shout. Of course, he will quarrel with you, and will endeavour to occupy the first place, as he insists that he, too, loves Jesus. But he is already advanced in years, and you are young; he is heavy on his feet, while you run swiftly; you will enter there first with Christ? Will you not?"

"Yes, I will not leave Jesus," John agreed.

On the same day Simon Peter referred the very same question to Judas. But fearing that his loud voice would be heard by the others, he led Judas out to the farthest corner behind the house.

"Well then, what is your opinion about it?" he asked anxiously. "You are wise; even the Master praises you for your intellect. And you will speak the truth."

"You, of course," answered Iscariot without hesitation. And Peter exclaimed with indignation, "I told him so!"

"But, of course, he will try even there to oust you from the first place."

"Certainly!"

"But what can he do, when you already occupy the place? Won't you be the first to go there with Jesus? You will not leave Him alone? Has He not named you the ROCK?"

Peter put his hand on Judas' shoulder, and said with warmth: "I tell you, Judas, you are the cleverest of us all. But why are you so sarcastic and malignant? The Master does not like it. Otherwise you might become the beloved disciple, equally with John. But to you neither," and Peter lifted his hand threateningly, "will I yield my place next to Jesus, neither on earth, nor there! Do you hear?"

Thus Judas endeavoured to make himself agreeable to all, but, at the same time, he cherished hidden thoughts in his mind. And while he remained ever the same modest, restrained and unobtrusive person, he knew how to make some especially pleasing remark to each. Thus to Thomas he said:

"The fool believeth every word: but the prudent taketh heed to his paths."

While to Matthew, who suffered somewhat from excess in

eating and drinking, and was ashamed of his weakness, he quoted the words of Solomon, the sage whom Matthew held in high estimation:

"'The righteous eateth to the satisfying of his soul: but the belly of the wicked shall want.'"

But his pleasant speeches were rare, which gave them the greater value. For the most part he was silent, listening attentively to what was said, and always meditating.

When reflecting, Judas had an unpleasant look, ridiculous and at the same time awe-inspiring. As long as his quick, crafty eye was in motion, he seemed simple and good-natured enough, but directly both eyes became fixed in an immovable stare, and the skin on his protruding forehead gathered into strange ridges and creases, a distressing surmise would force itself on one, that under that skull some very peculiar thoughts were working. So thoroughly apart, peculiar, and voiceless were the thoughts which enveloped Iscariot in the deep silence of secrecy, when he was in one of his reveries, that one would have preferred that he should begin to speak, to move, nay, even, to tell lies. For a lie, spoken by a human tongue, had been truth and light compared with that hopelessly deep and unresponsive silence.

"In the dumps again, Judas?" Peter would cry with his clear voice and bright smile, suddenly breaking in upon the sombre silence of Judas' thoughts, and banishing them to some dark corner. "What are you thinking about?"

"Of many things," Iscariot would reply with a quiet smile. And perceiving, apparently, what a bad impression his silence made upon the others, he began more frequently to shun the society of the disciples, and spent much time in solitary walks, or would betake himself to the flat roof and there sit still. And more than once he startled Thomas, who has unexpectedly stumbled in the darkness against a grey heap, out of which the hands and feet of Judas suddenly started, and his jeering voice was heard.

But one day, in a specially brusque and strange manner, Judas recalled his former character. This happened on the occasion of the quarrel for the first place in the kingdom of heaven. Peter and John were disputing together, hotly contending each for his own place nearest to Jesus. They reckoned up their services, they measured the degrees of their love for Jesus, they became heated and noisy, and even reviled one another without restraint. Peter roared, all red with anger. John was quiet and pale, with trembling hands and biting speech. Their quarrel had already passed the bounds of decency, and the Master had begun to frown, when Peter looked up by chance on Judas, and laughed self-complacently: John, too, looked at Judas, and also smiled. Each of them recalled what the cunning Judas had said to him. And foretasting the joy of approaching triumph, they, with silent consent, invited Judas to decide the matter.

Peter called out, "Come now, Judas the wise, tell us who will be first, nearest to Jesus, he or I?"

But Judas remained silent, breathing heavily, his eyes eagerly questioning the quiet, deep eyes of Jesus.

"Yes," John condescendingly repeated, "tell us who will be first, nearest to Jesus."

Without taking his eyes off Christ, Judas slowly rose, and answered quietly and gravely:

"I."

Jesus let His gaze fall slowly. And quietly striking himself on the breast with a bony finger, Iscariot repeated solemnly and sternly: "I, I shall be nearest to Jesus!" And he went out. Struck by his insolent freak, the disciples remained silent; but Peter suddenly recalling something, whispered to Thomas in an unexpectedly gentle voice:

"So that is what he is always thinking about! See?"

CHAPTER V

Just at this time Judas Iscariot took the first definite step towards the Betrayal. He visited the chief priest Annas secretly. He was very roughly received, but that did not disturb him in the least, and he demanded a long private interview. When he found himself alone with the dry, harsh old man, who looked at him with contempt from beneath his heavy overhanging eyelids, he stated that he was an honourable man who had become one of the disciples of Jesus of Nazareth with the sole purpose of exposing the impostor, and handing Him over to the arm of the law.

"But who is this Nazarene?" asked Annas contemptuously, making as though he heard the name of Jesus for the first time.

Judas on his part pretended to believe in the extraordinary ignorance of the chief priest, and spoke in detail of the preaching of Jesus, of His miracles, of His hatred for the Pharisees and the Temple, of His perpetual infringement of the Law, and eventually of His wish to wrest the power out of the hands of the priesthood, and to set up His own personal kingdom. And so cleverly did he mingle truth with lies, that Annas looked at him more attentively, and lazily remarked: "There are plenty of impostors and madmen in Judah."

"No! He is a dangerous person," Judas hotly contradicted. "He breaks the law. And it were better that one man should perish, rather than the whole people."

Annas, with an approving nod, said -

"But He, apparently, has many disciples."

"Yes, many."

"And they, it seems probable, have a great love for Him?"

"Yes, they say that they love Him, love Him much, more than themselves."

"But if we try to take Him, will they not defend Him? Will they not raise a tumult?"

Judas laughed long and maliciously. "What, they? Those cowardly dogs, who run if a man but stoop down to pick up a stone. They indeed!"

"Are they really so bad?" asked Annas coldly.

"But surely it is not the bad who flee from the good; is it not rather the good who flee from the bad? Ha! ha! They are good, and therefore they flee. They are good, and therefore they hide themselves. They are good, and therefore they will appear only in time to bury Jesus. They will lay Him in the tomb themselves; you have only to execute Him."

"But surely they love Him? You yourself said so."

"People always love their teacher, but better dead than alive. While a teacher's alive he may ask them questions which they will find difficult to answer. But, when a teacher dies, they become teachers themselves, and then others fare badly in turn. Ha! ha!"

Annas looked piercingly at the Traitor, and his lips puckered - which indicated that he was smiling.

"You have been insulted by them. I can see that."

"Can one hide anything from the perspicacity of the astute

Annas? You have pierced to the very heart of Judas. Yes, they insulted poor Judas. They said he had stolen from them three denarii - as though Judas were not the most honest man in Israel!"

They talked for some time longer about Jesus, and His disciples, and of His pernicious influence on the people of Israel, but on this occasion the crafty, cautious Annas gave no decisive answer. He had long had his eyes on Jesus, and in secret conclave with his own relatives and friends, with the authorities, and the Sadducees, had decided the fate of the Prophet of Galilee. But he did not trust Judas, who he had heard was a bad, untruthful man, and he had no confidence in his flippant faith in the cowardice of the disciples, and of the people. Annas believed in his own power, but he feared bloodshed, feared a serious riot, such as the insubordinate, irascible people of Jerusalem lent itself to so easily; he feared, in fact, the violent intervention of the Roman authorities. Fanned by opposition, fertilised by the red blood of the people, which vivifies everything on which it falls, the heresy would grow stronger, and stifle in its folds Annas, the government, and all his friends. So, when Iscariot knocked at his door a second time Annas was perturbed in spirit and would not admit him. But yet a third and a fourth time Iscariot came to him, persistent as the wind, which beats day and night against the closed door and blows in through its crevices.

"I see that the most astute Annas is afraid of something," said Judas when at last he obtained admission to the high priest.

"I am strong enough not to fear anything," Annas answered haughtily. And Iscariot stretched forth his hands and bowed abjectly.

"What do you want?"

"I wish to betray the Nazarene to you."

"We do not want Him."

Judas bowed and waited, humbly fixing his gaze on the high priest.

"Go away."

"But I am bound to return. Am I not, revered Annas?"

"You will not be admitted. Go away!"

But yet again and again Judas called on the aged Annas, and at last was admitted.

Dry and malicious, worried with thought, and silent, he gazed on the Traitor, and, as it were, counted the hairs on his knotted head. Judas also said nothing, and seemed in his turn to be counting the somewhat sparse grey hairs in the beard of the high priest.

"What? you here again?" the irritated Annas haughtily jerked out, as though spitting upon his head.

"I wish to betray the Nazarene to you."

Both held their peace, and continued to gaze attentively at each other. Iscariot's look was calm; but a quiet malice, dry and cold, began slightly to prick Annas, like the early morning rime of winter.

"How much do you want for your Jesus?"

"How much will you give?"

Annas, with evident enjoyment, insultingly replied: "You are nothing but a band of scoundrels. Thirty pieces - that's what we will give."

And he quietly rejoiced to see how Judas began to squirm and run about - agile and swift as though he had a whole dozen feet, not two.

"Thirty pieces of silver for Jesus!" he cried in a voice of wild madness, most pleasing to Annas. "For Jesus of Nazareth! You wish to buy Jesus for thirty pieces of silver? And you think that Jesus can be betrayed to you for thirty pieces of silver?" Judas turned quickly to the wall, and laughed in its smooth, white fence, lifting up his long hands. "Do you hear? Thirty pieces of silver! For Jesus!"

With the same quiet pleasure, Annas remarked indifferently:

"If you will not deal, go away. We shall find some one whose work is cheaper."

And like old-clothes men who throw useless rags from hand to hand in the dirty market-place, and shout, and swear and abuse each other, so they embarked on a rabid and fiery bargaining. Intoxicated with a strange rapture, running and turning about, and shouting, Judas ticked off on his fingers the merits of Him whom he was selling.

"And the fact that He is kind and heals the sick, is that worth nothing at all in your opinion? Ah, yes! Tell me, like an honest man!"

"If you - " began Annas, who was turning red, as he tried to get in a word, his cold malice quickly warming up under the burning words of Judas, who, however, interrupted him shamelessly:

"That He is young and handsome - like the Narcissus of Sharon, and the Lily of the Valley? What? Is that worth nothing? Perhaps you will say that He is old and useless, and that Judas is trying to dispose of an old bird? Eh?"

"If you - " Annas tried to exclaim; but Judas' stormy speech bore away his senile croak, like down upon the wind.

"Thirty pieces of silver! That will hardly work out to one obolus for each drop of blood! Half an obolus will not go to a tear! A quarter to a groan. And cries, and convulsions! And for the ceasing of His heartbeats? And the closing of His eyes? Is all this to be thrown in gratis?" sobbed Iscariot, advancing toward the high priest and enveloping him with an insane movement of his hands and fingers, and with intervolved words.

"Includes everything," said Annas in a choking voice.

"And how much will you make out of it yourself? Eh? You wish to rob Judas, to snatch the bit of bread from his children. No, I can't do it. I will go on to the market-place, and shout out: 'Annas has robbed poor Judas. Help!'"

Wearied, and grown quite dizzy, Annas wildly stamped about the floor in his soft slippers, gesticulating: "Be off, be off!"

But Judas on a sudden bowed down, stretching forth his hands submissively:

"But if you really.... But why be angry with poor Judas, who only desires his children's good. You also have children, young and handsome."

"We shall find some one else. Be gone!"

"But I - I did not say that I was unwilling to make a reduction. Did I ever say that I could not too yield? And do I not believe you, that possibly another may come and sell Jesus to you for fifteen oboli - nay, for two - for one?"

And bowing lower and lower, wriggling and flattering, Judas submissively consented to the sum offered to him. Annas shamefacedly, with dry, trembling hand, paid him the money, and silently looking round, as though scorched, lifted his head again and again towards the ceiling, and moving his lips rapidly, waited while Judas tested with his teeth all the silver pieces, one after another.

"There is now so much bad money about," Judas quickly explained.

"This money was devoted to the Temple by the pious," said Annas, glancing round quickly, and still more quickly turning the ruddy bald nape of his neck to Judas' view.

"But can pious people distinguish between good and bad money! Only rascals can do that."

Judas did not take the money home, but went beyond the city and hid it under a stone. Then he came back again quietly with heavy, dragging steps, as a wounded animal creeps slowly to its lair after a severe and deadly fight. Only Judas had no lair; but there was a house, and in the house he perceived Jesus. Weary and thin, exhausted with continual strife with the Pharisees, who surrounded Him every day in the Temple with a wall of white, shining, scholarly foreheads, He was sitting, leaning His cheek against the rough wall, apparently fast asleep. Through the open window drifted the restless noises of the city. On the other side of the wall Peter was hammering, as he put together a new table for the meal, humming the while a quiet Galilean song. But He heard nothing; he slept on peacefully and soundly. And this was He, whom they had bought for thirty pieces of silver.

Coming forward noiselessly, Judas, with the tender touch of a mother, who fears to wake her sick child - with the wonderment of a wild beast as it creeps from its lair suddenly, charmed by the sight of a white flowerlet - he gently touched His soft locks, and then quickly withdrew his hand. Once more he touched Him, and then silently crept out.

"Lord! Lord!" said he.

And going apart, he wept long, shrinking and wriggling and scratching his bosom with his nails and gnawing his shoulders. Then suddenly he ceased weeping and gnawing and gnashing his teeth, and fell into a sombre reverie, inclining his tear-stained face to one side in the attitude of one listening. And so he remained for a long time, doleful, determined, from every one apart, like fate itself.

. . . .

Judas surrounded the unhappy Jesus, during those last days of His short life, with quiet love and tender care and caresses. Bashful and timid like a maid in her first love, strangely sensitive and discerning, he divined the minutest unspoken wishes of Jesus, penetrating to the hidden depth of His feelings, His passing fits of sorrow, and distressing moments of weariness. And wherever Jesus stepped, His foot met something soft, and whenever He turned His gaze, it encountered something pleasing. Formerly Judas had not liked Mary Magdalene and the other women who were near Jesus. He had made rude jests at their expense, and done them little unkindnesses. But now he became their friend, their strange, awkward ally. With deep interest he would talk with them of the charming little idiosyncrasies of Jesus, and persistently asking the same questions, he would thrust money into their hands, their very palms - and they brought a box of very precious ointment, which Jesus liked so much, and anointed His feet. He himself bought for Jesus, after desperate bargaining, an expensive wine, and then was very angry when Peter drank nearly all of it up, with the indifference of a person who looks only to quantity; and in that rocky Jerusalem almost devoid of trees, flowers, and greenery he somehow managed to obtain young spring flowers and green grass, and through these same women to give them to Jesus.

For the first time in his life he would take up little children in his arms, finding them somewhere about the courts and streets, and unwillingly kiss them to prevent their crying; and often it would happen that some swarthy urchin with curly hair and dirty little nose, would climb up on the knees of the pensive Jesus, and imperiously demand to be petted. And while they enjoyed themselves together, Judas would walk up and down at one side like a severe jailor, who had himself, in springtime, let a butterfly in to a prisoner, and pretends to grumble at the breach of discipline.

On an evening, when together with the darkness, alarm took post as sentry by the window, Iscariot would cleverly turn the conversation to Galilee, strange to himself but dear to Jesus, with its still waters and green banks. And he would jog the heavy Peter till his dulled memory awoke, and in clear pictures in which everything was loud, distinct, full of colour, and solid, there arose before his eyes and ears the dear Galilean life. With eager attention, with half-open mouth in child-like fashion, and with eyes laughing in anticipation, Jesus would listen to his gusty, resonant, cheerful utterance, and sometimes laughed so at his jokes, that it was necessary to interrupt the story for some minutes. But John told tales even better than Peter. There was nothing ludicrous, nor startling, about his stories, but everything seemed so pensive, unusual, and beautiful, that tears would appear in Jesus' eyes, and He would sigh softly, while Judas nudged Mary Magdalene and excitedly whispered to her -

"What a narrator he is! Do you hear?"

"Yes, certainly."

"No, be more attentive. You women never make good listeners."

Then they would all quietly disperse to bed, and Jesus would kiss His thanks to John, and stroke kindly the shoulder of the tall Peter.

And without envy, but with a condescending contempt, Judas would witness these caresses. Of what importance were these tales and kisses and sighs compared with what he, Judas Iscariot, the red-haired, misshapen Judas, begotten among the rocks, could tell them if he chose?

CHAPTER VI

With one hand betraying Jesus, Judas tried hard with the other
to frustrate his own plans. He did not indeed endeavour to
dissuade Jesus from the last dangerous journey to Jerusalem, as
did the women; he even inclined rather to the side of the
relatives of Jesus, and of those amongst His disciples who
looked for a victory over Jerusalem as indispensable to the full
triumph of His cause. But he kept continually and obstinately
warning them of the danger, and in lively colours depicted the
threatening hatred of the Pharisees for Jesus, and their
readiness to commit any crime if, either secretly or openly,
they might make an end of the Prophet of Galilee. Each day
and every hour he kept talking of this, and there was not one
of the believers before whom Judas had not stood with uplifted
finger and uttered this serious warning:

"We must look after Jesus. We must defend for Jesus, when
the hour comes."

But whether it was the unlimited faith which the disciples had
in the miracle-working power of their Master, or the consciousness of their own uprightness, or whether it was simply
blindness, the alarming words of Judas were met with a smile,
and his continual advice provoked only a grumble. When
Judas procured, somewhere or other, two swords, and brought
them, only Peter approved of them, and gave Judas his meed
of praise, while the others complained:

"Are we soldiers that we should be made to gird on swords? Is
Jesus a captain of the host, and not a prophet?"

LEONID ANDREYEV

"But if they attempt to kill Him?"

"They will not dare when they perceive how all the people follow Him."

"But if they should dare! What then?"

John replied disdainfully -

"One would think, Judas, that you were the only one who loved Jesus!"

And eagerly seizing hold of these words, and not in the least offended, Judas began to question impatiently and hotly, with stern insistency:

"But you love Him, don't you?"

And there was not one of the believers who came to Jesus whom he did not ask more than once: "Do you love Him? Dearly love Him?"

And all answered that they loved Him.

He used often to converse with Thomas, and holding up his dry, hooked forefinger, with its long, dirty nail, in warning, would mysteriously say:

"Look here, Thomas, the terrible hour is drawing near. Are you prepared for it? Why did you not take the sword I brought you?"

Thomas would reply with deliberation:

"We are men unaccustomed to the use of arms. If we were to take issue with the Roman soldiery, they would kill us all, one after the other. Besides, you brought only two swords, and what could we do with only two?"

"We could get more. We could take them from the Roman soldiers," Judas impatiently objected, and even the serious Thomas smiled through his overhanging moustache.

"Ah! Judas! Judas! But where did you get these? They are like Roman swords."

"I stole them. I could have stolen more, only some one gave the alarm, and I fled."

Thomas considered a little, then said sorrowfully -

"Again you acted ill, Judas. Why do you steal?"

"There is no such thing as property."

"No, but to-morrow they will ask the soldiers: 'Where are your swords?' And when they cannot find them they will be punished though innocent."

The consequence was, that after the death of Jesus the disciples recalled these conversations of Judas, and determined that he had wished to destroy them, together with the Master, by inveigling them into an unequal and murderous conflict. And once again they cursed the hated name of Judas Iscariot the Traitor.

But the angry Judas, after each conversation, would go to the women and weep. They heard him gladly. The tender womanly element, that there was in his love for Jesus, drew him near to them, and made him simple, comprehensible, and even handsome in their eyes, although, as before, a certain amount of disdain was perceptible in his attitude towards them.

"Are they men?" he would bitterly complain of the disciples, fixing his blind, motionless eye confidingly on Mary Magdalene. "They are not men. They have not an oboles' worth of blood in their veins!"

"But then you are always speaking ill of others," Mary objected.

"Have I ever?" said Judas in surprise. "Oh, yes, I have indeed spoken ill of them; but is there not room for improvement in them? Ah! Mary, silly Mary, why are you not a man, to carry a sword?"

"It is so heavy, I could not lift it!" said Mary smilingly.

"But you will lift it, when men are too worthless. Did you give Jesus the lily that I found on the mountain? I got up early to find it, and this morning the sun was so beautiful, Mary! Was He pleased with it? Did He smile?"

"Yes, He was pleased. He said that its smell reminded Him of Galilee."

"But surely, you did not tell Him that it was Judas - Judas Iscariot - who got it for Him?"

"Why, you asked me not to tell Him."

"Yes, certainly, quite right," said Judas, with a sigh. "You might have let it out, though, women are such chatterers. But you did not let it out; no, you were firm. You are a good woman, Mary. You know that I have a wife somewhere. Now I should be glad to see her again; perhaps she is not a bad woman either. I don't know. She said, 'Judas was a liar and malignant,' so I left her. But she may be a good woman. Do you know?"

"How should I know, when I have never seen your wife?"

"True, true, Mary! But what think you, are thirty pieces of silver a large sum? Is it not rather a small one?"

"I should say a small one."

"Certainly, certainly. How much did you get when you were a harlot, five pieces of silver or ten? You were an expensive one, were you not?"

Mary Magdalene blushed, and dropped her head till her luxuriant, golden hair completely covered her face, so that nothing but her round white chin was visible.

"How bad you are, Judas; I want to forget about that, and you remind me of it!"

"No, Mary, you must not forget that. Why should you? Let others forget that you were a harlot, but you must remember. It is the others who should forget as soon as possible, but you should not. Why should you?"

"But it was a sin!"

"He fears who never committed a sin, but he who has committed it, what has he to fear? Do the dead fear death; is it not rather the living? No, the dead laugh at the living and their fears."

Thus by the hour would they sit and talk in friendly guise, he - already old, dried-up and misshapen, with his bulbous head and monstrous double-sided face; she - young, modest, tender, and charmed with life as with a story or a dream.

But time rolled by unconcernedly, while the thirty pieces of silver lay under the stone, and the terrible day of the Betrayal drew inevitably near. Already Jesus had ridden into Jerusalem on the ass's back, and the people, strewing their garments in the way, had greeted Him with enthusiastic cries of "Hosanna! Hosanna! He that cometh in the name of the Lord!"

So great was the exultation, so unrestrainedly did their loving cries rend the skies, that Jesus wept, but His disciples proudly said:

"Is not this the Son of God with us?"

And they themselves cried out with enthusiasm: "Hosanna! Hosanna! He that cometh in the name of the Lord!"

That evening it was long before they went to bed, recalling the enthusiastic and joyful reception. Peter was like a madman, as though possessed by the demon of merriment and pride. He shouted, drowning all voices with his leonine roar; he laughed, hurling his laughter at their heads, like great round stones; he kept kissing John and James, and even gave a kiss to Judas. He noisily confessed that he had had great fears for Jesus, but that he feared nothing now, that he had seen the love of the people for Him.

Swiftly moving his vivid, watchful eye, Judas glanced in surprise from side to side. He meditated, and then again listened, and looked. Then he took Thomas aside, and pinning him, as it were, to the wall with his keen gaze, he asked in doubt and fear, but with a certain confused hopefulness:

"Thomas! But what if He is right? What if He be founded upon a rock, and we upon sand? What then?"

"Of whom are you speaking?"

"How, then, would it be with Judas Iscariot? Then I should be obliged to strangle Him in order to do right. Who is deceiving Judas? You or he himself? Who is deceiving Judas? Who?"

"I don't understand you, Judas. You speak very unintelligently. 'Who is deceiving Jesus?' 'Who is right?'"

And Judas nodded his head and repeated like an echo:

"Who is deceiving Judas? Who?"

And the next day, in the way in which Judas raised his hand with thumb bent back,[1] and by the way in which he looked at Thomas, the same strange question was implied:

"Who is deceiving Judas? Who is right?"

[1] Does our author refer to the Roman sign of disapprobation, vertere, or convertere, pollicem? - Tr.

And still more surprised, and even alarmed, was Thomas,
when suddenly in the night he heard the loud, apparently glad
voice of Judas:

"Then Judas Iscariot will be no more. Then Jesus will be no
more. Then there will be Thomas, the stupid Thomas! Did
you ever wish to take the earth and lift it? And then, possibly
hurl it away?"

"That's impossible. What are you talking about, Judas?"

"It's quite possible," said Iscariot with conviction, "and we will
lift it up some day when you are asleep, stupid Thomas. Go to
sleep. I'm enjoying myself. When you sleep your nose plays the
Galilean pipe. Sleep!"

But now the believers were already dispersed about Jerusalem,
hiding in houses and behind walls, and the faces of those that
met them looked mysterious. The exultation had died down.
Confused reports of danger found their way in; Peter, with
gloomy countenance, tested the sword given to him by Judas,
and the face of the Master became even more melancholy and
stern. So swiftly the time passed, and inevitably approached
the terrible day of the Betrayal. Lo! the Last Supper was over,
full of grief and confused dread, and already had the obscure
words of Jesus sounded concerning some one who should
betray Him.

"You know who will betray Him?" asked Thomas, looking at
Judas with his straight-forward, clear, almost transparent eyes.

" Yes, I know," Judas replied harshly and decidedly. "You,

Thomas, will betray Him. But He Himself does not believe what He says! It is full time! Why does He not call to Him the strong, magnificent Judas?"

No longer by days, but by short, fleeting hours, was the inevitable time to be measured. It was evening; and evening stillness and long shadows lay upon the ground - the first sharp darts of the coming night of mighty contest - when a harsh, sorrowful voice was heard. It said:

"Dost Thou know whither I go, Lord? I go to betray Thee into the hands of Thine enemies."

And there was a long silence, evening stillness, and swift black shadows.

"Thou art silent, Lord? Thou commandest me to go?"

And again silence.

"Allow me to remain. But perhaps Thou canst not? Or darest not? Or wilt not?"

And again silence, stupendous, like the eyes of eternity.

"But indeed Thou knowest that I love Thee. Thou knowest all things. Why lookest Thou thus at Judas? Great is the mystery of Thy beautiful eyes, but is mine less? Order me to remain! But Thou art silent. Thou art ever silent. Lord, Lord, is it for this that in grief and pains have I sought Thee all my life, sought and found! Free me! Remove the weight; it is heavier than even mountains of lead. Dost Thou hear how the bosom of Judas Iscariot is cracking under it?"

And the last silence was abysmal, like the last glance of eternity.

"I go."

But the evening stillness woke not, neither uttered cry nor plaint, nor did its subtle air vibrate with the slightest tinkle - so soft was the fall of the retreating steps. They sounded for a time, and then were silent. And the evening stillness became pensive, stretched itself out in long shadows, and then grew dark; - and suddenly night, coming to meet it, all atremble with the rustle of sadly brushed-up leaves, heaved a last sigh and was still.

There was a bustle, a jostle, a rattle of other voices, as though some one had untied a bag of lively resonant voices, and they were falling out on the ground, by one and two, and whole heaps. It was the disciples talking. And drowning them all, reverberating from the trees and walls, and tripping up over itself, thundered the determined, powerful voice of Peter - he was swearing that never would he desert his Master.

"Lord," said he, half in anger, half in grief: "Lord! I am ready to go with Thee to prison and to death."

And quietly, like the soft echo of retiring footsteps, came the inexorable answer:

"I tell thee, Peter, the cock will not crow this day before thou dost deny Me thrice."

CHAPTER VII

The moon had already risen when Jesus prepared to go to the Mount of Olives, where He had spent all His last nights. But He tarried, for some inexplicable reason, and the disciples, ready to start, were hurrying Him. Then He said suddenly:

"He that hath a purse, let him take it, and likewise his scrip; and he that hath no sword, let him sell his garment and buy one. For I say unto you that this that is written must yet be accomplished in me: 'And he was reckoned among the transgressors.'"

The disciples were surprised and looked at one another in confusion. Peter replied:

"Lord, we have two swords here."

He looked searchingly into their kind faces, lowered His head, and said softly:

"It is enough."

The steps of the disciples resounded loudly in the narrow streets, and they were frightened by the sounds of their own footsteps; on the white wall, illumined by the moon, their black shadows appeared - and they were frightened by their own shadows. Thus they passed in silence through Jerusalem, which was absorbed in sleep, and now they came out of the gates of the city, and in the valley, full of fantastic, motionless shadows, the stream of Kedron stretched before them. Now they were frightened by everything. The soft murmuring and splashing of the water on the stones sounded to them like voices of people approaching them stealthily; the monstrous shades of the rocks and the trees, obstructing the road, disturbed them, and their motionlessness seemed to them to stir. But as they were ascending the mountain and approaching the garden, where they had safely and quietly passed so many nights before, they were growing ever bolder. From time to time they looked back at Jerusalem, all white in the moonlight, and they spoke to one another about the fear that had passed; and those who walked in the rear heard, in fragments, the soft words of Jesus. He spoke about their forsaking Him.

In the garden they paused soon after they had entered it. The majority of them remained there, and, speaking softly, began to make ready for their sleep, outspreading their cloaks over the transparent embroidery of the shadows and the moonlight. Jesus, tormented with uneasiness, and four of His disciples went further into the depth of the garden. There they seated themselves on the ground, which had not yet cooled off from the heat of the day, and while Jesus was silent, Peter and John lazily exchanged words almost devoid of any meaning. Yawning from fatigue, they spoke about the coolness of the night; about the high price of meat in Jerusalem, and about the fact that no fish was to be had in the city. They tried to determine the exact number of pilgrims that had gathered in Jerusalem for the festival, and Peter, drawling his words and yawning loudly, said that they numbered 20,000, while John and his brother Jacob assured him just as lazily that they did not number more than 10,000. Suddenly Jesus rose quickly.

"My soul is exceedingly sorrowful, even unto death; tarry ye here and watch with Me," He said, and departed hastily to the grove and soon disappeared amid its motionless shades and light.

"Where did He go?" said John, lifting himself on his elbow. Peter turned his head in the direction of Jesus and answered fatiguedly:

"I do not know."

And he yawned again loudly, then threw himself on his back and became silent. The others also became silent, and their motionless bodies were soon absorbed in the sound sleep of fatigue. Through his heavy slumber Peter vaguely saw something white bending over him, some one's voice resounded and died away, leaving no trace in his dimmed consciousness.

"Simon, are you sleeping?"

And he slept again, and again some soft voice reached his ear and died away without leaving any trace.

"You could not watch with me even one hour?"

"Oh, Master! if you only knew how sleepy I am," he thought in his slumber, but it seemed to him that he said it aloud. And he slept again. And a long time seemed to have passed, when suddenly the figure of Jesus appeared near him, and a loud, rousing voice instantly awakened him and the others:

"You are still sleeping and resting? It is ended, the hour has come - the Son of Man is betrayed into the hands of the sinners."

The disciples quickly sprang to their feet, confusedly seizing their cloaks and trembling from the cold of the sudden awakening. Through the thicket of the trees a multitude of warriors and temple servants was seen approaching noisily, illumining their way with torches. And from the other side the disciples came running, quivering from cold, their sleepy faces frightened; and not yet understanding what was going on, they asked hastily:

"What is it? Who are these people with torches?"

Thomas, pale faced, his moustaches in disorder, his teeth chattering from chilliness, said to Peter:

"They have evidently come after us."

Now a multitude of warriors surrounded them, and the smoky, quivering light of the torches dispelled the soft light of the moon. In front of the warriors walked Judas Iscariot quickly, and sharply turning his quick eye, searched for Jesus. He found Him, rested his look for an instant upon His tall, slender figure, and quickly whispered to the priests:

"Whomsoever I shall kiss, that same is He. Take Him and lead Him cautiously. Lead Him cautiously, do you hear?"

Then he moved quickly to Jesus, who waited for him in silence, and he directed his straight, sharp look, like a knife, into His calm, darkened eyes.

"Hail, Master!" he said loudly, charging his words of usual greeting with a strange and stern meaning.

But Jesus was silent, and the disciples looked at the traitor with horror, not understanding how the soul of a man could contain so much evil. Iscariot threw a rapid glance at their confused ranks, noticed their quiver, which was about to turn into a loud, trembling fear, noticed their pallor, their senseless smiles, the drowsy movements of their hands, which seemed as though fettered in iron at the shoulders - and a mortal sorrow began to burn in his heart, akin to the sorrow Christ had experienced before. Outstretching himself into a hundred ringing, sobbing strings, he rushed over to Jesus and kissed His cold cheek tenderly. He kissed it so softly, so tenderly, with such painful love and sorrow, that if Jesus had been a flower upon a thin stalk it would not have shaken from this kiss and would not have dropped the pearly dew from its pure petals.

"Judas," said Jesus, and with the lightning of His look He illumined that monstrous heap of shadows which was Iscariot's soul, but he could not penetrate into the bottomless depth. "Judas! Is it with a kiss you betray the Son of Man?"

And He saw how that monstrous chaos trembled and stirred. Speechless and stern, like death in its haughty majesty, stood Judas Iscariot, and within him a thousand impetuous and fiery voices groaned and roared:

"Yes! We betray Thee with the kiss of love! With the kiss of love we betray Thee to outrage, to torture, to death! With the voice of love we call together the hangmen from their dark holes, and we place a cross - and high over the top of the earth we lift love, crucified by love upon a cross."

Thus stood Judas, silent and cold, like death, and the shouting and the noise about Jesus answered the cry of His soul. With the rude irresoluteness of armed force, with the awkwardness of a vaguely understood purpose, the soldiers seized Him and dragged Him off - mistaking their irresoluteness for resistance, their fear for derision and mockery. Like a flock of frightened lambs, the disciples stood huddled together, not interfering, yet disturbing everybody, even themselves. Only a few of them resolved to walk and act separately. Jostled from all sides, Peter drew out the sword from its sheath with difficulty, as though he had lost all his strength, and faintly lowered it upon the head of one of the priests - without causing him any harm. Jesus, observing this, ordered him to throw away the useless weapon, and it fell under foot with a dull thud, and so evidently had it lost its sharpness and destructive power that it did not occur to any one to pick it up. So it rolled about under foot, until several days afterwards it was found on the same spot by some children at play, who made a toy of it.

The soldiers kept dispersing the disciples, but they gathered together again and stupidly got under the soldiers' feet, and this went on so long that at last a contemptuous rage mastered the soldiery. One of them with frowning brow went up to the shouting John; another rudely pushed from his shoulder the hand of Thomas, who was arguing with him about something or other, and shook a big fist right in front of his straight-forward, transparent eyes. John fled, and Thomas and James fled, and all the disciples, as many as were present, forsook

Jesus and fled. Losing their cloaks, knocking themselves against the trees, tripping up against stones and falling, they fled to the hills terror-driven, while in the stillness of the moonlight night the ground rumbled loudly beneath the tramp of many feet. Some one, whose name did not transpire, just risen from his bed (for he was covered only with a blanket), rushed excitedly into the crowd of soldiers and servants. When they tried to stop him, and seized hold of his blanket, he gave a cry of terror, and took to flight like the others, leaving his garment in the hands of the soldiers. And so he ran stark-naked, with desperate leaps, and his bare body glistened strangely in the moonlight.

When Jesus was led away, Peter, who had hidden himself behind the trees, came out and followed his Master at a distance. Noticing another man in front of him, who walked silently, he thought that it was John, and he called him softly:

"John, is that you?"

"And is that you, Peter?" answered the other, pausing, and by the voice Peter recognised the traitor. "Peter, why did you not run away together with the others?"

Peter stopped and said with contempt:

"Leave me, Satan!"

Judas began to laugh, and paying no further attention to Peter, he advanced where the torches were flashing dimly and where the clanking of the weapons mingled with the footsteps. Peter followed him cautiously, and thus they entered the court of the high priest almost simultaneously and mingled in the crowd of the priests who were warming themselves at the bonfires. Judas warmed his bony hands morosely at the bonfire and heard Peter saying loudly somewhere behind him:

"No, I do not know Him."

But it was evident that they were insisting there that he was one of the disciples of Jesus, for Peter repeated still louder: "But I do not understand what you are saying."

Without turning around, and smiling involuntarily, Judas shook his head affirmatively and muttered:

"That's right, Peter! Do not give up the place near Jesus to any one."

And he did not see the frightened Peter walk away from the courtyard. And from that night until the very death of Jesus, Judas did not see a single one of the disciples of Jesus near Him; and amid all that multitude there were only two, inseparable until death, strangely bound together by sufferings - He who had been betrayed to abuse and torture and he who had betrayed Him. Like brothers, they both, the Betrayed and the betrayer, drank out of the same cup of sufferings, and the fiery liquid burned equally the pure and the impure lips.

Gazing fixedly at the wood-fire, which imparted a feeling of warmth to his eyes, stretching out his long, shaking hands to the flame, his hands and feet forming a confused outline in the trembling light and shade, Iscariot kept mumbling in hoarse complaint:

"How cold! My God, how cold it is!"

So, when the fishermen go away at night leaving an expiring fire of drift-wood upon the shore, from the dark depth of the sea might something creep forth, crawl up towards the fire, look at it with wild intentness, and dragging all its limbs up to it, mutter in hoarse complaint:

"How cold! My God, how cold it is!"

Suddenly Judas heard behind him a burst of loud voices, the cries and laughter of the soldiers full of the usual sleepy, greedy malice; and lashes, short frequent strokes upon a living body.

He turned round, a momentary anguish running through his whole frame - his very bones. They were scourging Jesus.

Has it come to that?

He had seen the soldiers lead Jesus away with them to their guardroom. The night was already nearly over, the fires had sunk down and were covered with ashes, but from the guardroom was still borne the sound of muffled cries, laughter, and invectives. They were scourging Jesus.

As one who has lost his way, Iscariot ran nimbly about the empty courtyard, stopped in his course, lifted his head and ran on again, and was surprised when he came into collision with heaps of embers, or with the walls.

Then he clung to the wall of the guardroom, stretched himself out to his full height, and glued himself to the window and the crevices of the door, eagerly examining what they were doing. He saw a confined stuffy room, dirty, like all guardrooms in the world, with bespitten floor, and walls as greasy and stained as though they had been trodden and rolled upon. And he saw the Man whom they were scourging. They struck Him on the face and head, and tossed Him about like a soft bundle from one end of the room to the other. And since He neither cried out nor resisted, after looking intently, it actually appeared at moments as though it was not a living human being, but a soft effigy without bones or blood. It bent itself strangely like a doll, and in falling, knocking its head against the stone floor it did not give the impression of a hard substance striking against a hard substance, but of something soft and devoid of feeling. And when one looked long, it became like some strange, endless game - and sometimes it became almost a complete illusion.

After one hard kick, the man or effigy fell slowly on its knees before a sitting soldier, he in turn flung it away, and turning over, it dropped down before the next, and so on and on. A loud guffaw arose, and Judas smiled too, - as though the strong hand of some one with iron fingers had torn his mouth asunder. It was the mouth of Judas that was deceived.

Night dragged on, and the fires were still smouldering. Judas threw himself from the wall, and crawled to one of the fires, poked up the ashes, rekindled it, and although he no longer felt the cold, he stretched his slightly trembling hands over the flames, and began to mutter dolefully:

"Ah! how painful, my Son, my Son! How painful!"

Then he went again to the window, which was gleaming yellow with a dull light between the thick grating, and once more began to watch them scourging Jesus. Once before the very eyes of Judas appeared His swarthy countenance, now marred out of human semblance, and covered with a forest of dishevelled hair. Then some one's hand plunged into those locks, threw the Man down, and rhythmically turning His head from one side to the other, began to wipe the filthy floor with His face. Right under the window a soldier was sleeping, his open mouth revealing his glittering white teeth; and some one's broad back, with naked, brawny neck, barred the window, so that nothing more could be seen. And suddenly the noise ceased.

"What's that? Why are they silent? Have they suddenly divined the truth?"

Momentarily the whole head of Judas, in all its parts, was filled with the rumbling, shouting and roaring of a thousand maddened thoughts! Had they divined? They understood that this was the very best of men - it was so simple, so clear! Lo! He is coming out, and behind Him they are abjectly crawling. Yes, He is coming here, to Judas, coming out a victor, a hero, arbiter of the truth, a god....

"Who is deceiving Judas? Who is right?"

But no. Once more noise and shouting. They are scourging

Him again. They do not understand, they have not guessed, they are beating Him harder, more cruelly than ever. The fires burn out, covered with ashes, and the smoke above them is as transparently blue as the air, and the sky as bright as the moon. It is the day approaching.

"What is day?" asks Judas.

And lo! everything begins to glow, to scintillate, to grow young again, and the smoke above is no longer blue, but rose-coloured. It is the sun rising.

"What is the sun?" asks Judas.

CHAPTER VIII

They pointed the finger at Judas, and some in contempt, others with hatred and fear, said:

"Look, that is Judas the Traitor!"

This already began to be the opprobrious title, to which he had doomed himself throughout the ages. Thousands of years may pass, nation may supplant nation, and still the air will resound with the words, uttered with contempt and fear by good and bad alike:

"Judas the Traitor!"

But he listened imperturbably to what was said of him, dominated by a feeling of burning, all-subduing curiosity. Ever since the morning when they led forth Jesus from the guard-room, after scourging Him, Judas had followed Him, strangely enough feeling neither grief nor pain nor joy - only an unconquerable desire to see and hear everything. Though he had had no sleep the whole night, his body felt light; when he was crushed and prevented from advancing, he elbowed his way through the crowd and adroitly wormed himself into the front place; and not for a moment did his vivid quick eye remain at rest. At the examination of Jesus before Caiaphas, in order not to lose a word, he hollowed his hand round his ear, and nodded his head in affirmation, murmuring:

"Just so! Thou hearest, Jesus?"

But he was a prisoner, like a fly tied to a thread, which,

buzzing, flies hither and thither, but cannot for one moment free itself from the tractable but unyielding thread.

Certain stony thoughts lay at the back of his head, and to these he was firmly bound; he knew not, as it were, what these thoughts were; he did not wish to stir them up, but he felt them continually. At times they would come to him all of a sudden, oppress him more and more, and begin to crush him with their unimaginable weight, as though the vault of a rocky cavern were slowly and terribly descending upon his head.

Then he would grip his heart with his hand, and strive to set his whole body in motion, as though he were perishing with cold, and hasten to shift his eyes to a fresh place, and again to another. When they led Jesus away from Caiaphas, he met His weary eyes quite close, and, somehow or other, unconsciously he gave Him several friendly nods.

"I am here, my Son, I am here," he muttered hurriedly, and maliciously poked to some gaper in the back who stood in his way.

And now, in a huge shouting crowd, they all moved on to Pilate for the last examination and trial, and with the same insupportable curiosity Judas searched the faces of the ever swelling multitude. Many were quite unknown to him; Judas had never seen them before, but some were there who had cried, "Hosanna!" to Jesus, and at each step the number of them seemed to increase.

"Well, well!" thought Judas, and his head spun round as if he were drunk, "the worst is over. Directly they will be crying: 'He is ours, He is Jesus! What are you about?' and all will understand, and - "

But the believers walked in silence. Some hypocritically smiled, as if to say: "The affair is none of ours!" Others spoke with constraint, but their low voices were drowned in the rumbling of movement, and the loud delirious shouts of His enemies.

And Judas felt better again. Suddenly he noticed Thomas cautiously slipping through the crowd not far off, and struck by a sudden thought, he was about to go up to him. At the sight of the traitor, Thomas was frightened, and tried to hide himself. But in a little narrow street, between two walls, Judas overtook him.

"Thomas, wait a bit!"

Thomas stopped, and stretching both hands out in front of him solemnly pronounced the words:

"Avaunt, Satan!"

Iscariot made an impatient movement of the hands.

"What a fool you are, Thomas! I thought that you had more sense than the others. Satan indeed! That requires proof."

Letting his hands fall, Thomas asked in surprise:

"But did not you betray the Master? I myself saw you bring the soldiers, and point Him out to them. If this is not treachery, I should like to know what is!"

"Never mind that," hurriedly said Judas. "Listen, there are many of you here. You must all gather together, and loudly demand: 'Give up Jesus. He is ours!' They will not refuse you, they dare not. They themselves will understand."

"What do you mean! What are you thinking of!" said Thomas, with a decisive wave of his hands. "Have you not seen what a number of armed soldiers and servants of the Temple there are here? Moreover, the trial has not yet taken place, and we must not interfere with the court. Surely he understands that Jesus is innocent, and will order His release without delay."

"You, then, think so too," said Judas thoughtfully. "Thomas, Thomas, what if it be the truth? What then? Who is right?

Who has deceived Judas?"

"We were all talking last night, and came to the conclusion that the court cannot condemn the innocent. But if it does, why then - "

"What then!"

"Why, then it is no court. And it will be the worse for them when they have to give an account before the real Judge."

"Before the real! Is there any 'real' left?" sneered Judas.

"And all of our party cursed you; but since you say that you were not the traitor, I think you ought to be tried."

Judas did not want to hear him out; but turned right about, and hurried down the street in the wake of the retreating crowd. He soon, however, slackened his pace, mindful of the fact that a crowd always travels slowly, and that a single pedestrian will inevitably overtake it.

When Pilate led Jesus out from his palace, and set Him before the people, Judas, crushed against a column by the heavy backs of the soldiers, furiously turning his head about to see something between two shining helmets, suddenly felt clearly that the worst was over. He saw Jesus in the sunshine, high above the heads of the crowd, blood-stained, pale with a crown of thorns, the sharp spikes of which pressed into His forehead.

He stood on the edge of an elevation, visible from His head to His small, sunburnt feet, and waited so calmly, was so serene in His immaculate purity, that only a blind man, who perceived not the very sun, could fail to see, only a madman would not understand. And the people held their peace - it was so still, that Judas heard the breathing of the soldier in front of him, and how, at each breath, a strap creaked somewhere about his body.

"Yes, it will soon be over! They will understand immediately," thought Judas, and suddenly something strange, like the dazzling joy of falling from a giddy height into a blue sparkling abyss, arrested his heart-beats.

Contemptuously drawing his lips down to his rounded well-shaven chin, Pilate flung to the crowd the dry, curt words - as one throws bones to a pack of hungry hounds - thinking to cheat their longing for fresh blood and living, palpitating flesh:

"You have brought this Man before me as a corrupter of the people, and behold I have examined Him before you, and I find this Man guiltless of that of which you accuse Him...."

Judas closed his eyes. He was waiting.

All the people began to shout, to sob, to howl with a thousand voices of wild beasts and men:

"Put Him to death! Crucify Him! Crucify Him!" And as though in self-mockery, as though wishing in one moment to plumb the very depths of all possible degradation, madness and shame, the crowd cries out, sobs, and demands with a thousand voices of wild beasts and men:

"Release unto us Barabbas! But crucify Him! Crucify Him!"

But the Roman had evidently not yet said his last word. Over his proud, shaven countenance there passed convulsions of disgust and anger. He understood! He has understood all along! He speaks quietly to his attendants, but his voice is not heard in the roar of the crowd. What does he say? Is he ordering them to bring swords, and to smite those maniacs?

"Bring water."

"Water? What water? What for?"

Ah , lo! he washes his hands. Why does he wash his clean white hands all adorned with rings? He lifts them and cries angrily to the people, whom surprise holds in silence:

"I am innocent of the blood of this Just Person. See ye to it."

While the water is still dripping from his fingers on to the marble pavement, something soft prostrates itself at his feet, and sharp, burning lips kiss his hand, which he is powerless to withdraw, glue themselves to it like tentacles, almost bite and draw blood. He looks down in disgust and fear, and sees a great squirming body, a strangely twofold face, and two immense eyes so queerly diverse from one another that, as it were, not one being but a number of them clung to his hands and feet. He heard a broken, burning whisper:

"O wise and noble... wise and noble."

And with such a truly satanic joy did that wild face blaze, that, with a cry, Pilate kicked him away, and Judas fell backwards. And there he lay upon the stone flags like an overthrown demon, still stretching out his hand to the departing Pilate, and crying as one passionately enamoured:

"O wise, O wise and noble...."

Then he gathered himself up with agility, and ran away followed by the laughter of the soldiery. Evidently there was yet hope. When they come to see the cross, and the nails, then they will understand, and then.... What then? He catches sight of the panic-stricken Thomas in passing, and for some reason or other reassuringly nods to him; he overtakes Jesus being led to execution. The walking is difficult, small stones roll under the feet, and suddenly Judas feels that he is tired. He gives himself up wholly to the trouble of deciding where best to plant his feet, he looks dully around, and sees Mary Magdalene weeping, and a number of women weeping - hair dishevelled, eyes red, lips distorted - all the excessive grief of a tender woman's soul when submitted to outrage. Suddenly he revives, and seizing the moment, runs up to Jesus:

LEONID ANDREYEV

"I go with Thee," he hurriedly whispers.

The soldiers drive him away with blows of their whips, and squirming so as to avoid the blows, and showing his teeth at the soldiers, he explains hurriedly:

"I go with Thee. Thither. Thou understandest whither."

He wipes the blood from his face, shakes his fist at one of the soldiers, who turns round and smiles, and points him out to the others. Then he looks for Thomas, but neither he nor any of the disciples are in the crowd that accompanies Jesus. Again he is conscious of fatigue, and drags one foot with difficulty after the other, as he attentively looks out for the sharp, white, scattered pebbles.

When the hammer was uplifted to nail Jesus' left hand to the tree, Judas closed his eyes, and for a whole age neither breathed, nor saw, nor lived, but only listened.

But lo! with a grating sound, iron strikes against iron, time after time, dull, short blows, and then the sharp nail penetrating the soft wood and separating its particles is distinctly heard.

One hand. It is not yet too late!

The other hand. It is not yet too late!

A foot, the other foot! Is all lost?

He irresolutely opens his eyes, and sees how the cross is raised, and rocks, and is set fast in the trench. He sees how the hands of Jesus are convulsed by the tension, how painfully His arms stretch, how the wounds grow wider, and how the exhausted abdomen disappears under the ribs. The arms stretch more and more, grow thinner and whiter, and become dislocated from the shoulders, and the wounds of the nails redden and lengthen gradually - lo! in a moment they will be torn away.

No. It stopped. All stopped. Only the ribs move up and down with the short, deep breathing.

On the very crown of the hill the cross is raised, and on it is the crucified Jesus. The horror and the dreams of Judas are realised, he gets up from his knees on which, for some reason, he has knelt, and gazes around coldly.

Thus does a stern conqueror look, when he has already determined in his heart to surrender everything to destruction and death, and for the last time throws a glance over a rich foreign city, still alive with sound, but already phantom-like under the cold hand of death. And suddenly, as clearly as his terrible victory, Iscariot saw its ominous precariousness. What if they should suddenly understand? It is not yet too late! Jesus still lives. There He gazes with entreating, sorrowing eyes.

What can prevent the thin film which covers the eyes of mankind, so thin that it hardly seems to exist at all, what can prevent it from rending? What if they should understand? What if suddenly, in all their threatening mass of men, women and children, they should advance, silently, without a cry, and wipe out the soldiery, plunging them up to their ears in their own blood, should tear from the ground the accursed cross, and by the hands of all who remain alive should lift up the liberated Jesus above the summit of the hill! Hosanna! Hosanna!

Hosanna? No! Better that Judas should lie on the ground. Better that he should lie upon the ground, and gnashing his teeth like a dog, should watch and wait until all these should rise up.

But what has come to Time? Now it almost stands still, so that one would wish to push it with the hands, to kick it, beat it with a whip like a lazy ass. Now it rushes madly down some mountain, and catches its breath, and stretches out its hand in vain to stop itself. There weeps the mother of Jesus. Let them weep. What avail her tears now? nay, the tears of all the mothers in the world?

"What are tears?" asks Judas, and madly pushes unyielding Time, beats it with his fists, curses it like a slave. It belongs to some one else, and therefore is unamenable to discipline. Oh! if only it belonged to Judas! But it belongs to all these people who are weeping, laughing, chattering as in the market. It belongs to the sun; it belongs to the cross; to the heart of Jesus, which is dying so slowly.

What an abject heart has Judas! He lays his hand upon it, but it cries out: "Hosanna," so loud that all may hear. He presses it to the ground, but it cries, "Hosanna, Hosanna!" like a babbler who scatters holy mysteries broadcast through the street.

"Be still! Be still!"

Suddenly a loud broken lamentation, dull cries, the last hurried movements towards the cross. What is it? Have they understood at last?

No, Jesus is dying. But can this be? Yes, Jesus is dying. His pale hands are motionless, but short convulsions run over His face, and breast, and legs. But can this be? Yes, He is dying. His breathing becomes less frequent. It ceases. No, there is yet one sigh, Jesus is still upon the earth. But is there another? No, no, no. Jesus is dead.

It is finished. Hosanna! Hosanna!

His horror and his dreams are realised. Who will now snatch the victory from the hands of Iscariot?

It is finished. Let all people on earth stream to Golgotha, and shout with their million throats, "Hosanna! Hosanna!" And let a sea of blood and tears be poured out at its foot, and they will find only the shameful cross and a dead Jesus!

Calmly and coldly Iscariot surveys the dead, letting his gaze rest for a moment on that neck, which he had kissed only yesterday with a farewell kiss; and slowly goes away. Now all Time belongs to him, and he walks without hurry; now all the World belongs to him, and he steps firmly, like a ruler, like a king, like one who is infinitely and joyfully alone in the world. He observes the mother of Jesus, and says to her sternly:

"Thou weepest, mother? Weep, weep, and long will all the mothers upon earth weep with thee: until I come with Jesus and destroy death."

What does he mean? Is he mad, or is he mocking - this Traitor? He is serious, and his face is stern, and his eyes no longer dart about in mad haste. Lo! he stands still, and with cold attention views a new, diminished earth.

It has become small, and he feels the whole of it under his feet. He looks at the little mountains, quietly reddening under the last rays of the sun, and he feels the mountains under his feet.

He looks at the sky opening wide its azure mouth; he looks at the small round disc of the sun, which vainly strives to singe and dazzle, and he feels the sky and the sun under his feet. Infinitely and joyfully alone, he proudly feels the impotence of all forces which operate in the world, and has cast them all into the abyss.

He walks farther on, with quiet, masterful steps. And Time goes neither forward nor back: obediently it marches in step with him in all its invisible immensity.

It is the end.

CHAPTER IX

As an old cheat, coughing, smiling fawningly, bowing incessantly, Judas Iscariot the Traitor appeared before the Sanhedrin. It was the day after the murder of Jesus, about midday. There they were all, His judges and murderers: the aged Annas with his sons, exact and disgusting likenesses of their father, and his son-in-law Caiaphas, devoured by ambition, and all the other members of the Sanhedrin, whose names have been snatched from the memory of mankind - rich and distinguished Sadducees, proud in their power and knowledge of the Law.

In silence they received the Traitor, their haughty faces remaining motionless, as though no one had entered. And even the very least, and most insignificant among them, to whom the others paid no attention, lifted up his bird-like face and looked as though no one had entered.

Judas bowed and bowed and bowed, and they looked on in silence: as though it were not a human being that had entered, but only an unclean insect that had crept in, and which they had not observed. But Judas Iscariot was not the man to be perturbed: they kept silence, and he kept on bowing, and thought that if it was necessary to go on bowing till evening, he could do so.

At length Caiaphas inquired impatiently:

"What do you want?"

Judas bowed once more, and said in a loud voice -

"It is I, Judas Iscariot, who betrayed to you Jesus of Nazareth."

"Well, what of that? You have received your due. Go away!" ordered Annas; but Judas appeared unconscious of the command, and continued bowing. Glancing at him, Caiaphas asked Annas:

"How much did you give?"

"Thirty pieces of silver."

Caiaphas laughed, and even the grey-bearded Annas laughed, too, and over all their proud faces there crept a smile of enjoyment; and even the one with the bird-like face laughed. Judas, perceptibly blanching, hastily interrupted with the words:

"That's right! Certainly it was very little; but is Judas discontented, does Judas call out that he has been robbed? He is satisfied. Has he not contributed to a holy cause - yes, a holy? Do not the most sage people now listen to Judas, and think: He is one of us, this Judas Iscariot; he is our brother, our friend, this Judas Iscariot, the Traitor! Does not Annas want to kneel down and kiss the hand of Judas? Only Judas will not allow it; he is a coward, he is afraid they will bite him."

Caiaphas said:

"Drive the dog out! What's he barking about?"

"Get along with you. We have no time to listen to your babbling," said Annas imperturbably.

Judas drew himself up and closed his eyes. The hypocrisy, which he had carried so lightly all his life, suddenly became an insupportable burden, and with one movement of his eyelashes he cast it from him. And when he looked at Annas again, his glance was simple, direct, and terrible in its naked truthfulness.

But they paid no attention to this either.

"You want to be driven out with sticks!" cried Caiaphas.

Panting under the weight of the terrible words, which he was lifting higher and higher, in order to hurl them hence upon the heads of the judges, Judas hoarsely asked:

"But you know... you know... who He was... He, whom you condemned yesterday and crucified?"

"We know. Go away!"

With one word he would straightway rend that thin film which was spread over their eyes, and all the earth would stagger beneath the weight of the merciless truth! They had a soul, they should be deprived of it; they had a life, they should lose their life; they had light before their eyes, eternal darkness and horror should cover them. Hosanna! Hosanna!

And these words, these terrible words, were tearing his throat asunder -

"He was no deceiver. He was innocent and pure. Do you hear? Judas deceived you. He betrayed to you an innocent man."

He waits. He hears the aged, unconcerned voice of Annas, saying:

"And is that all you want to say?"

"You do not seem to have understood me," says Judas, with dignity, turning pale. "Judas deceived you. He was innocent. You have slain the innocent."

He of the bird-like face smiles; but Annas is indifferent, Annas yawns. And Caiaphas yawns, too, and says wearily:

"What did they mean by talking to me about the intellect of

Judas Iscariot? He is simply a fool, and a bore, too."

"What?" cries Judas, all suffused with dark madness. "But who are you, the clever ones! Judas deceived you - hear! It was not He that he betrayed - but you - you wiseacres, you, the powerful, you he betrayed to a shameful death, which will not end, throughout the ages. Thirty pieces of silver! Well, well. But that is the price of YOUR blood - blood filthy as the dishwater which the women throw out of the gates of their houses. Oh! Annas, old, grey, stupid Annas, chock-full of the Law, why did you not give one silver piece, just one obolus more? At this price you will go down through the ages!"

"Be off!" cries Caiaphas, growing purple in the face. But Annas stops him with a motion of the hand, and asks Judas as unconcernedly as ever:

"Is that all?"

"Verily, if I were to go into the desert, and cry to the wild beasts: 'Wild beasts, have ye heard the price at which men valued their Jesus?' - what would the wild beasts do? They would creep out of the lairs, they would howl with anger, they would forget their fear of mankind, and would all come here to devour you! If I were to say to the sea: 'Sea, knowest thou the price at which men valued their Jesus?' If I were to say to the mountains: 'Mountains, know ye the price at which men valued their Jesus?' Then the sea and the mountains would leave their places, assigned to them for ages, and would come here and fall upon your heads!"

"Does Judas wish to become a prophet? He speaks so loud!" mockingly remarks he of the bird-like face, with an ingratiating glance at Caiaphas.

"To-day I saw a pale sun. It was looking at the earth, and saying: 'Where is the Man?' To-day I saw a scorpion. It was sitting upon a stone and laughingly said: 'Where is the Man?' I went near and looked into its eyes. And it laughed and said:

'Where is the Man? I do not see Him!' Where is the Man? I ask you, I do not see Him - or is Judas become blind, poor Judas Iscariot!"

And Iscariot begins to weep aloud.

He was, during those moments, like a man out of his mind, and Caiaphas turned away, making a contemptuous gesture with his hand. But Annas considered for a time, and then said:

"I perceive, Judas, that you really have received but little, and that disturbs you. Here is some more money; take it and give it to your children."

He threw something, which rang shrilly. The sound had not died away, before another, like it, strangely prolonged the clinking.

Judas had hastily flung the pieces of silver and the oboles into the faces of the high priest and of the judges, returning the price paid for Jesus. The pieces of money flew in a curved shower, falling on their faces, and on the table, and rolling about the floor.

Some of the judges closed their hands with the palms outwards; others leapt from their places, and shouted and scolded. Judas, trying to hit Annas, threw the last coin, after which his trembling hand had long been fumbling in his wallet, spat in anger, and went out.

"Well, well," he mumbled, as he passed swiftly through the streets, scaring the children. "It seems that thou didst weep, Judas? Was Caiaphas really right when he said that Judas Iscariot was a fool? He who weeps in the day of his great revenge is not worthy of it - know'st thou that, Judas? Let not thine eyes deceive thee; let not thine heart lie to thee; flood not the fire with tears, Judas Iscariot!"

The disciples were sitting in mournful silence, listening to what was going on without. There was still danger that the vengeance of Jesus' enemies might not confine itself to Him, and so they were all expecting a visit from the guard, and perhaps more executions. Near to John, to whom, as the beloved disciple, the death of Jesus was especially grievous, sat Mary Magdalene, and Matthew trying to comfort him in an undertone. Mary, whose face was swollen with weeping, softly stroked his luxurious curling hair with her hand, while Matthew said didactically, in the words of Solomon:

"'The long suffering is better than a hero; and he that ruleth his own spirit than one who taketh a city.'"

At this moment Judas knocked loudly at the door, and entered. All started up in terror, and at first were not sure who it was; but when they recognised the hated countenance, the red-haired, bulbous head, they uttered a simultaneous cry.

Peter raised both hands and shouted:

"Get out of here, Traitor! Get out, or I will kill you."

But the others looked more carefully at the face and eyes of the Traitor, and said nothing, merely whispering in terror:

"Leave him alone, leave him alone! He is possessed with a devil."

Judas waited until they had quite done, and then cried out in a loud voice:

"Hail, ye eyes of Judas Iscariot! Ye have just seen the cold-blooded murderers. Lo! Where is Jesus? I ask you, where is Jesus?"

There was something compelling in the hoarse voice of Judas, and Thomas replied obediently -

" You know yourself, Judas, that our Master was

crucified yesterday."

"But how came you to permit it? Where was your love? Thou, Beloved Disciple, and thou, Rock, where were you all when they were crucifying your Friend on the tree?"

"What could we do, judge thou?" said Thomas, with a gesture of protest.

"Thou asketh that, Thomas? Very well!" and Judas threw his head back, and fell upon him angrily. "He who loves does not ask what can be done - he goes and does it - he weeps, he bites, he throttles the enemy, and breaks his bones! He, that is, who loves! If your son were drowning would you go into the city and inquire of the passers by: 'What must I do? My son is drowning!' No, you would rather throw yourself into the water and drown with him. One who loved would!"

Peter replied grimly to the violent speech of Judas:

"I drew a sword, but He Himself forbade."

"Forbade? And you obeyed!" jeered Judas. "Peter, Peter, how could you listen to Him? Does He know anything of men, and of fighting?"

"He who does not submit to Him goes to hell fire."

"Then why did you not go, Peter? Hell fire! What's that? Now, supposing you had gone - what good's your soul to you, if you dare not throw it into the fire, if you want to?"

"Silence!" cried John, rising. "He Himself willed this sacrifice. His sacrifice is beautiful!"

"Is a sacrifice ever beautiful, Beloved Disciple? Wherever there is a sacrifice, then there is an executioner, and there traitors! Sacrifice - that is suffering for one and disgrace for all the others! Traitors, traitors, what have ye done with the world?

Now they look at it from above and below, and laugh and cry: 'Look at that world, upon it they crucified Jesus!' And they spit on it - as I do!"

Judas angrily spat on the ground.

"He took upon Him the sin of all mankind. His sacrifice is beautiful," John insisted.

"No! you have taken all sin upon yourselves. You, Beloved Disciple, will not a race of traitors take their beginning from you, a pusillanimous and lying breed? O blind men, what have ye done with the earth? You have done your best to destroy it, ye will soon be kissing the cross on which ye crucified Jesus! Yes, yes, Judas gives ye his word that ye will kiss the cross!"

"Judas, don't revile!" roared Peter, pushing. "How could we slay all His enemies? They are so many!"

"And thou, Peter!" exclaimed John in anger, "dost thou not perceive that he is possessed of Satan? Leave us, Tempter! Thou'rt full of lies. The Teacher forbade us to kill."

"But did He forbid you to die? Why are you alive, when He is dead? Why do your feet walk, why does your tongue talk trash, why do your eyes blink, when He is dead, motionless, speechless? How do your cheeks dare to be red, John, when His are pale? How can you dare to shout, Peter, when He is silent? What could you do? You ask Judas? And Judas answers you, the magnificent, bold Judas Iscariot replies: 'Die!' You ought to have fallen on the road, to have seized the soldiers by the sword, by the hands, and drowned them in a sea of your own blood - yes, die, die! Better had it been, that His Father should have cause to cry out with horror, when you all enter there!"

Judas ceased with raised head. Suddenly he noticed the remains of a meal upon the table. With strange surprise, curiously, as though for the first time in his life he looked on food, he examined it, and slowly asked:

"What is this? You have been eating? Perhaps you have also been sleeping?"

Peter, who had begun to feel Judas to be some one, who could command obedience, drooping his head, tersely replied: "I slept, I slept and ate!"

Thomas said, resolutely and firmly:

"This is all untrue, Judas. Just consider: if we had all died, who would have told the story of Jesus? Who would have conveyed His teaching to mankind if we had all died, Peter and John and I?"

"But what is the truth itself in the mouths of traitors? Does it not become a lie? Thomas, Thomas, dost thou not understand, that thou art now only a sentinel at the grave of dead Truth? The sentinel falls asleep, and the thief cometh and carries away the truth; say, where is the truth? Cursed be thou, Thomas! Fruitless, and a beggar shalt thou be throughout the ages, and all you with him, accursed ones!"

"Accursed be thou thyself, Satan!" cried John, and James and Matthew and all the other disciples repeated his cry; only Peter held his peace.

"I am going to Him," said Judas, stretching his powerful hand on high. "Who will follow Iscariot to Jesus?"

"I - I also go with thee," cried Peter, rising.

But John and the others stopped him in horror, saying:

"Madman! Thou hast forgotten, that he betrayed the Master into the hands of His enemies."

Peter began to lament bitterly, striking his breast with his fist:

"Whither, then, shall I go? O Lord! whither shall I go?"

. . . .

Judas had long ago, during his solitary walks, marked the place where he intended to make an end of himself after the death of Jesus.

It was upon a hill high above Jerusalem. There stood but one tree, bent and twisted by the wind, which had torn it on all sides, half withered. One of its broken, crooked branches stretched out towards Jerusalem, as though in blessing or in threat, and this one Judas had chosen on which to hang a noose.

But the walk to the tree was long and tedious, and Judas Iscariot was very weary. The small, sharp stones, scattered under his feet, seemed continually to drag him backwards, and the hill was high, stern, and malign, exposed to the wind. Judas was obliged to sit down several times to rest, and panted heavily, while behind him, through the clefts of the rock, the mountain breathed cold upon his back.

"Thou too art against me, accursed one!" said Judas contemptuously, as he breathed with difficulty, and swayed his heavy head, in which all the thoughts were now petrifying.

Then he raised it suddenly, and opening wide his now fixed eyes, angrily muttered:

"No, they were too bad for Judas. Thou hearest Jesus? Wilt Thou trust me now? I am coming to Thee. Meet me kindly, I am weary - very weary. Then Thou and I, embracing like brothers, shall return to earth. Shall we not?"

Again he swayed his petrifying head, and again he opened his eyes, mumbling:

"But maybe Thou wilt be angry with Judas when he arrives?

And Thou wilt not trust him? And wilt send him to hell? Well! What then! I will go to hell. And in Thy hell fire I will weld iron, and weld iron, and demolish Thy heaven. Dost approve? Then Thou wilt believe in me. Then Thou wilt come back with me to earth, wilt Thou not, Jesus?"

Eventually Judas reached the summit and the crooked tree, and there the wind began to torment him. And when Judas rebuked it, it began to blow soft and low, and took leave and flew away.

"Right! But as for them, they are curs!" said Judas, making a slip-knot. And since the rope might fail him and break, he hung it over a precipice, so that if it broke, he would be sure to meet his death upon the stones. And before he shoved himself off the brink with his foot, and hanged himself, Judas Iscariot once more anxiously prepared Jesus for his coming:

"Yes, meet me kindly, Jesus. I am very weary."

He leapt. The rope strained, but held. His neck stretched, but his hands and feet were crossed, and hung down as though damp.

He died. Thus, in the course of two days, one after another, Jesus of Nazareth and Judas Iscariot, the Traitor, left the world.

All the night through, like some monstrous fruit, Judas swayed over Jerusalem, and the wind kept turning his face now to the city, and now to the desert - as though it wished to exhibit Judas to both city and desert. But in whichever direction his face, distorted by death, was turned, his red eyes suffused with blood, and now as like one another as two brothers, incessantly looked towards the sky. In the morning some sharp-sighted person perceived Judas hanging above the city, and cried out in horror.

People came and took him down, and knowing who he was,

threw him into a deep ravine, into which they were in the habit of throwing dead horses and cats and other carrion.

The same evening all the believers knew of the terrible death of the Traitor, and the next day it was known to all Jerusalem. Stony Judaea knew of it and green Galilee; and from one sea to the other, distant as it was, the news flew of the death of the Traitor.

Neither faster nor slower, but with equal pace with Time itself, it went, and as there is no end to Time so will there be no end to the stories about the Traitor Judas and his terrible death.

And all - both good and bad - will equally anathematise his shameful memory; and among all peoples, past and present, will he remain alone in his cruel destiny - Judas Iscariot, the Traitor.

"THE MAN WHO FOUND THE TRUTH"

CHAPTER I

I was twenty-seven years old and had just maintained my thesis for the degree of Doctor of Mathematics with unusual success, when I was suddenly seized in the middle of the night and thrown into this prison. I shall not narrate to you the details of the monstrous crime of which I was accused - there are events which people should neither remember nor even know, that they may not acquire a feeling of aversion for themselves; but no doubt there are many people among the living who remember that terrible case and "the human brute," as the newspapers called me at that time. They probably remember how the entire civilised society of the land unanimously demanded that the criminal be put to death, and it is due only to the inexplicable kindness of the man at the head of the Government at the time that I am alive, and I now write these lines for the edification of the weak and the wavering.

I shall say briefly: My father, my elder brother, and my sister were murdered brutally, and I was supposed to have committed the crime for the purpose of securing a really enormous inheritance.

I am an old man now; I shall die soon, and you have not the slightest ground for doubting when I say that I was entirely innocent of the monstrous and horrible crime, for which twelve honest and conscientious judges unanimously sentenced me to death. The death sentence was finally commuted to imprisonment for life in solitary confinement.

It was merely a fatal linking of circumstances, of grave and insignificant events, of vague silence and indefinite words, which gave me the appearance and likeness of the criminal, innocent though I was. But he who would suspect me of being ill-disposed toward my strict judges would be profoundly mistaken. They were perfectly right, perfectly right. As people who can judge things and events only by their appearance, and who are deprived of the ability to penetrate their own mysterious being, they could not act differently, nor should they have acted differently.

It so happened that in the game of circumstances, the truth concerning my actions, which I alone knew, assumed all the features of an insolent and shameless lie; and however strange it may seem to my kind and serious reader, I could establish the truth of my innocence only by falsehood, and not by the truth.

Later on, when I was already in prison, in going over in detail the story of the crime and the trial, and picturing myself in the place of one of my judges, I came to the inevitable conclusion each time that I was guilty. Then I produced a very interesting and instructive work; having set aside entirely the question of truth and falsehood on general principles, I subjected the facts and the words to numerous combinations, erecting structures, even as small children build various structures with their wooden blocks; and after persistent efforts I finally succeeded in finding a certain combination of facts which, though strong in principle, seemed so plausible that my actual innocence became perfectly clear, exactly and positively established.

To this day I remember the great feeling of astonishment, mingled with fear, which I experienced at my strange and unexpected discovery; by telling the truth I lead people into error and thus deceive them, while by maintaining falsehood I lead them, on the contrary, to the truth and to knowledge.

I did not yet understand at that time that, like Newton and his famous apple, I discovered unexpectedly the great law upon which the entire history of human thought rests, which seeks not the truth, but verisimilitude, the appearance of truth - that is, the harmony between that which is seen and that which is conceived, based on the strict laws of logical reasoning. And instead of rejoicing, I exclaimed in an outburst of naive, juvenile despair: "Where, then, is the truth? Where is the truth in this world of phantoms and falsehood?" (See my "Diary of a Prisoner" of June 29, 18 - .)

I know that at the present time, when I have but five or six more years to live, I could easily secure my pardon if I but asked for it. But aside from my being accustomed to the prison and for several other important reasons, of which I shall speak later, I simply have no right to ask for pardon, and thus break the force and natural course of the lawful and entirely justified verdict. Nor would I want to hear people apply to me the words, "a victim of judicial error," as some of my gentle visitors expressed themselves, to my sorrow. I repeat, there was no error, nor could there be any error in a case in which a combination of definite circumstances inevitably lead a normally constructed and developed mind to the one and only conclusion.

I was convicted justly, although I did not commit the crime - such is the simple and clear truth, and I live joyously and peacefully my last few years on earth with a sense of respect for this truth.

The only purpose by which I was guided in writing these modest notes is to show to my indulgent reader that under the most painful conditions, where it would seem that there remains no room for hope or life - a human being, a being of the highest order, possessing a mind and a will, finds both hope and life. I want to show how a human being, condemned to death, looked with free eyes upon the world, through the grated window of his prison, and discovered the great purpose, harmony, and beauty of the universe - to the disgrace of those fools who, being free, living a life of plenty and happiness, slander life disgustingly.

Some of my visitors reproach me for being "haughty"; they ask me where I secured the right to teach and to preach; cruel in their reasoning, they would like to drive away even the smile from the face of the man who has been imprisoned for life as a murderer.

No. Just as the kind and bright smile will not leave my lips, as an evidence of a clear and unstained conscience, so my soul will never be darkened, my soul, which has passed firmly through the defiles of life, which has been carried by a mighty will power across these terrible abysses and bottomless pits, where so many daring people have found their heroic, but, alas! fruitless, death.

And if the tone of my confessions may sometimes seem too positive to my indulgent reader, it is not at all due to the absence of modesty in me, but it is due to the fact that I firmly believe that I am right, and also to my firm desire to be useful to my neighbour as far as my faint powers permit.

Here I must apologise for my frequent references to my "Diary of a Prisoner," which is unknown to the reader; but the fact is that I consider the complete publication of my "Diary" too premature and perhaps even dangerous. Begun during the remote period of cruel disillusions, of the shipwreck of all my beliefs and hopes, breathing boundless despair, my note book bears evidence in places that its author was, if not in a state of complete insanity, on the brink of insanity. And if we recall how contagious that illness is, my caution in the use of my "Diary" will become entirely clear.

O, blooming youth! With an involuntary tear in my eye I recall your magnificent dreams, your daring visions and outbursts, your impetuous, seething power - but I should not want your return, blooming youth! Only with the greyness of the hair comes clear wisdom, and that great aptitude for unprejudiced reflection which makes of all old men philosophers and often even sages.

CHAPTER II

Those of my kind visitors who honour me by expressing their delight and even - may this little indiscretion be forgiven me! - even their adoration of my spiritual clearness, can hardly imagine what I was when I came to this prison. The tens of years which have passed over my head and which have whitened my hair cannot muffle the slight agitation which I experience at the recollection of the first moments when, with the creaking of the rusty hinges, the fatal prison doors opened and then closed behind me forever.

Not endowed with literary talent, which in reality is an indomitable inclination to invent and to lie, I shall attempt to introduce myself to my indulgent reader exactly as I was at that remote time.

I was a young man, twenty-seven years of age - as I had occasion to mention before - unrestrained, impetuous, given to abrupt deviations. A certain dreaminess, peculiar to my age; a self-respect which was easily offended and which revolted at the slightest insignificant provocation; a passionate impetuosity in solving world problems; fits of melancholy alternated by equally wild fits of merriment - all this gave the young mathematician a character of extreme unsteadiness, of sad and harsh discord.

I must also mention the extreme pride, a family trait, which I inherited from my mother, and which often hindered me from taking the advice of riper and more experienced people than myself; also my extreme obstinacy in carrying out my purposes, a good quality in itself, which becomes dangerous, however, when the purpose in question is not sufficiently well founded and considered.

Thus, during the first days of my confinement, I behaved like all other fools who are thrown into prison. I shouted loudly and, of course, vainly about my innocence; I demanded violently my immediate freedom and even beat against the door and the walls with my fists. The door and the walls naturally remained mute, while I caused myself a rather sharp pain. I remember I even beat my head against the wall, and for hours I lay unconscious on the stone floor of my cell; and for some time, when I had grown desperate, I refused food, until the persistent demands of my organism defeated my obstinacy.

I cursed my judges and threatened them with merciless vengeance. At last I commenced to regard all human life, the whole world, even Heaven, as an enormous injustice, a derision and a mockery. Forgetting that in my position I could hardly be unprejudiced, I came with the self-confidence of youth, with the sickly pain of a prisoner, gradually to the complete negation of life and its great meaning.

Those were indeed terrible days and nights, when, crushed by the walls, getting no answer to any of my questions, I paced my cell endlessly and hurled one after another into the dark abyss all the great valuables which life has bestowed upon us: friendship, love, reason and justice.

In some justification to myself I may mention the fact that during the first and most painful years of my imprisonment a series of events happened which reflected themselves rather painfully upon my psychic nature. Thus I learned with the profoundest indignation that the girl, whose name I shall not mention and who was to become my wife, married another man. She was one of the few who believed in my innocence; at the last parting she swore to me to remain faithful to me unto death, and rather to die than betray her love for me - and within one year after that she married a man I knew, who possessed certain good qualities, but who was not at all a sensible man. I did not want to understand at that time that such a marriage was natural on the part of a young, healthy, and beautiful girl. But, alas! We all forget our natural science when we are deceived by the woman we love - may this little jest be forgiven me! At the present time Mme. N. is a happy and respected mother, and this proves better than anything else how wise and entirely in accordance with the demands of nature and life was her marriage at that time, which vexed me so painfully.

I must confess, however, that at that time I was not at all calm. Her exceedingly amiable and kind letter in which she notified me of her marriage, expressing profound regret that changed circumstances and a suddenly awakened love compelled her to break her promise to me - that amiable, truthful letter, scented with perfume, bearing the traces of her tender fingers, seemed to me a message from the devil himself.

The letters of fire burned my exhausted brains, and in a wild ecstasy I shook the doors of my cell and called violently:

"Come! Let me look into your lying eyes! Let me hear your lying voice! Let me but touch with my fingers your tender throat and pour into your death rattle my last bitter laugh!"

From this quotation my indulgent reader will see how right were the judges who convicted me for murder; they had really foreseen in me a murderer.

My gloomy view of life at the time was aggravated by several other events. Two years after the marriage of my fiancee, consequently three years after the first day of my imprisonment, my mother died - she died, as I learned, of profound grief for me. However strange it may seem, she remained firmly convinced to the end of her days that I had committed the monstrous crime. Evidently this conviction was an inexhaustible source of grief to her, the chief cause of the gloomy melancholy which fettered her lips in silence and caused her death through paralysis of the heart. As I was told, she never mentioned my name nor the names of those who died so tragically, and she bequeathed the entire enormous fortune, which was supposed to have served as the motive for the murder, to various charitable organisations. It is characteristic that even under such terrible conditions her motherly instinct did not forsake her altogether; in a postscript to the will she left me a considerable sum, which secures my existence whether I am in prison or at large.

Now I understand that, however great her grief may have been, that alone was not enough to cause her death; the real cause was her advanced age and a series of illnesses which had undermined her once strong and sound organism. In the name of justice, I must say that my father, a weak-charactered man, was not at all a model husband and family man; by numerous betrayals, by falsehood and deception he had led my mother to despair, constantly offending her pride and her strict, unbribable truthfulness. But at that time I did not understand it; the death of my mother seemed to me one of the most cruel manifestations of universal injustice, and called forth a new stream of useless and sacrilegious curses.

I do not know whether I ought to tire the attention of the reader with the story of other events of a similar nature. I shall mention but briefly that one after another my friends, who remained my friends from the time when I was happy and free, stopped visiting me. According to their words, they believed in my innocence, and at first warmly expressed to me their sympathy. But our lives, mine in prison and theirs at liberty, were so different that gradually under the pressure of perfectly natural causes, such as forgetfulness, official and other duties, the absence of mutual interests, they visited me ever more and more rarely, and finally ceased to see me entirely. I cannot recall without a smile that even the death of my mother, even the betrayal of the girl I loved did not arouse in me such a hopelessly bitter feeling as these gentlemen, whose names I remember but vaguely now, succeeded in wresting from my soul.

LEONID ANDREYEV

"What horror! What pain! My friends, you have left me alone! My friends, do you understand what you have done? You have left me alone. Can you conceive of leaving a human being alone? Even a serpent has its mate, even a spider has its comrade - and you have left a human being alone! You have given him a soul - and left him alone! You have given him a heart, a mind, a hand for a handshake, lips for a kiss - and you have left him alone! What shall he do now that you have left him alone?"

Thus I exclaimed in my "Diary of a Prisoner," tormented by woeful perplexities. In my juvenile blindness, in the pain of my young, senseless heart, I still did not want to understand that the solitude, of which I complained so bitterly, like the mind, was an advantage given to man over other creatures, in order to fence around the sacred mysteries of his soul from the stranger's gaze.

Let my serious reader consider what would have become of life if man were robbed of his right, of his duty to be alone. In the gathering of idle chatterers, amid the dull collection of transparent glass dolls, that kill each other with their sameness; in the wild city where all doors are open, and all windows are open - passers-by look wearily through the glass walls and observe the same evidences of the hearth and the alcove. Only the creatures that can be alone possess a face; while those that know no solitude - the great, blissful, sacred solitude of the soul - have snouts instead of faces.

And in calling my friends "perfidious traitors" I, poor youth that I was, could not understand the wise law of life, according to which neither friendship, nor love, nor even the tenderest attachment of sister and mother, is eternal. Deceived by the lies of the poets, who proclaimed eternal friendship and love, I did not want to see that which my indulgent reader observes from the windows of his dwelling - how friends, relatives, mother and wife, in apparent despair and in tears, follow their dead to the cemetery, and after a lapse of some time return from there. No one buries himself together with the dead, no one asks the dead to make room in the coffin, and if the grief-stricken wife exclaims, in an outburst of tears, "Oh, bury me together with him!" she is merely expressing symbolically the extreme degree of her despair - one could easily convince himself of this by trying, in jest, to push her down into the grave. And those who restrain her are merely expressing symbolically their sympathy and understanding, thus lending the necessary aspect of solemn grief to the funeral custom.

Man must subject himself to the laws of life, not of death, nor to the fiction of the poets, however beautiful it may be. But can the fictitious be beautiful? Is there no beauty in the stern truth of life, in the mighty work of its wise laws, which subjects to itself with great disinterestedness the movements of the heavenly luminaries, as well as the restless linking of the tiny creatures called human beings?

CHAPTER III

Thus I lived sadly in my prison for five or six years.

The first redeeming ray flashed upon me when I least expected it.

Endowed with the gift of imagination, I made my former fiancee the object of all my thoughts. She became my love and my dream.

Another circumstance which suddenly revealed to me the ground under my feet was, strange as it may seem, the conviction that it was impossible to make my escape from prison.

During the first period of my imprisonment, I, as a youthful and enthusiastic dreamer, made all kinds of plans for escape, and some of them seemed to me entirely possible of realisation. Cherishing deceptive hopes, this thought naturally kept me in a state of tense alarm and hindered my attention from concentrating itself on more important and substantial matters. As soon as I despaired of one plan I created another, but of course I did not make any progress - I merely moved within a closed circle. It is hardly necessary to mention that each transition from one plan to another was accompanied by cruel sufferings, which tormented my soul, just as the eagle tortured the body of Prometheus.

One day, while staring with a weary look at the walls of my cell, I suddenly began to feel how irresistibly thick the stone was, how strong the cement which kept it together, how skilfully and mathematically this severe fortress was constructed. It is true, my first sensation was extremely painful; it was, perhaps, a horror of hopelessness.

I cannot recall what I did and how I felt during the two or three months that followed. The first note in my diary after a long period of silence does not explain very much. Briefly I state only that they made new clothes for me and that I had grown stout.

The fact is that, after all my hopes had been abandoned, the consciousness of the impossibility of my escape once for all extinguished also my painful alarm and liberated my mind, which was then already inclined to lofty contemplation and the joys of mathematics.

But the following is the day I consider as the first real day of my liberation. It was a beautiful spring morning (May 6) and the balmy, invigourating air was pouring into the open window; while walking back and forth in my cell I unconsciously glanced, at each turn, with a vague interest, at the high window, where the iron grate outlined its form sharply and distinctly against the background of the azure, cloudless sky.

"Why is the sky so beautiful through these bars?" I reflected as I walked. "Is not this the effect of the aesthetic law of contrasts, according to which azure stands out prominently beside black? Or is it not, perhaps, a manifestation of some other, higher law, according to which the infinite may be conceived by the human mind only when it is brought within certain boundaries, for instance, when it is enclosed within a square?"

When I recalled that at the sight of a wide open window, which was not protected by bars, or of the sky, I had usually experienced a desire to fly, which was painful because of its uselessness and absurdity - I suddenly began to experience a feeling of tenderness for the bars; tender gratitude, even love. Forged by hand, by the weak human hand of some ignorant blacksmith, who did not even give himself an account of the profound meaning of his creation; placed in the wall by an equally ignorant mason, it suddenly represented in itself a model of beauty, nobility and power. Having seized the infinite within its iron squares, it became congealed in cold and proud peace, frightening the ignorant, giving food for thought to the intelligent and delighting the sage!

CHAPTER IV

In order to make the further narrative clearer to my indulgent reader, I am compelled to say a few words about the exclusive, quite flattering, and, I fear, not entirely deserved, position which I occupy in our prison. On one hand, my spiritual clearness, my rare and perfect view of life, and the nobility of my feelings, which impress all those who speak to me; and, on the other hand, several rather unimportant favours which I have done to the Warden, have given me a series of privileges, of which I avail myself, rather moderately, of course, not desiring to upset the general plan and system of our prison.

Thus, during the weekly visiting days, my visitors are not limited to any special time for their interviews, and all those who wish to see me are admitted, sometimes forming quite a large audience. Not daring to accept altogether the assurances made somewhat ironically by the Warden, to the effect that I would be "the pride of any prison," I may say, nevertheless, without any false modesty, that my words are treated with proper respect, and that among my visitors I number quite a few warm and enthusiastic admirers, both men and women. I shall mention that the Warden himself and some of his assistants honour me by their visits, drawing from me strength and courage for the purpose of continuing their hard work. Of course I use the prison library freely, and even the archives of the prison; and if the Warden politely refused to grant my request for an exact plan of the prison, it is not at all because of his lack of confidence in me, but because such a plan is a state secret....

Our prison is a huge five-story building. Situated in the

LEONID ANDREYEV

outskirts of the city, at the edge of a deserted field, overgrown with high grass, it attracts the attention of the wayfarer by its rigid outlines, promising him peace and rest after his endless wanderings. Not being plastered, the building has retained its natural dark red colour of old brick, and at close view, I am told, it produces a gloomy, even threatening, impression, especially on nervous people, to whom the red bricks recall blood and bloody lumps of human flesh. The small, dark, flat windows with iron bars naturally complete the impression and lend to the whole a character of gloomy harmony, or stern beauty. Even during good weather, when the sun shines upon our prison, it does not lose any of its dark and grim importance, and is constantly reminding the people that there are laws in existence and that punishment awaits those who break them.

My cell is on the fifth story, and my grated window commands a splendid view of the distant city and a part of the deserted field to the right. On the left, beyond the boundary of my vision, are the outskirts of the city, and, as I am told, the church and the cemetery adjoining it. Of the existence of the church and even the cemetery I had known before from the mournful tolling of the bells, which custom requires during the burial of the dead.

Quite in keeping with the external style of architecture, the interior arrangement of our prison is also finished harmoniously and properly constructed. For the purpose of conveying to the reader a clearer idea of the prison, I will take the liberty of giving the example of a fool who might make up his mind to run away from our prison. Admitting that the brave fellow possessed supernatural, Herculean strength and broke the lock of his room - what would he find? The corridor, with numerous grated doors, which could withstand cannonading - and armed keepers. Let us suppose that he kills all the keepers, breaks all the doors, and comes out into the yard - perhaps he may think that he is already free. But what of the walls? The walls which encircle our prison, with three rings of stone?

I omitted the guard advisedly. The guard is indefatigable. Day and night I hear behind my doors the footsteps of the guard; day and night his eye watches me through the little window in my door, controlling my movements, reading on my face my thoughts, my intentions and my dreams. In the daytime I could deceive his attention with lies, assuming a cheerful and carefree expression on my face, but I have rarely met the man who could lie even in his sleep. No matter how much I would be on my guard during the day, at night I would betray myself by an involuntary moan, by a twitch of the face, by an expression of fatigue or grief, or by other manifestations of a guilty and uneasy conscience. Only very few people of unusual will power are able to lie even in their sleep, skilfully managing the features of their faces, sometimes even preserving a courteous and bright smile on their lips, when their souls, given over to dreams, are quivering from the horrors of a monstrous nightmare - but, as exceptions, these cannot be taken into consideration. I am profoundly happy that I am not a criminal, that my conscience is clear and calm.

"Read, my friend, read," I say to the watchful eye as I lay myself down to sleep peacefully. "You will not be able to read anything on my face!"

And it was I who invented the window in the prison door.

I feel that my reader is astonished and smiles incredulously, mentally calling me an old liar, but there are instances in which modesty is superfluous and even dangerous. Yes, this simple and great invention belongs to me, just as Newton's system belongs to Newton, and as Kepler's laws of the revolution of the planets belong to Kepler.

Later on, encouraged by the success of my invention, I devised and introduced in our prison a series of little innovations, which were concerned only with details; thus the form of chains and locks used in our prison has been changed.

The little window in the door was my invention, and, if any

LEONID ANDREYEV

one should dare deny this, I would call him a liar and a scoundrel.

I came upon this invention under the following circumstances: One day, during the roll call, a certain prisoner killed with the iron leg of his bed the Inspector who entered his cell. Of course the rascal was hanged in the yard of our prison, and the administration light mindedly grew calm, but I was in despair - the great purpose of the prison proved to be wrong since such horrible deeds were possible. How is it that no one had noticed that the prisoner had broken off the leg of his bed? How is it that no one had noticed the state of agitation in which the prisoner must have been before committing the murder?

By taking up the question so directly I thus approached considerably the solution of the problem; and indeed, after two or three weeks had elapsed I arrived simply and even unexpectedly at my great discovery. I confess frankly that before telling my discovery to the Warden of the prison I experienced moments of a certain hesitation, which was quite natural in my position of prisoner. To the reader who may still be surprised at this hesitation, knowing me to be a man of a clear, unstained conscience, I will answer by a quotation from my "Diary of a Prisoner," relating to that period:

"How difficult is the position of the man who is convicted, though innocent, as I am. If he is sad, if his lips are sealed in silence, and his eyes are lowered, people say of him: 'He is repenting; he is suffering from pangs of conscience.'

"If in the innocence of his heart he smiles brightly and kindly, the keeper thinks: 'There, by a false and feigned smile, he wishes to hide his secret.'

"No matter what he does, he seems guilty - such is the force of the prejudice against which it is necessary to struggle. But I am innocent, and I shall be myself, firmly confident that my spiritual clearness will destroy the malicious magic of prejudice."

And on the following day the Warden of the prison pressed my hand warmly, expressing his gratitude to me, and a month later little holes were made in all doors in every prison in the land, thus opening a field for wide and fruitful observation.

The entire system of our prison life gives me deep satisfaction. The hours for rising and going to bed, for meals and walks are arranged so rationally, in accordance with the real require-ments of nature, that soon they lose the appearance of compulsion and become natural, even dear habits. Only in this way can I explain the interesting fact that when I was free I was a nervous and weak young man, susceptible to colds and illness, whereas in prison I have grown considerably stronger and that for my sixty years I am enjoying an enviable state of health. I am not stout, but I am not thin, either; my lungs are in good condition and I have saved almost all my teeth, with the exception of two on the left side of the jaw; I am good natured, even tempered; my sleep is sound, almost without any dreams. In figure, in which an expression of calm power and self-confidence predominates, and in face, I resemble some-what Michaelangelo's "Moses" - that is, at least what some of my friendly visitors have told me.

But even more than by the regular and healthy regime, the strengthening of my soul and body was helped by the wonder-ful, yet natural, peculiarity of our prison, which eliminates entirely the accidental and the unexpected from its life. Having neither a family nor friends, I am perfectly safe from the shocks, so injurious to life, which are caused by treachery, by the illness or death of relatives - let my indulgent reader recall how many people have perished before his eyes not of their own fault, but because capricious fate had linked them to people unworthy of them. Without changing my feeling of love into trivial personal attachments, I thus make it free for the broad and mighty love for all mankind; and as mankind is immortal, not subjected to illness, and as a harmonious whole it is undoubtedly progressing toward perfection, love for it becomes the surest guarantee of spiritual and physical soundness.

My day is clear. So are also my days of the future, which are coming toward me in radiant and even order. A murderer will not break into my cell for the purpose of robbing me, a mad automobile will not crush me, the illness of a child will not torture me, cruel treachery will not steal its way to me from the darkness. My mind is free, my heart is calm, my soul is clear and bright.

The clear and rigid rules of our prison define everything that I must not do, thus freeing me from those unbearable hesitations, doubts, and errors with which practical life is filled. True, sometimes there penetrates even into our prison, through its high walls, something which ignorant people call chance, or even Fate, and which is only an inevitable reflection of the general laws; but the life of the prison, agitated for a moment, quickly goes back to its habitual rut, like a river after an overflow. To this category of accidents belong the abovementioned murder of the Inspector, the rare and always unsuccessful attempts at escape, and also the executions, which take place in one of the remotest yards of our prison.

There is still another peculiarity in the system of our prison, which I consider most beneficial, and which gives to the whole thing a character of stern and noble justice. Left to himself, and only to himself, the prisoner cannot count upon support, or upon that spurious, wretched pity which so often falls to the lot of weak people, disfiguring thereby the fundamental purposes of nature.

I confess that I think, with a certain sense of pride, that if I am now enjoying general respect and admiration, if my mind is strong, my will powerful, my view of life clear and bright, I owe it only to myself, to my power and my perseverance. How many weak people would have perished in my place as victims of madness, despair, or grief? But I have conquered everything! I have changed the world. I gave to my soul the form which my mind desired. In the desert, working alone, exhausted with fatigue, I have erected a stately structure in which I now live joyously and calmly, like a king. Destroy it - and to-morrow I shall begin to build a new structure, and in my bloody sweat I shall erect it! For I must live!

Forgive my involuntary pathos in the last lines, which is so unbecoming to my balanced and calm nature. But it is hard to restrain myself when I recall the road I have travelled. I hope, however, that in the future I shall not darken the mood of my reader with any outbursts of agitated feelings. Only he shouts who is not confident of the truth of his words; calm firmness and cold simplicity are becoming to the truth.

P.S. - I do not remember whether I told you that the criminal who murdered my father has not been found as yet.

CHAPTER V

Deviating from time to time from the calm form of a historical narrative I must pause on current events. Thus I will permit myself to acquaint my readers in a few lines with a rather interesting specimen of the human species which I have found accidentally in our prison.

One afternoon a few days ago the Warden came to me for the usual chat, and among other things told me there was a very unfortunate man in prison at the time upon whom I could exert a beneficent influence. I expressed my willingness in the most cordial manner, and for several days in succession I have had long discussions with the artist K., by permission of the Warden. The spirit of hostility, even of obstinacy, with which, to my regret, he met me at his first visit, has now disappeared entirely under the influence of my discussion. Listening willingly and with interest to my ever pacifying words he gradually told me his rather unusual story after a series of persistent questions.

He is a man of about twenty-six or twenty-eight, of pleasant appearance, and rather good manners, which show that he is a well-bred man. A certain quite natural unrestraint in his speech, a passionate vehemence with which he talks about himself, occasionally a bitter, even ironical laughter, followed by painful pensiveness, from which it is difficult to arouse him even by a touch of the hand - these complete the make-up of my new acquaintance. Personally to me he is not particularly sympathetic, and however strange it may seem I am especially annoyed by his disgusting habit of constantly moving his thin, emaciated fingers and clutching helplessly the hand of the person with whom he speaks.

K. told me very little of his past life.

"Well, what is there to tell? I was an artist, that's all," he repeated, with a sorrowful grimace, and refused to talk about the "immoral act" for which he was condemned to solitary confinement.

"I don't want to corrupt you, grandpa - live honestly," he would jest in a somewhat unbecoming familiar tone, which I tolerated simply because I wished to please the Warden of the prison, having learned from the prisoner the real cause of his sufferings, which sometimes assumed an acute form of violence and threats. During one of these painful minutes, when K.'s will power was weak, as a result of insomnia, from which he was suffering, I seated myself on his bed and treated him in general with fatherly kindness, and he blurted out everything to me right there and then.

Not desiring to tire the reader with an exact reproduction of his hysterical outbursts, his laughter and his tears, I shall give only the facts of his story.

K.'s grief, at first not quite clear to me, consists of the fact that instead of paper or canvas for his drawings he was given a large slate and a slate pencil. (By the way, the art with which he mastered the material, which was new to him, is remarkable. I have seen some of his productions, and it seems to me that they could satisfy the taste of the most fastidious expert of graphic arts. Personally I am indifferent to the art of painting, preferring live and truthful nature.) Thus, owing to the nature of the material, before commencing a new picture, K. had to destroy the previous one by wiping it off his slate, and this seemed to lead him every time to the verge of madness.

"You cannot imagine what it means," he would say, clutching my hands with his thin, clinging fingers. "While I draw, you know, I forget entirely that it is useless; I am usually very cheerful and I even whistle some tune, and once I was even incarcerated for that, as it is forbidden to whistle in this cursed prison. But that is a trifle - for I had at least a good sleep there. But when I finish my picture - no, even when I approach the end of the picture, I am seized with a sensation so terrible that I feel like tearing the brain from my head and trampling it with my feet. Do you understand me?"

"I understand you, my friend, I understand you perfectly, and I sympathise with you."

"Really? Well, then, listen, old man. I make the last strokes with so much pain, with such a sense of sorrow and hopelessness, as though I were bidding good-bye to the person I loved best of all. But here I have finished it. Do you understand what it means? It means that it has assumed life, that it lives, that there is a certain mysterious spirit in it. And yet it is already doomed to death, it is dead already, dead like a herring. Can you understand it at all? I do not understand it. And, now, imagine, I - fool that I am - I nevertheless rejoice, I cry and rejoice. No, I think, this picture I shall not destroy; it is so good that I shall not destroy it. Let it live. And it is a fact that at such times I do not feel like drawing anything new, I have not the slightest desire for it. And yet it is dreadful. Do you understand me?"

"Perfectly, my friend. No doubt the drawing ceases to please you on the following day - "

"Oh, what nonsense you are prating, old man! (That is exactly what he said. 'Nonsense.') How can a dying child cease to please you? Of course, if he lived, he might have become a scoundrel, but when he is dying - No, old man, that isn't it. For I am killing it myself. I do not sleep all night long, I jump up, I look at it, and I love it so dearly that I feel like stealing it. Stealing it from whom? What do I know? But when morning sets in I feel that I cannot do without it, that I must take up that cursed pencil again and create anew. What a mockery! To create! What am I, a galley slave?"

"My friend, you are in a prison."

"My dear old man! When I begin to steal over to the slate with the sponge in my hand I feel like a murderer. It happens that I go around it for a day or two. Do you know, one day I bit off a finger of my right hand so as not to draw any more, but that, of course, was only a trifle, for I started to learn drawing with my left hand. What is this necessity for creating! To create by all means, create for suffering - create with the knowledge that it will all perish! Do you understand it?"

"Finish it, my friend, don't be agitated; then I will expound to you my views."

Unfortunately, my advice hardly reached the ears of K. In one of those paroxysms of despair, which frighten the Warden of our prison, K. began to throw himself about in his bed, tear his clothes, shout and sob, manifesting in general all the symptoms of extreme mortification. I looked at the sufferings of the unfortunate youth with deep emotion (compared with me he was a youth), vainly endeavouring to hold his fingers which were tearing his clothes. I knew that for this breach of discipline new incarceration awaited him.

"O, impetuous youth," I thought when he had grown somewhat calmer, and I was tenderly unfolding his fine hair which had become entangled, "how easily you fall into despair! A bit of drawing, which may in the end fall into the hands of a dealer in old rags, or a dealer in old bronze and cemented porcelain, can cause you so much suffering!" But, of course, I did not tell this to my youthful friend, striving, as any one should under similar circumstances, not to irritate him by unnecessary contradictions.

"Thank you, old man," said K., apparently calm now. "To tell the truth you seemed very strange to me at first; your face is so venerable, but your eyes. Have you murdered anybody, old man?"

I deliberately quote the malicious and careless phrase to show how in the eyes of lightminded and shallow people the stamp of a terrible accusation is transformed into the stamp of the crime itself. Controlling my feeling of bitterness, I remarked calmly to the impertinent youth:

"You are an artist, my child; to you are known the mysteries of the human face, that flexible, mobile and deceptive masque, which, like the sea, reflects the hurrying clouds and the azure ether. Being green, the sea turns blue under the clear sky and black when the sky is black, when the heavy clouds are dark. What do you want of my face, over which hangs an accusation of the most cruel crime?"

But, occupied with his own thoughts, the artist apparently paid no particular attention to my words and continued in a broken voice:

"What am I to do? You saw my drawing. I destroyed it, and it is already a whole week since I touched my pencil. Of course," he resumed thoughtfully, rubbing his brow, "it would be better to break the slate; to punish me they would not give me another one - "

"You had better return it to the authorities."

"Very well, I may hold out another week, but what then? I know myself. Even now that devil is pushing my hand: 'Take the pencil, take the pencil.'"

At that moment, as my eyes wandered distractedly over his cell, I suddenly noticed that some of the artist's clothes hanging on the wall were unnaturally stretched, and one end was skilfully fastened by the back of the cot. Assuming an air that I was tired and that I wanted to walk about in the cell, I staggered as from a quiver of senility in my legs, and pushed the clothes aside. The entire wall was covered with drawings!

The artist had already leaped from his cot, and thus we stood facing each other in silence. I said in a tone of gentle reproach:

"How did you allow yourself to do this, my friend? You know the rules of the prison, according to which no inscriptions or drawing on the walls are permissible?"

"I know no rules," said K. morosely.

"And then," I continued, sternly this time, "you lied to me, my friend. You said that you did not take the pencil into your hands for a whole week."

"Of course I didn't," said the artist, with a strange smile, and even a challenge. Even when caught red-handed, he did not betray any signs of repentance, and looked rather sarcastic than guilty. Having examined more closely the drawings on the wall, which represented human figures in various positions, I became interested in the strange reddish-yellow colour of an unknown pencil.

"Is this iodine? You told me that you had a pain and that you secured iodine."

"No. It is blood."

"Blood?"

"Yes."

I must say frankly that I even liked him at that moment.

"How did you get it?"

"From my hand."

"From your hand? But how did you manage to hide yourself from the eye that is watching you?"

He smiled cunningly, and even winked.

"Don't you know that you can always deceive if only you want to do it?"

My sympathies for him were immediately dispersed. I saw before me a man who was not particularly clever, but in all probability terribly spoiled already, who did not even admit the thought that there are people who simply cannot lie. Recalling, however, the promise I had made to the Warden, I assumed a calm air of dignity and said to him tenderly, as only a mother could speak to her child:

"Don't be surprised and don't condemn me for being so strict, my friend. I am an old man. I have passed half of my life in this prison; I have formed certain habits, like all old people, and submitting to all rules myself, I am perhaps overdoing it somewhat in demanding the same of others. You will of course wipe off these drawings yourself - although I feel sorry for them, for I admire them sincerely - and I will not say anything to the administration. We will forget all this, as if nothing had happened. Are you satisfied?"

He answered drowsily:

"Very well."

"In our prison, where we have the sad pleasure of being confined, everything is arranged in accordance with a most purposeful plan and is most strictly subjected to laws and rules. And the very strict order, on account of which the existence of your creations is so short lived, and, I may say, ephemeral, is full of the profoundest wisdom. Allowing you to perfect yourself in your art, it wisely guards other people against the perhaps injurious influence of your productions, and in any case it completes logically, finishes, enforces, and makes clear the meaning of your solitary confinement. What does solitary confinement in our prison mean? It means that the prisoner should be alone. But would he be alone if by his productions he would communicate in some way or other with other people outside?"

By the expression of K.'s face I noticed with a sense of profound joy that my words had produced on him the proper impression, bringing him back from the realm of poetic inventions to the land of stern but beautiful reality. And, raising my voice, I continued:

"As for the rule you have broken, which forbids any inscription or drawing on the walls of our prison, it is not less logical. Years will pass; in your place there may be another prisoner like you - and he may see that which you have drawn. Shall this be tolerated? Just think of it! And what would become of the walls of our prison if every one who wished it were to leave upon them his profane marks?"

"To the devil with it!"

This is exactly how K. expressed himself. He said it loudly, even with an air of calmness.

"What do you mean to say by this, my youthful friend?"

"I wish to say that you may perish here, my old friend, but I shall leave this place."

"You can't escape from our prison," I retorted, sternly.

"Have you tried?"

"Yes, I have tried."

He looked at me incredulously and smiled. He smiled!

"You are a coward, old man. You are simply a miserable coward."

I - a coward! Oh, if that self-satisfied puppy knew what a tempest of rage he had aroused in my soul he would have squealed for fright and would have hidden himself on the bed. I - a coward! The world has crumbled upon my head, but has

LEONID ANDREYEV

not crushed me, and out of its terrible fragments I have created a new world, according to my own design and plan; all the evil forces of life - solitude, imprisonment, treachery, and falsehood - all have taken up arms against me, but I have subjected them all to my will. And I who have subjected to myself even my dreams - I am a coward?

But I shall not tire the attention of my indulgent reader with these lyrical deviations, which have no bearing on the matter. I continue.

After a pause, broken only by K.'s loud breathing, I said to him sadly:

"I - a coward! And you say this to the man who came with the sole aim of helping you? Of helping you not only in word but also in deed?"

"You wish to help me? In what way?"

"I will get you paper and pencil."

The artist was silent. And his voice was soft and timid when he asked, hesitatingly:

"And - my drawings - will remain?"

"Yes; they will remain."

It is hard to describe the vehement delight into which the exalted young man was thrown; naive and pure-hearted youth knows no bounds either in grief or in joy. He pressed my hand warmly, shook me, disturbing my old bones; he called me friend, father, even "dear old phiz" (!) and a thousand other endearing and somewhat naive names. To my regret our conversation lasted too long, and, notwithstanding the entreaties of the young man, who would not part with me, I hurried away to my cell.

I did not go to the Warden of the prison, as I felt somewhat agitated. At that remote time I paced my cell until late in the night, striving to understand what means of escaping from our prison that rather foolish young man could have discovered. Was it possible to run away from our prison? No, I could not admit and I must not admit it. And gradually conjuring up in my memory everything I knew about our prison, I understood that K. must have hit upon an old plan, which I had long discarded, and that he would convince himself of its impracticability even as I convinced myself. It is impossible to escape from our prison.

But, tormented by doubts, I measured my lonely cell for a long time, thinking of various plans that might relieve K.'s position and thus divert him from the idea of making his escape. He must not run away from our prison under any circumstances. Then I gave myself to peaceful and sound sleep, with which benevolent nature has rewarded those who have a clear conscience and a pure soul.

By the way, lest I forget, I shall mention the fact that I destroyed my "Diary of a Prisoner" that night. I had long wished to do it, but the natural pity and faint-hearted love which we feel for our blunders and our shortcomings restrained me; besides, there was nothing in my "Diary" that could have compromised me in any way. And if I have destroyed it now it is due solely to my desire to throw my past into oblivion and to save my reader from the tediousness of long complaints and moans, from the horror of sacrilegious cursings. May it rest in peace!

CHAPTER VI

Having conveyed to the Warden of our prison the contents of my conversation with K., I asked him not to punish the young man for spoiling the walls, which would thus betray me, and I, to save the youth, suggested the following plan, which was accepted by the Warden after a few purely formal objections.

"It is important for him," I said, "that his drawings should be preserved, but it is apparently immaterial to him in whose possession these drawings are. Let him, then, avail himself of his art, paint your portrait, Mr. Warden, and after that the portraits of the entire staff of your officials. To say nothing of the honour you would show him by this condescension - an honour which he will surely know how to appreciate - the painting may be useful to you as a very original ornament in your drawing room or study. Besides, nothing will prevent us from destroying the drawings if we should not care for them, for the naive and somewhat selfish young man apparently does not even admit the thought that anybody's hand would destroy his productions."

Smiling, the Warden suggested, with a politeness that flattered me extremely, that the series of portraits should commence with mine. I quote word for word that which the Warden said to me:

"Your face actually calls for reproduction on canvas. We shall hang your portrait in the office."

The zeal of creativeness - these are the only words I can apply to the passionate, silent agitation in which K. reproduced my features. Usually talkative, he now maintained silence for hours, leaving unanswered my jests and remarks.

"Be silent, old man, be silent - you are at your best when you are silent," he repeated persistently, calling forth an involuntary smile by his zeal as a professional.

My portrait would remind you, my indulgent reader, of that mysterious peculiarity of artists, according to which they very often transmit their own feelings, even their external features, to the subject upon which they are working. Thus, reproducing with remarkable likeness, the lower part of my face, where kindness and the expression of authoritativeness and calm dignity are so harmoniously blended, K. undoubtedly introduced into my eyes his own suffering and even his horror. Their fixed, immobile gaze; madness glimmering somewhere in their depth; the painful eloquence of a deep and infinitely lonely soul - all that was not mine.

"Is this I?" I exclaimed, laughing, when from the canvas this terrible face, full of wild contradictions, stared at me. "My friend, I do not congratulate you on this portrait. I do not think it is successful."

"It is you, old man, you! It is well drawn. You criticise it wrongly. Where will you hang it?"

He grew talkative again like a magpie, that amiable young man, and all because his wretched painting was to be preserved for some time. O impetuous, O happy youth! Here I could not restrain myself from a little jest for the purpose of teaching a lesson to the self-confident youngster, so I asked him, with a smile:

"Well, Mr. Artist, what do you think? Am I murderer or not?"

The artist, closing one eye, examined me and the portrait critically. Then whistling a polka, he answered recklessly: "The devil knows you, old man!"

I smiled. K. understood my jest at last, burst out laughing and then said with sudden seriousness:

"You are speaking of the human face but do you know that there is nothing worse in the world than the human face? Even when it tells the truth, when it shouts about the truth, it lies, it lies, old man, for it speaks its own language. Do you know, old man, a terrible incident happened to me? It was in one of the picture galleries in Spain. I was examining a portrait of Christ, when suddenly - Christ, you understand, Christ - great eyes, dark, terrible suffering, sorrow, grief, love - well, in a word - Christ. Suddenly I was struck with something; suddenly it seemed to me that it was the face of the greatest wrongdoer, tormented by the greatest unheard-of woes of repentance - Old man, why do you look at me so! Old man!"

Nearing my eyes to the very face of the artist, I asked him in a cautious whisper, as the occasion required, dividing each word from the other:

"Don't you think that when the devil tempted Him in the desert He did not renounce him, as He said later, but consented, sold Himself - that He did not renounce the devil, but sold Himself. Do you understand? Does not that passage in the Gospels seem doubtful to you?"

Extreme fright was expressed on the face of my young friend. Forcing the palms of his hands against my chest, as if to push me away, he ejaculated in a voice so low that I could hardly hear his indistinct words:

"What? You say Jesus sold Himself? What for?"

I explained softly:

"That the people, my child, that the people should believe Him."

"Well?"

I smiled. K.'s eyes became round, as if a noose was strangling him. Suddenly, with that lack of respect for old age which was one of his characteristics, he threw me down on the bed with a sharp thrust and jumped away into a corner. When I was slowly getting up from the awkward position into which the unrestraint of that young man had forced me - I fell backward, with my head between the pillow and the back of the bed - he cried to me loudly:

"Don't you dare! Don't you dare get up, you Devil."

But I did not think of rising to my feet. I simply sat down on the bed, and, thus seated, with an involuntary smile at the passionate outburst of the youth, I shook my head good naturedly and laughed.

"Oh, young man, young man! You yourself have drawn me into this theological conversation."

But he stared at me stubbornly, wide eyed, and kept repeating:

"Sit there, sit there! I did not say this. No, no!"

"You said it, you, young man - you. Do you remember Spain, the picture gallery! You said it and now you deny it, mocking my clumsy old age. Oh!"

K. suddenly lowered his hands and admitted in a low voice:

"Yes. I said it. But you, old man - "

I do not remember what he said after that - it is so hard to recall all the childish chatter of this kind, but unfortunately too light-minded young man. I remember only that we parted as friends, and he pressed my hand warmly, expressing to me his sincere gratitude, even calling me, so far as I can remember, his "saviour."

By the way, I succeeded in convincing the Warden that the

portrait of even such a man as I, after all a prisoner, was out of place in such a solemn official room as the office of our prison. And now the portrait hangs on the wall of my cell, pleasantly breaking the cold monotony of the pure white walls.

Leaving for a time our artist, who is now carried away by the portrait of the Warden, I shall continue my story.

CHAPTER VII

My spiritual clearness, as I had the pleasure of informing the reader before, has built up for me a considerable circle of men and women admirers. With self-evident emotion I shall tell of the pleasant hours of our hearty conversations, which I modestly call "My talks."

It is difficult for me to explain how I deserved it, but the majority of those who come to me regard me with a feeling of the profoundest respect, even adoration, and only a few come for the purpose of arguing with me, but these arguments are usually of a moderate and proper character. I usually seat myself in the middle of the room, in a soft and deep armchair, which is furnished me for this occasion by the Warden; my hearers surround me closely, and some of them, the more enthusiastic youths and maidens, seat themselves at my feet.

Having before me an audience more than half of which is composed of women, and entirely disposed in my favour, I always appeal not so much to the mind as to the sensitive and truthful heart. Fortunately I possess a certain oratorical power, and the customary effects of the oratorical art, to which all preachers, beginning in all probability with Mohammed, have resorted, and which I can handle rather cleverly, allow me to influence my hearers in the desired direction. It is easily understood that to the dear ladies in my audience I am not so much the sage, who has solved the mystery of the iron grate, as a great martyr of a righteous cause, which they do not quite understand. Shunning abstract discussions, they eagerly hang on every word of compassion and kindness, and respond with the same. Allowing them to love me and to believe in my immutable knowledge of life, I afford them the happy opportunity to depart at least for a time from the coldness of life, from its painful doubts and questions.

I say openly without any false modesty, which I despise even as I despise hypocrisy, there were lectures at which I myself being in a state of exaltation, called forth in my audience, especially in my nervous lady visitors, a mood of intense agitation, which turned into hysterical laughter and tears. Of course I am not a prophet; I am merely a modest thinker, but no one would succeed in convincing my lady admirers that there is no prophetic meaning and significance in my speeches.

I remember one such lecture which took place two months ago. The night before I could not sleep as soundly as I usually slept; perhaps it was simply because of the full moon, which affects sleep, disturbing and interrupting it. I vaguely remember the strange sensation which I experienced when the pale crescent of the moon appeared in my window and the iron squares cut it with ominous black lines into small silver squares....

When I started for the lecture I felt exhausted and rather inclined to silence than to conversation; the vision of the night before disturbed me. But when I saw those dear faces, those eyes full of hope and ardent entreaty for friendly advice; when I saw before me that rich field, already ploughed, waiting only for the good seed to be sown, my heart began to burn with delight, pity and love. Avoiding the customary formalities which accompany the meetings of people, declining the hands outstretched to greet me, I turned to the audience, which was agitated at the very sight of me, and gave them my blessing with a gesture to which I know how to lend a peculiar majesty.

"Come unto me," I exclaimed; "come unto me; you who have gone away from that life. Here, in this quiet abode, under the sacred protection of the iron grate, at my heart overflowing with love, you will find rest and comfort. My beloved children, give me your sad soul, exhausted from suffering, and I shall clothe it with light. I shall carry it to those blissful lands where the sun of eternal truth and love never sets."

Many had begun to cry already, but, as it was too early for tears, I interrupted them with a gesture of fatherly impatience, and continued:

"You, dear girl, who came from the world which calls itself free - what gloomy shadows lie on your charming and beautiful face! And you, my daring youth, why are you so pale? Why do I see, instead of the ecstasy of victory, the fear of defeat in your lowered eyes? And you, honest mother, tell me, what wind has made your eyes so red? What furious rain has lashed your wizened face? What snow has whitened your hair, for it used to be dark?"

But the weeping and the sobs drowned the end of my speech, and besides, I admit it without feeling ashamed of it, I myself brushed away more than one treacherous tear from my eyes. Without allowing the agitation to subside completely, I called in a voice of stern and truthful reproach:

"Do not weep because your soul is dark, stricken with misfortunes, blinded by chaos, clipped of its wings by doubts; give it to me and I shall direct it toward the light, toward order and reason. I know the truth. I have conceived the world! I have discovered the great principle of its purpose! I have solved the sacred formula of the iron grate! I demand of you - swear to me by the cold iron of its squares that henceforth you will confess to me without shame or fear all your deeds, your errors and doubts, all the secret thoughts of your soul and the dreams and desires of your body!"

"We swear! We swear! We swear! Save us! Reveal to us the truth! Take our sins upon yourself! Save us! Save us!" numerous exclamations resounded.

I must mention the sad incident which occurred during that same lecture. At the moment when the excitement reached its height and the hearts had already opened, ready to unburden themselves, a certain youth, looking morose and embittered, exclaimed loudly, evidently addressing himself to me:

"Liar! Do not listen to him. He is lying!"

The indulgent reader will easily believe that it was only by a great effort that I succeeded in saving the incautious youth from the fury of the audience. Offended in that which is most precious to a human being, his faith in goodness and the divine purpose of life, my women admirers rushed upon the foolish youth in a mob and would have beaten him cruelly. Remembering, however, that there was more joy to the pastor in one sinner who repents than in ten righteous men, I took the young man aside where no one could hear us, and entered into a brief conversation with him.

"Did you call me a liar, my child?"

Moved by my kindness, the poor young man became confused and answered hesitatingly:

"Pardon me for my harshness, but it seems to me that you are not telling the truth."

"I understand you, my friend. You must have been agitated by the intense ecstasy of the women, and you, as a sensible man, not inclined to mysticism, suspected me of fraud, of a hideous fraud. No, no, don't excuse yourself. I understand you. But I wish you would understand me. Out of the mire of superstitions, out of the deep gulf of prejudices and unfounded beliefs, I want to lead their strayed thoughts and place them upon the solid foundation of strictly logical reasoning. The iron grate, which I mentioned, is not a mystical sign; it is only a formula, a simple, sober, honest, mathematical formula. To you, as a sensible man, I will willingly explain this formula. The grate is the scheme in which are placed all the laws guiding the universe, which do away with chaos, substituting in its place strict, iron, inviolable order, forgotten by mankind.

As a brightminded man you will easily understand - "

"Pardon me. I did not understand you, and if you will permit me I - But why do you make them swear?"

"My friend, the soul of man, believing itself free and constantly suffering from this spurious freedom, is demanding fetters for itself - to some these fetters are an oath, to others a vow, to still others simply a word of honour. You will give me your word of honour, will you not?"

"I will."

"And by this you are simply striving to enter the harmony of the world, where everything is subjected to a law. Is not the falling of a stone the fulfilment of a vow, of the vow called the law of gravitation?"

I shall not go into detail about this conversation and the others that followed. The obstinate and unrestrained youth, who had insulted me by calling me liar, became one of my warmest adherents.

I must return to the others. During the time that I talked with the young man, the desire for penitence among my charming proselytes reached its height. Not patient enough to wait for me, they commenced in a state of intense ecstasy to confess to one another, giving to the room an appearance of a garden where dozens of birds of paradise were twittering at the same time. When I returned, each of them separately unfolded her agitated soul to me....

I saw how, from day to day, from hour to hour, terrible chaos was struggling in their souls with an eager inclination for harmony and order; how in the bloody struggle between eternal falsehood and immortal truth, falsehood, through inconceivable ways, passed into truth, and truth became falsehood. I found in the human soul all the forces in the world, and none of them was dormant, and in the mad whirlpool each soul became like a fountain, whose source is the abyss of the sea and whose summit the sky. And every human being, as I have learned and seen, is like the rich and powerful master who gave a masquerade ball at his castle and illuminated it with many lights; and strange masks came from everywhere and the master greeted them, bowing courteously, and vainly asking them who they were; and new, ever stranger, ever more terrible, masks were arriving, and the master bowed to them ever more courteously, staggering from fatigue and fear. And they were laughing and whispering strange words about the eternal chaos, whence they came, obeying the call of the master. And lights were burning in the castle - and in the distance lighted windows were visible, reminding him of the festival, and the exhausted master kept bowing ever lower, ever more courteously, ever more cheerfully. My indulgent reader will easily understand that in addition to a certain sense of fear which I experienced, the greatest delight and even joyous emotion soon came upon me - for I saw that eternal chaos was defeated and the triumphant hymn of bright harmony was rising to the skies....

Not without a sense of pride I shall mention the modest offerings by which my kind admirers were striving to express to me their feelings of love and adoration. I am not afraid of calling out a smile on the lips of my readers, for I feel how comical it is - I will say that among the offerings brought me at first were fruit, cakes, all kinds of sweet-meats. But I am afraid, however, that no one will believe me when I say that I have actually declined these offerings, preferring the observance of the prison regime in all its rigidness.

At the last lecture, a kind and honourable lady brought me a basketful of live flowers. To my regret, I was compelled to decline this present, too.

"Forgive me, madam, but flowers do not enter into the system of our prison. I appreciate very much your magnanimous attention - I kiss your hands, madam - " I said, "but I am compelled to decline the flowers. Travelling along the thorny road to self-renunciation, I must not caress my eyes with the ephemeral and illusionary beauty of these charming lilies and roses. All flowers perish in our prison, madam."

Yesterday another lady brought me a very valuable crucifix of ivory, a family heirloom, she said. Not afflicted with the sin of hypocrisy, I told my generous lady frankly that I do not believe in miracles.

"But at the same time," I said, "I regard with the profoundest respect Him who is justly called the Saviour of the world, and I honour greatly His services to mankind.

"If I should tell you, madam, that the Gospel has long been my favourite book, that there is not a day in my life that I do not open this great Book, drawing from it strength and courage to be able to continue my hard course - you will understand that your liberal gift could not have fallen into better hands. Henceforth, thanks to you, the sad solitude of my cell will vanish; I am not alone. I bless you, my daughter."

I cannot forego mentioning the strange thoughts brought out by the crucifix as it hung there beside my portrait. It was twilight; outside the wall the bell was tolling heavily in the invisible church, calling the believers together; in the distance, over the deserted field, overgrown with high grass, an unknown wanderer was plodding along, passing into the unknown distance, like a little black dot. It was as quiet in our prison as in a sepulchre. I looked long and attentively at the features of Jesus, which were so calm, so joyous compared with him who looked silently and dully from the wall beside Him. And with my habit, formed during the long years of solitude, of addressing inanimate things aloud, I said to the motionless crucifix:

"Good evening, Jesus. I am glad to welcome You in our prison. There are three of us here: You, I, and the one who is looking from the wall, and I hope that we three will manage to live in peace and in harmony. He is looking silently, and You are silent, and Your eyes are closed - I shall speak for the three of us, a sure sign that our peace will never be broken."

They were silent, and, continuing, I addressed my speech to the portrait:

"Where are you looking so intently and so strangely, my unknown friend and roommate? In your eyes I see mystery and reproach. Is it possible that you dare reproach Him? Answer!"

And, pretending that the portrait answered, I continued in a different voice with an expression of extreme sternness and boundless grief:

"Yes, I do reproach Him. Jesus, Jesus! Why is Your face so pure, so blissful? You have passed only over the brink of human sufferings, as over the brink of an abyss, and only the foam of the bloody and miry waves have touched You. Do You command me, a human being, to sink into the dark depth? Great is Your Golgotha, Jesus, but too reverent and joyous, and one small but interesting stroke is missing - the horror of aimlessness!"

Here I interrupted the speech of the Portrait, with an expression of anger.

"How dare you," I exclaimed; "how dare you speak of aimlessness in our prison?"

They were silent; and suddenly Jesus, without opening His eyes - He even seemed to close them more tightly - answered:

"Who knows the mysteries of the heart of Jesus?"

I burst into laughter, and my esteemed reader will easily understand this laughter. It turned out that I, a cool and sober mathematician, possessed a poetic talent and could compose very interesting comedies.

I do not know how all this would have ended, for I had already prepared a thundering answer for my roommate when the appearance of the keeper, who brought me food, suddenly interrupted me. But apparently my face bore traces of excitement, for the man asked me with stern sympathy:

"Were you praying?"

I do not remember what I answered.

CHAPTER VIII

Last Sunday a great misfortune occurred in our prison: The artist K., whom the reader knows already, ended his life in suicide by flinging himself from the table with his head against the stone floor. The fall and the force of the blow had been so skilfully calculated by the unfortunate young man that his skull was split in two. The grief of the Warden was indescribable. Having called me to the office, the Warden, without shaking hands with me, reproached me in angry and harsh terms for having deceived him, and he regained his calm, only after my hearty apologies and promises that such accidents would not happen again. I promised to prepare a project for watching the criminals which would render suicide impossible. The esteemed wife of the Warden, whose portrait remained unfinished, was also grieved by the death of the artist.

Of course, I had not expected this outcome, either, although a few days before committing suicide, K. had provoked in me a feeling of uneasiness. Upon entering his cell one morning, and greeting him, I noticed with amazement that he was sitting before his slate once more drawing human figures.

"What does this mean, my friend?" I inquired cautiously. "And how about the portrait of the second assistant?"

"The devil take it!"

"But you - "

"The devil take it!"

After a pause I remarked distractedly:

"Your portrait of the Warden is meeting with great success. Although some of the people who have seen it say that the right moustache is somewhat shorter than the left - "

"Shorter?"

"Yes, shorter. But in general they find that you caught the likeness very successfully."

K. had put aside his slate pencil and, perfectly calm, said:

"Tell your Warden that I am not going to paint that prison riffraff any more."

After these words there was nothing left for me to do but leave him, which I decided to do. But the artist, who could not get along without giving vent to his effusions, seized me by the hand and said with his usual enthusiasm:

"Just think of it, old man, what a horror! Every day a new repulsive face appears before me. They sit and stare at me with their froglike eyes. What am I to do? At first I laughed - I even liked it - but when the froglike eyes stared at me every day I was seized with horror. I was afraid they might start to quack - qua-qua!"

Indeed there was a certain fear, even madness, in the eyes of the artist - the madness which shortly led him to his untimely grave.

"Old man, it is necessary to have something beautiful. Do you understand me?"

"And the wife of the Warden? Is she not - "

I shall pass in silence the unbecoming expressions with which he spoke of the lady in his excitement. I must, however, admit that to a certain extent the artist was right in his complaints. I had been present several times at the sittings, and noticed that all who had posed for the artist behaved rather unnaturally. Sincere and naive, conscious of the importance of their position, convinced that the features of their faces perpetuated upon the canvas would go down to posterity, they exaggerated somewhat the qualities which are so characteristic of their high and responsible office in our prison. A certain bombast of pose, an exaggerated expression of stern authority, an obvious consciousness of their own importance, and a noticeable contempt for those on whom their eyes were directed - all this disfigured their kind and affable faces. But I cannot understand what horrible features the artist found where there should have been a smile. I was even indignant at the superficial attitude with which an artist, who considered himself talented and sensible, passed the people without noticing that a divine spark was glimmering in each one of them. In the quest after some fantastic beauty he light-mindedly passed by the true beauties with which the human soul is filled. I cannot help feeling sorry for those unfortunate people who, like K., because of a peculiar construction of their brains, always turn their eyes toward the dark side, whereas there is so much joy and light in our prison!

When I said this to K. I heard, to my regret, the same stereotyped and indecent answer:

"The devil take it!"

All I could do was to shrug my shoulders. Suddenly changing his tone and bearing, the artist turned to me seriously with a question which, in my opinion, was also indecent:

"Why do you lie, old man?"

I was astonished, of course.

"I lie?"

"Well, let it be the truth, if you like, but why? I am looking and thinking. Why did you say that? Why?"

My indulgent reader, who knows well what the truth has cost me, will readily understand my profound indignation. I deliberately mention this audacious and other calumnious phrases to show in what an atmosphere of malice, distrust, and disrespect I have to plod along the hard road of suffering. He insisted rudely:

"I have had enough of your smiles. Tell me plainly, why do you speak so?"

Then, I admit, I flared up:

"You want to know why I speak the truth? Because I hate falsehood and I commit it to eternal anathema! Because fate has made me a victim of injustice, and as a victim, like Him who took upon Himself the great sin of the world and its great sufferings, I wish to point out the way to mankind. Wretched egoist, you know only yourself and your miserable art, while I love mankind."

My anger grew. I felt the veins on my forehead swelling.

"Fool, miserable dauber, unfortunate schoolboy, in love with colours! Human beings pass before you, and you see only their froglike eyes. How did your tongue turn to say such a thing ? Oh, if you only looked even once into the human soul! What treasures of tenderness, love, humble faith, holy humility, you would have discovered there! And to you, bold man, it would have seemed as if you entered a temple - a bright, illuminated temple. But it is said of people like you - 'do not cast your pearls before swine.'"

The artist was silent, crushed by my angry and unrestrained speech. Finally he sighed and said:

"Forgive me, old man; I am talking nonsense, of course, but I am so unfortunate and so lonely. Of course, my dear old man, it is all true about the divine spark and about beauty, but a polished boot is also beautiful. I cannot, I cannot! Just think of it! How can a man have such moustaches as he has ? And yet he is complaining that the left moustache is shorter!"

He laughed like a child, and, heaving a sigh, added:

"I'll make another attempt. I will paint the lady. There is really something good in her. Although she is after all - a cow."

He laughed again, and, fearing to brush away with his sleeve the drawing on the slate, he cautiously placed it in the corner.

Here I did that which my duty compelled me to do. Seizing the slate, I smashed it to pieces with a powerful blow. I thought that the artist would rush upon me furiously, but he did not. To his weak mind my act seemed so blasphemous, so supernaturally horrible, that his deathlike lips could not utter a word.

"What have you done?" he asked at last in a low voice. "You have broken it?"

And raising my hand I replied solemnly:

"Foolish youth, I have done that which I would have done to my heart if it wanted to jest and mock me! Unfortunate youth, can you not see that your art has long been mocking you, that from that slate of yours the devil himself was making hideous faces at you?"

"Yes. The devil!"

"Being far from your wonderful art, I did not understand you at first, nor your longing, your horror of aimlessness. But when I entered your cell to-day and noticed you at your ruinous occupation, I said to myself: It is better that he should not create at all than to create in this manner. Listen to me."

I then revealed for the first time to this youth the sacred formula of the iron grate, which, dividing the infinite into squares, thereby subjects it to itself. K. listened to my words with emotion, looking with the horror of an ignorant man at the figures which must have seemed to him to be cabalistic, but which were nothing else than the ordinary figures used in mathematics.

"I am your slave, old man," he said at last, kissing my hand with his cold lips.

"No, you will be my favourite pupil, my son. I bless you."

And it seemed to me that the artist was saved. True, he regarded me with great joy, which could easily be explained by the extreme respect with which I inspired him, and he painted the portrait of the Warden's wife with such zeal and enthusiasm that the esteemed lady was sincerely moved. And, strange to say, the artist succeeded in making so strangely beautiful the features of this woman, who was stout and no longer young, that the Warden, long accustomed to the face of his wife, was greatly delighted by its new expression. Thus everything went on smoothly, when suddenly this catastrophe occurred, the entire horror of which I alone knew.

Not desiring to call forth any unnecessary disputes, I concealed from the Warden the fact that on the eve of his death the artist had thrown a letter into my cell, which I noticed only in the morning. I did not preserve the note, nor do I remember all that the unfortunate youth told me in his farewell message; I think it was a letter of thanks for my effort to save him. He wrote that he regretted sincerely that his failing strength did not permit him to avail himself of my instructions. But one phrase impressed itself deeply in my memory, and you will understand the reason for it when I repeat it in all its terrifying simplicity.

"I am going away from your prison," thus read the phrase.

And he really did go away. Here are the walls, here is the little window in the door, here is our prison, but he is not there; he has gone away. Consequently I, too, could go away. Instead of having wasted dozens of years on a titanic struggle, instead of being tormented by the throes of despair, instead of growing enfeebled by horror in the face of unsolved mysteries, of striving to subject the world to my mind and my will, I could have climbed the table and - one instant of pain - I would be free; I would be triumphant over the lock and the walls, over truth and falsehood, over joys and sufferings. I will not say that I had not thought of suicide before as a means of escaping from our prison, but now for the first time it appeared before me in all its attractiveness. In a fit of base faint-heartedness, which I shall not conceal from my reader, even as I do not conceal from him my good qualities; perhaps even in a fit of temporary insanity I momentarily forgot all I knew about our prison and its great purpose. I forgot - I am ashamed to say - even the great formula of the iron grate, which I conceived and mastered with such difficulty, and I prepared a noose made of my towel for the purpose of strangling myself. But at the last moment, when all was ready, and it was but necessary to push away the taburet, I asked myself, with my habit of reasoning which did not forsake me even at that time: But where am I going? The answer was: I am going to death. But what is death? And the answer was: I do not know.

These brief reflections were enough for me to come to myself, and with a bitter laugh at my cowardice I removed the fatal noose from my neck. Just as I had been ready to sob for grief a minute before, so now I laughed - I laughed like a madman, realising that another trap, placed before me by derisive fate, had so brilliantly been evaded by me. Oh, how many traps there are in the life of man! Like a cunning fisherman, fate catches him now with the alluring bait of some truth, now with the hairy little worm of dark falsehood, now with the phantom of life, now with the phantom of death.

My dear young man, my fascinating fool, my charming silly fellow - who told you that our prison ends here, that from one prison you did not fall into another prison, from which it will hardly be possible for you to run away? You were too hasty, my friend, you forgot to ask me something else - I would have told it to you. I would have told you that omnipotent law reigns over that which you call non-existence and death just as it reigns over that which you call life and existence. Only the fools, dying, believe that they have made an end of themselves - they have ended but one form of themselves, in order to assume another form immediately.

Thus I reflected, laughing at the foolish suicide, the ridiculous destroyer of the fetters of eternity. And this is what I said addressing myself to my two silent roommates hanging motionlessly on the white wall of my cell:

"I believe and confess that our prison is immortal. What do you say to this, my friends?"

But they were silent. And having burst into good-natured laughter - What quiet roommates I have! I undressed slowly and gave myself to peaceful sleep. In my dream I saw another majestic prison, and wonderful jailers with white wings on their backs, and the Chief Warden of the prison himself. I do not remember whether there were any little windows in the doors or not, but I think there were. I recall that something like an angel's eye was fixed upon me with tender attention and love. My indulgent reader will, of course, guess that I am jesting. I did not dream at all. I am not in the habit of dreaming.

Without hoping that the Warden, occupied with pressing official affairs, would understand me thoroughly and appreciate my idea concerning the impossibility of escaping from our prison, I confined myself, in my report, to an indication of several ways in which suicides could be averted. With magnanimous shortsightedness peculiar to busy and trusting people, the Warden failed to notice the weak points of my project and clasped my hand warmly, expressing to me his gratitude in the name of our entire prison.

On that day I had the honour, for the first time, to drink a glass of tea at the home of the Warden, in the presence of his kind wife and charming children, who called me "Grandpa." Tears of emotion which gathered in my eyes could but faintly express the feelings that came over me.

At the request of the Warden's wife, who took a deep interest in me, I related in detail the story of the tragic murders which led me so unexpectedly and so terribly to the prison. I could not find expressions strong enough - there are no expressions strong enough in the human language - to brand adequately the unknown criminal, who not only murdered three helpless people, but who mocked them brutally in a fit of blind and savage rage.

As the investigation and the autopsy showed, the murderer dealt the last blows after the people had been dead. It is very possible, however - even murderers should be given their due - that the man, intoxicated by the sight of blood, ceased to be a human being and became a beast, the son of chaos, the child of dark and terrible desires. It was characteristic that the murderer, after having committed the crime, drank wine and ate biscuits - some of these were left on the table together with the marks of his blood-stained fingers. But there was something so horrible that my mind could neither understand nor explain: the murderer, after lighting a cigar himself, apparently moved by a feeling of strange kindness, put a lighted cigar between the closed teeth of my father.

I had not recalled these details in many years. They had almost been erased by the hand of time, and now while relating them to my shocked listeners, who would not believe that such horrors were possible, I felt my face turning pale and my hair quivering on my head. In an outburst of grief and anger I rose from my armchair, and straightening myself to my full height, I exclaimed:

"Justice on earth is often powerless, but I implore heavenly justice, I implore the justice of life which never forgives, I implore all the higher laws under whose authority man lives. May the guilty one not escape his deserved punishment! His punishment!"

Moved by my sobs, my listeners there and then expressed their zeal and readiness to work for my liberation, and thus at least partly redeem the injustice heaped upon me. I apologised and returned to my cell.

Evidently my old organism cannot bear such agitation any longer; besides, it is hard even for a strong man to picture in his imagination certain images without risking the loss of his reason. Only in this way can I explain the strange hallucination which appeared before my fatigued eyes in the solitude of my cell. As though benumbed I gazed aimlessly at the tightly closed door, when suddenly it seemed to me that some one was standing behind me. I had felt this deceptive sensation before, so I did not turn around for some time. But when I turned around at last I saw - in the distance, between the crucifix and my portrait, about a quarter of a yard above the floor - the body of my father, as though hanging in the air. It is hard for me to give the details, for twilight had long set in, but I can say with certainty that it was the image of a corpse, and not of a living being, although a cigar was smoking in its mouth. To be more exact, there was no smoke from the cigar, but a faintly reddish light was seen. It is characteristic that I did not sense the odour of tobacco either at that time or later - I had long given up smoking. Here - I must confess my weakness, but the illusion was striking - I commenced to speak to the hallucination. Advancing as closely as possible - the body did not retreat as I approached, but remained perfectly motionless - I said to the ghost:

"I thank you, father. You know how your son is suffering, and you have come - you have come to testify to my innocence. I thank you, father. Give me your hand, and with a firm filial hand-clasp I will respond to your unexpected visit. Don't you want to? Let me have your hand. Give me your hand, or I will call you a liar!"

I stretched out my hand, but of course the hallucination did not deem it worth while to respond, and I was forever deprived of the opportunity of feeling the touch of a ghost. The cry which I uttered and which so upset my friend, the jailer, creating some confusion in the prison, was called forth by the sudden disappearance of the phantom - it was so sudden that the space in the place where the corpse had been seemed to me more terrible than the corpse itself.

Such is the power of human imagination when, excited, it creates phantoms and visions, peopling the bottomless and ever silent emptiness with them. It is sad to admit that there are people, however, who believe in ghosts and build upon this belief nonsensical theories about certain relations between the world of the living and the enigmatic land inhabited by the dead. I understand that the human ear and eye can be deceived - but how can the great and lucid human mind fall into such coarse and ridiculous deception?

I asked the jailer:

"I feel a strange sensation, as though there were the odour of cigar smoke in my cell. Don't you smell it?"

The jailer sniffed the air conscientiously and replied:

"No I don't. You only imagined it."

If you need any confirmation, here is a splendid proof that all I had seen, if it existed at all, existed only in the net of my eye.

CHAPTER IX

Something altogether unexpected has happened; the efforts of my friends, the Warden and his wife, were crowned with success, and for two months I have been free, out of prison.

I am happy to inform you that immediately upon my leaving the prison I occupied a very honourable position, to which I could hardly have aspired, conscious of my humble qualities. The entire press met me with unanimous enthusiasm. Numerous journalists, photographers, even caricaturists (the people of our time are so fond of laughter and clever witticisms), in hundreds of articles and drawings reproduced the story of my remarkable life. With striking unanimity the newspapers assigned to me the name of "Master," a highly flattering name, which I accepted, after some hesitation, with deep gratitude. I do not know whether it is worth mentioning the few hostile notices called forth by irritation and envy - a vice which so frequently stains the human soul. In one of these notices, which appeared, by the way, in a very filthy little newspaper, a certain scamp, guided by wretched gossip and baseless rumours about my chats in our prison, called me a "zealot and liar." Enraged by the insolence of the miserable scribbler, my friends wanted to prosecute him, but I persuaded them not to do it. Vice is its own proper punishment.

The fortune which my kind mother had left me and which had grown considerably during the time I was in prison has enabled me to settle down to a life of luxury in one of the most aristocratic hotels. I have a large retinue of servants at my command and an automobile - a splendid invention with which I now became acquainted for the first time - and I have skilfully arranged my financial affairs. Live flowers brought to me in abundance by my charming lady visitors give to my nook the appearance of a flower garden or even a bit of a tropical forest. My servant, a very decent young man, is in a state of despair. He says that he had never seen such a variety of flowers and had never smelled such a variety of odours at the same time. If not for my advanced age and the strict and serious propriety with which I treat my visitors, I do not know how far they would have gone in the expression of their feelings. How many perfumed notes! How many languid sighs and humbly imploring eyes! There was even a fascinating stranger with a black veil - three times she appeared mysteriously, and when she learned that I had visitors she disappeared just as mysteriously.

I will add that at the present time I have had the honour of being elected an honourary member of numerous humanitarian organisations such as "The League of Peace," "The League for Combating Juvenile Criminality," "The Society of the Friends of Man," and others. Besides, at the request of the editor of one of the most widely read newspapers, I am to begin next month a series of public lectures, for which purpose I am going on a tour together with my kind impresario.

I have already prepared my material for the first three lectures and, in the hope that my reader may be interested, I shall give the synopsis of these lectures.

FIRST LECTURE

Chaos or order? The eternal struggle between chaos and order. The eternal revolt and the defeat of chaos, the rebel. The triumph of law and order.

SECOND LECTURE

What is the soul of man? The eternal conflict in the soul of man between chaos, whence it came, and harmony, whither it strives irresistibly. Falsehood, as the offspring of chaos, and

Truth, as the child of harmony. The triumph of truth and the downfall of falsehood.

THIRD LECTURE

THE EXPLANATION OF THE SACRED FORMULA OF THE IRON GRATE

As my indulgent reader will see, justice is after all not an empty sound, and I am getting a great reward for my sufferings. But not daring to reproach fate which was so merciful to me, I nevertheless do not feel that sense of contentment which, it would seem, I ought to feel. True, at first I was positively happy, but soon my habit for strictly logical reasoning, the clearness and honesty of my views, gained by contemplating the world through a mathematically correct grate, have led me to a series of disillusions.

I am afraid to say it now with full certainty, but it seems to me that all their life of this so-called freedom is a continuous self-deception and falsehood. The life of each of these people, whom I have seen during these days, is moving in a strictly defined circle, which is just as solid as the corridors of our prison, just as closed as the dial of the watches which they, in the innocence of their mind, lift every minute to their eyes, not understanding the fatal meaning of the eternally moving hand, which is eternally returning to its place, and each of them feels this, even as the circus horse probably feels it, but in a state of strange blindness each one assures us that he is perfectly free and moving forward. Like the stupid bird which is beating itself to exhaustion against the transparent glass obstacle, without understanding what it is that obstructs its way, these people are helplessly beating against the walls of their glass prison.

I was greatly mistaken, it seems, also in the significance of the greetings which fell to my lot when I left the prison. Of course I was convinced that in me they greeted the representative of our prison, a leader hardened by experience, a master, who came to them only for the purpose of revealing to them the great mystery of purpose. And when they congratulated me upon the freedom granted to me I responded with thanks, not suspecting what an idiotic meaning they placed on the word. May I be forgiven this coarse expression, but I am powerless now to restrain my aversion for their stupid life, for their thoughts, for their feelings.

Foolish hypocrites, fearing to tell the truth even when it adorns them! My hardened truthfulness was cruelly taxed in the midst of these false and trivial people. Not a single person believed that I was never so happy as in prison. Why, then, are they so surprised at me, and why do they print my portraits? Are there so few idiots that are unhappy in prison? And the most remarkable thing, which only my indulgent reader will be able to appreciate, is this: Often distrusting me completely, they nevertheless sincerely go into raptures over me, bowing before me, clasping my hands and mumbling at every step, "Master! Master!"

If they only profited by their constant lying - but, no; they are perfectly disinterested, and they lie as though by some one's higher order; they lie in the fanatical conviction that falsehood is in no way different from the truth. Wretched actors, even incapable of a decent makeup, they writhe from morning till night on the boards of the stage, and, dying the most real death, suffering the most real sufferings, they bring into their deathly convulsions the cheap art of the harlequin. Even their crooks are not real; they only play the roles of crooks, while remaining honest people; and the role of honest people is played by rogues, and played poorly, and the public sees it, but in the name of the same fatal falsehood it gives them wreaths and bouquets. And if there is really a talented actor who can wipe away the boundary between truth and deception, so that even they begin to believe, they go into raptures, call him great, start a subscription for a monument, but do not give any money. Desperate cowards, they fear themselves most of all, and admiring delightedly the reflection of their spuriously made-up faces in the mirror, they howl with fear and rage when some one incautiously holds up the mirror to their soul.

My indulgent reader should accept all this relatively, not forgetting that certain grumblings are natural in old age. Of course, I have met quite a number of most worthy people, absolutely truthful, sincere, and courageous; I am proud to admit that I found among them also a proper estimate of my personality. With the support of these friends of mine I hope to complete successfully my struggle for truth and justice. I am sufficiently strong for my sixty years, and, it seems, there is no power that could break my iron will.

At times I am seized with fatigue owing to their absurd mode of life. I have not the proper rest even at night.

The consciousness that while going to bed I may absent-mindedly have forgotten to lock my bedroom door compels me to jump from my bed dozens of times and to feel the lock with a quiver of horror.

Not long ago it happened that I locked my door and hid the key under my pillow, perfectly confident that my room was locked, when suddenly I heard a knock, then the door opened, and my servant entered with a smile on his face. You, dear reader, will easily understand the horror I experienced at this unexpected visit - it seemed to me that some one had entered my soul. And though I have absolutely nothing to conceal, this breaking into my room seems to me indecent, to say the least.

I caught a cold a few days ago - there is a terrible draught in their windows - and I asked my servant to watch me at night. In the morning I asked him, in jest:

"Well, did I talk much in my sleep?"

"No, you didn't talk at all."

"I had a terrible dream, and I remember I even cried."

"No, you smiled all the time, and I thought - what fine dreams our Master must see!"

The dear youth must have been sincerely devoted to me, and I am deeply moved by such devotion during these painful days.

To-morrow I shall sit down to prepare my lectures. It is high time!

CHAPTER X

My God! What has happened to me? I do not know how I shall tell my reader about it. I was on the brink of the abyss, I almost perished. What cruel temptations fate is sending me! Fools, we smile, without suspecting anything, when some murderous hand is already lifted to attack us; we smile, and the very next instant we open our eyes wide with horror. I - I cried. I cried. Another moment and deceived, I would have hurled myself down, thinking that I was flying toward the sky.

It turned out that "the charming stranger" who wore a dark veil, and who came to me so mysteriously three times, was no one else than Mme. N., my former fiancee, my love, my dream and my suffering.

But order! order! May my indulgent reader forgive the involuntary incoherence of the preceding lines, but I am sixty years old, and my strength is beginning to fail me, and I am alone. My unknown reader, be my friend at this moment, for I am not of iron, and my strength is beginning to fail me. Listen, my friend; I shall endeavour to tell you exactly and in detail, as objectively as my cold and clear mind will be able to do it, all that has happened. You must understand that which my tongue may omit.

I was sitting, engaged upon the preparation of my lecture, seriously carried away by the absorbing work, when my servant announced that the strange lady in the black veil was there again, and that she wished to see me. I confess I was irritated, that I was ready to decline to see her, but my curiosity, coupled with my desire not to offend her, led me to receive the

unexpected guest. Assuming the expression of majestic nobleness with which I usually greet my visitors, and softening that
expression somewhat by a smile in view of the romantic
character of the affair, I ordered my servant to open the door.

"Please be seated, my dear guest," I said politely to the
stranger, who stood as dazed before me, still keeping the veil
on her face.

She sat down.

"Although I respect all secrecy," I continued jestingly, "I would
nevertheless ask you to remove this gloomy cover which
disfigures you. Does the human face need a mask?"

The strange visitor declined, in a state of agitation.

"Very well, I'll take it off, but not now - later. First I want to
see you well."

The pleasant voice of the stranger did not call forth any
recollections in me. Deeply interested and even flattered, I
submitted to my strange visitor all the treasures of my mind,
experience and talent. With enthusiasm I related to her the
edifying story of my life, constantly illuminating every detail
with a ray of the Great Purpose. (In this I availed myself partly
of the material on which I had just been working, preparing
my lectures.) The passionate attention with which the strange
lady listened to my words, the frequent, deep sighs, the
nervous quiver of her thin fingers in her black gloves, her
agitated exclamations - inspired me.

Carried away by my own narrative, I confess, I did not pay
proper attention to the queer behaviour of my strange visitor.
Having lost all restraint, she now clasped my hands, now
pushed them away, she cried and availing herself of each pause
in my speech, she implored:

"Don't, don't, don't! Stop speaking! I can't listen to it!"

And at the moment when I least expected it she tore the veil from her face, and before my eyes - before my eyes appeared her face, the face of my love, of my dream, of my boundless and bitter sorrow. Perhaps because I lived all my life dreaming of her alone, with her alone I was young, with her I had developed and grown old, with her I was advancing to the grave - her face seemed to me neither old nor faded - it was exactly as I had pictured it in my dreams - it seemed endlessly dear to me.

What has happened to me? For the first time in tens of years I forgot that I had a face - for the first time in tens of years I looked helplessly, like a youngster, like a criminal caught red-handed, waiting for some deadly blow.

"You see! You see! It is I. It is I! My God, why are you silent? Don't you recognise me?"

Did I recognise her? It were better not to have known that face at all! It were better for me to have grown blind rather than to see her again!

"Why are you silent ? How terrible you are! You have forgotten me!"

"Madam - "

Of course, I should have continued in this manner; I saw how she staggered. I saw how with trembling fingers, almost falling, she was looking for her veil; I saw that another word of courageous truth, and the terrible vision would vanish never to appear again. But some stranger within me - not I - not I - uttered the following absurd, ridiculous phrase, in which, despite its chilliness, rang so much jealousy and hopeless sorrow:

"Madam, you have deceived me. I don't know you. Perhaps you entered the wrong door. I suppose your husband and your children are waiting for you. Please, my servant will take you down to the carriage."

Could I think that these words, uttered in the same stern and cold voice, would have such a strange effect upon the woman's heart? With a cry, all the bitter passion of which I could not describe, she threw herself before me on her knees, exclaiming:

"So you do love me!"

Forgetting that our life had already been lived, that we were old, that all had been ruined and scattered like dust by Time, and that it can never return again; forgetting that I was grey, that my shoulders were bent, that the voice of passion sounds strangely when it comes from old lips - I burst into impetuous reproaches and complaints.

"Yes, I did deceive you!" her deathly pale lips uttered. "I knew that you were innocent - "

"Be silent. Be silent."

"Everybody laughed at me - even your friends, your mother whom I despised for it - all betrayed you. Only I kept repeating: 'He is innocent!'"

Oh, if this woman knew what she was doing to me with her words! If the trumpet of the angel, announcing the day of judgment, had resounded at my very ear, I would not have been so frightened as now. What is the blaring of a trumpet calling to battle and struggle to the ear of the brave? It was as if an abyss had opened at my feet. It was as if an abyss had opened before me, and as though blinded by lightning, as though dazed by a blow, I shouted in an outburst of wild and strange ecstasy:

"Be silent! I - "

If that woman were sent by God, she would have become silent. If she were sent by the devil, she would have become silent even then. But there was neither God nor devil in her, and interrupting me, not permitting me to finish the phrase, she went on:

"No, I will not be silent. I must tell you all. I have waited for you so many years. Listen, listen!"

But suddenly she saw my face and she retreated, seized with horror.

"What is it? What is the matter with you? Why do you laugh? I am afraid of your laughter! Stop laughing! Don't! Don't!"

But I was not laughing at all, I only smiled softly. And then I said very seriously, without smiling:

"I am smiling because I am glad to see you. Tell me about yourself."

And, as in a dream, I saw her face and I heard her soft terrible whisper:

"You know that I love you. You know that all my life I loved you alone. I lived with another and was faithful to him. I have children, but you know they are all strangers to me - he and the children and I myself. Yes, I deceived you, I am a criminal, but I do not know how it happened. He was so kind to me, he made me believe that he was convinced of your innocence - later I learned that he did not tell the truth, and with this, just think of it, with this he won me."

"You lie!"

"I swear to you. For a whole year he followed me and spoke only of you. One day he even cried when I told him about you, about your sufferings, about your love."

"But he was lying!"

"Of course he was lying. But at that time he seemed so dear to me, so kind that I kissed him on the forehead. Then we used to bring you flowers to the prison. One day as we were returning from you - listen - he suddenly proposed that we should go out driving. The evening was so beautiful - "

"And you went! How did you dare go out with him? You had just seen my prison, you had just been near me, and yet you dared go with him. How base!"

"Be silent. Be silent. I know I am a criminal. But I was so exhausted, so tired, and you were so far away. Understand me."

She began to cry, wringing her hands.

"Understand me. I was so exhausted. And he - he saw how I felt - and yet he dared kiss me."

"He kissed you! And you allowed him ? On the lips?"

"No, no! Only on the cheek."

"You lie!"

"No, no. I swear to you."

I began to laugh.

"You responded? And you were driving in the forest - you, my fiancee, my love, my dream! And all this for my sake? Tell me! Speak!"

In my rage I wrung her arms, and wriggling like a snake, vainly trying to evade my look, she whispered:

"Forgive me; forgive me."

"How many children have you?"

"Forgive me."

But my reason forsook me, and in my growing rage I cried, stamping my foot:

"How many children have you? Speak, or I will kill you!"

I actually said this. Evidently I was losing my reason completely if I could threaten to kill a helpless woman. And she, surmising apparently that my threats were mere words, answered with feigned readiness:

"Kill me! You have a right to do it! I am a criminal. I deceived you. You are a martyr, a saint! When you told me - is it true that even in your thoughts you never deceived me - even in your thoughts!"

And again an abyss opened before me. Everything trembled, everything fell, everything became an absurd dream, and in the last effort to save my extinguishing reason I shouted:

"But you are happy! You cannot be unhappy; you have no right to be unhappy! Otherwise I shall lose my mind."

But she did not understand. With a bitter laugh, with a senseless smile, in which her suffering mingled with bright, heavenly joy, she said:

"I am happy! I - happy! Oh, my friend, only near you I can find happiness. From the moment you left the prison I began to despise my home. I am alone there; I am a stranger to all. If you only knew how I hate that scoundrel! You are sensible; you must have felt that you were not alone in prison, that I was always with you there - "

"And he?"

"Be silent! Be silent! If you only heard with what delight I called him scoundrel!"

She burst into laughter, frightening me by the wild expression on her face.

"Just think of it! All his life he embraced only a lie. And when, deceived, happy, he fell asleep, I looked at him with wide-open eyes, I gnashed my teeth softly, and I felt like pinching him, like sticking him with a pin."

She burst into laughter again. It seemed to me that she was driving wedges into my brain. Clasping my head, I cried:

"You lie! You lie to me!"

Indeed, it was easier for me to speak to the ghost than to the woman. What could I say to her? My mind was growing dim. And how could I repulse her when she, full of love and passion, kissed my hands, my eyes, my face? It was she, my love, my dream, my bitter sorrow!

"I love you! I love you!"

And I believed her - I believed her love. I believed everything. And once more I felt that my locks were black, and I saw myself young again. And I knelt before her and wept for a long time, and whispered to her about my sufferings, about the pain of solitude, about a heart cruelly broken, about offended, disfigured, mutilated thoughts. And, laughing and crying, she stroked my hair. Suddenly she noticed that it was grey, and she cried strangely:

"What is it? And life? I am an old woman already."

On leaving me she demanded that I escort her to the threshold, like a young man; and I did. Before going she said to me:

"I am coming back to-morrow. I know my children will deny me - my daughter is to marry soon. You and I will go away. Do you love me?"

"I do."

"We will go far, far away, my dear. You wanted to deliver some lectures. You should not do it. I don't like what you say about that iron grate. You are exhausted, you need a rest. Shall it be so?"

"Yes."

"Oh, I forgot my veil. Keep it, keep it as a remembrance of this day. My dear!"

In the vestibule, in the presence of the sleepy porter, she kissed me. There was the odour of some new perfume, unlike the perfume with which her letter was scented. And her coquettish laugh was like a sob as she disappeared behind the glass door.

That night I aroused my servant, ordered him to pack our things, and we went away. I shall not say where I am at present, but last night and to-night trees were rustling over my head and the rain was beating against my windows. Here the windows are small, and I feel much better. I wrote her a rather long letter, the contents of which I shall not reproduce. I shall never see her again.

But what am I to do? May the reader pardon these incoherent questions. They are so natural in a man in my condition. Besides, I caught an acute rheumatism while travelling, which is most painful and even dangerous for a man of my age, and which does not permit me to reason calmly. For some reason or another I think very often about my young friend K., who went to an untimely grave. How does he feel in his new prison?

To-morrow morning, if my strength will permit me, I intend to pay a visit to the Warden of our prison and to his esteemed wife. Our prison -

CHAPTER XI

I am profoundly happy to inform my dear reader that I have completely recovered my physical as well as my spiritual powers. A long rest out in the country, amid nature's soothing beauties; the contemplation of village life, which is so simple and bright; the absence of the noise of the city, where hundreds of wind-mills are stupidly flapping their long arms before your very nose, and finally the complete solitude, undisturbed by anything - all these have restored to my unbalanced view of the world all its former steadiness and its iron, irresistible firmness. I look upon my future calmly and confidently, and although it promises me nothing but a lonely grave and the last journey to an unknown distance, I am ready to meet death just as courageously as I lived my life, drawing strength from my solitude, from the consciousness of my innocence and my uprightness.

After long hesitations, which are not quite intelligible to me now, I finally resolved to establish for myself the system of our prison in all its rigidness. For that purpose, finding a small house in the outskirts of the city, which was to be leased for a long term of years, I hired it. Then with the kind assistance of the Warden of our prison, (I cannot express my gratitude to him adequately enough in words,) I invited to the new place one of the most experienced jailers, who is still a young man, but already hardened in the strict principles of our prison. Availing myself of his instruction, and also of the suggestions of the obliging Warden, I have engaged workmen who transformed one of the rooms into a cell. The measurements as well as the form and all the details of my new, and, I hope, my last dwelling are strictly in accordance with my plan. My cell is 8 by 4 yards, 4 yards high, the walls are painted grey at the bottom, the upper part of the walls and the ceiling are white, and near the ceiling there is a square window 1 1/2 by 1 1/2 yards, with a massive iron grate, which has already become rusty with age. In the door, locked with a heavy and strong lock, which issues a loud creak at each turn of the key, there is a small hole for observation, and below it a little window, through which the food is brought and received. The furnishing of the cell: a table, a chair, and a cot fastened to the wall; on the wall a crucifix, my portrait, and the rules concerning the conduct of the prisoners, in a black frame; and in the corner a closet filled with books. This last, being a violation of the strict harmony of my dwelling, I was compelled to do by extreme and sad necessity; the jailer positively refused to be my librarian and to bring the books according to my order, and to engage a special librarian seemed to me to be an act of unnecessary eccentricity. Aside from this, in elaborating my plans, I met with strong opposition not only from the local population, which simply declared me to be insane, but even from the enlightened people. Even the Warden endeavoured for some time to dissuade me, but finally he clasped my hand warmly, with an expression of sincere regret at not being in a position to offer me a place in our prison.

I cannot recall the first day of my confinement without a bitter smile. A mob of impertinent and ignorant idlers yelled from morning till night at my window, with their heads lifted high (my cell is situated in the second story), and they heaped upon me senseless abuse; there were even efforts - to the disgrace of my townspeople - to storm my dwelling, and one heavy stone almost crushed my head. Only the police, which arrived in time, succeeded in averting the catastrophe. When, in the evening, I went out for a walk, hundreds of fools, adults and children, followed me, shouting and whistling, heaping abuse upon me, and even hurling mud at me. Thus, like a persecuted prophet, I wended my way without fear amidst the maddened crowd, answering their blows and curses with proud silence.

What has stirred these fools? In what way have I offended their empty heads? When I lied to them, they kissed my hands; now, when I have re-established the sacred truth of my life in all its strictness and purity, they burst into curses, they branded me with contempt, they hurled mud at me. They were disturbed because I dared to live alone, and because I did not ask them for a place in the "common cell for rogues." How difficult it is to be truthful in this world!

True, my perseverance and firmness finally defeated them. With the naivete of savages, who honour all they do not understand, they commenced, in the second year, to bow to me, and they are making ever lower bows to me, because their amazement is growing ever greater, their fear of the inexplicable is growing ever deeper. And the fact that I never respond to their greetings fills them with delight, and the fact that I never smile in response to their flattering smiles, fills them with a firm assurance that they are guilty before me for some grave wrong, and that I know their guilt. Having lost confidence in their own and other people's words, they revere my silence, even as people revere every silence and every mystery. If I were to start to speak suddenly, I would again become human to them and would disillusion them bitterly, no matter what I would say; in my silence I am to them like their eternally silent God. For these strange people would cease believing their God as soon as their God would commence to speak. Their women are already regarding me as a saint. And the kneeling women and sick children that I often find at the threshold of my dwelling undoubtedly expect of me a trifle - to heal them, to perform a miracle. Well, another year or two will pass, and I shall commence to perform miracles as well as those of whom they speak with such enthusiasm. Strange people, at times I feel sorry for them, and I begin to feel really angry at the devil who so skilfully mixed the cards in their game that only the cheat knows the truth, his little cheating truth about the marked queens and the marked kings. They bow too low, however, and this hinders me from developing a sense of mercy, otherwise - smile at my jest, indulgent reader - I would not restrain myself from the temptation of performing two or three small, but effective miracles.

I must go back to the description of my prison.

Having constructed my cell completely, I offered my jailer the following alternative: He must observe with regard to me the rules of the prison regime in all its rigidness, and in that case he would inherit all my fortune according to my will, or he would receive nothing if he failed to do his duty. It seemed that in putting the matter before him so clearly I would meet with no difficulties. Yet at the very first instance, when I should have been incarcerated for violating some prison regulation, this naive and timid man absolutely refused to do it; and only when I threatened to get another man immediately, a more conscientious jailer, was he compelled to perform his duty. Though he always locked the door punctually, he at first neglected his duty of watching me through the peephole; and when I tried to test his firmness by suggesting a change in some rule or other to the detriment of common sense he yielded willingly and quickly. One day, on trapping him in this way, I said to him:

"My friend, you are simply foolish. If you will not watch me and guard me properly I shall run away to another prison, taking my legacy along with me. What will you do then?"

I am happy to inform you that at the present time all these misunderstandings have been removed, and if there is anything I can complain of it is rather excessive strictness than mildness. Now that my jailer has entered into the spirit of his position this honest man treats me with extreme sternness, not for the sake of the profit but for the sake of the principle . Thus, in the beginning of this week he incarcerated me for twenty-four hours for violating some rule, of which, it seemed to me, I was not guilty; and protesting against this seeming injustice I had the unpardonable weakness to say to him:

"In the end I will drive you away from here. You must not forget that you are my servant."

"Before you drive me away I will incarcerate you," replied this worthy man.

"But how about the money?" I asked with astonishment. "Don't you know that you will be deprived of it?"

"Do I need your money? I would give up all my own money if I could stop being what I am. But what can I do if you violate the rule and I must punish you by incarcerating you?"

I am powerless to describe the joyous emotion which came over me at the thought that the consciousness of duty had at last entered his dark mind, and that now, even if in a moment of weakness I wanted to leave my prison, my conscientious jailer would not permit me to do it. The spark of firmness which glittered in his round eyes showed me clearly that no matter where I might run away he would find me and bring me back; and that the revolver which he often forgot to take before, and which he now cleans every day, would do its work in the event I decided to run away.

And for the first time in all these years I fell asleep on the stone floor of my dark cell with a happy smile, realising that my plan was crowned with complete success, passing from the realm of eccentricity to the domain of stern and austere reality. And the fear which I felt while falling asleep in the presence of my jailer, my fear of his resolute look, of his revolver; my timid desire to hear a word of praise from him, or to call forth perhaps a smile on his lips, re-echoed in my soul as the harmonious clanking of my eternal and last chains.

Thus I pass my last years. As before, my health is sound and my free spirit is clear. Let some call me a fool and laugh at me; in their pitiful blindness let others regard me as a saint and expect me to perform miracles; an upright man to some people, to others - a liar and a deceiver - I myself know who I am, and I do not ask them to understand me. And if there are people who will accuse me of deception, of baseness, even of the lack of simple honour - for there are scoundrels who are convinced to this day that I committed murder - no one will dare accuse me of cowardice, no one will dare say that I could not perform my painful duty to the end. From the beginning till the end I remained firm and unbribable; and though a bugbear, a fanatic, a dark horror to some people, I may awaken in others a heroic dream of the infinite power of man.

I have long discontinued to receive visitors, and with the death of the Warden of our prison, my only true friend, whom I visited occasionally, my last tie with this world was broken. Only I and my ferocious jailer, who watches every movement of mine with mad suspicion, and the black grate which has caught in its iron embrace and muzzled the infinite - this is my life. Silently accepting the low bows, in my cold estrangement from the people I am passing my last road.

I am thinking of death ever more frequently, but even before death I do not bend my fearless look. Whether it brings me eternal rest or a new unknown and terrible struggle, I am humbly prepared to accept it.

Farewell, my dear reader! Like a vague phantom you appeared before my eyes and passed, leaving me alone before the face of life and death. Do not be angry because at times I deceived you and lied - you, too, would have lied perhaps in my place. Nevertheless I loved you sincerely, and sincerely longed for your love; and the thought of your sympathy for me was quite a support to me in my moments and days of hardship. I am sending you my last farewell and my sincere advice. Forget about my existence, even as I shall henceforth forget about yours forever.

- - - - -

A deserted field, overgrown with high grass, devoid of an echo, extends like a deep carpet to the very fence of our prison, whose majestic outlines subdue my imagination and my mind. When the dying sun illumines it with its last rays, and our prison, all in red, stands like a queen, like a martyr, with the dark wounds of its grated windows, and the sun rises silently and proudly over the plain - with sorrow, like a lover, I send my complaints and my sighs and my tender reproach and vows to her, to my love, to my dream, to my bitter and last sorrow. I wish I could forever remain near her, but here I look back - and black against the fiery frame of the sunset stands my jailer, stands and waits.

With a sigh I go back in silence, and he moves behind me noiselessly, about two steps away, watching every move of mine.

Our prison is beautiful at sunset.

Choose from Thousands of 1stWorldLibrary Classics By

Adolphus WilliamWard
Aesop
Agatha Christie
Alexander Aaronsohn
Alexander Kielland
Alexandre Dumas
Alfred Gatty
Alfred Ollivant
Alice Duer Miller
Alice Turner Curtis
Alice Dunbar
Ambrose Bierce
Amelia E. Barr
Andrew Lang
Andrew McFarland Davis
Anna Sewell
Annie Besant
Annie Hamilton Donnell
Annie Payson Call
Anton Chekhov
Arnold Bennett
Arthur Conan Doyle
Arthur Ransome
Atticus
B. M. Bower
Basil King
Bayard Taylor
Ben Macomber
Booth Tarkington
Bram Stoker
C. Collodi
C. E. Orr
C. M. Ingleby
Carolyn Wells
Catherine Parr Traill
Charles A. Eastman
Charles Dickens
Charles Dudley Warner
Charles Farrar Browne
Charles Ives
Charles Kingsley
Charles Lathrop Pack
Charles Whibley
Charles Willing Beale
Charlotte M. Braeme
Charlotte M.Yonge
Clair W. Hayes
Clarence Day Jr.
Clarence E. Mulford

Clemence Housman
Confucius
Cornelis DeWitt Wilcox
Cyril Burleigh
D. H. Lawrence
Daniel Defoe
David Garnett
Don Carlos Janes
Donald Keyhole
Dorothy Kilner
Dougan Clark
E. Nesbit
E.P.Roe
E. Phillips Oppenheim
Edgar Allan Poe
Edgar Rice Burroughs
Edith Wharton
Edward J. O'Biren
John Cournos
Edwin L. Arnold
Eleanor Atkins
Elizabeth Cleghorn
Gaskell
Elizabeth Von Arnim
Ellem Key
Emily Dickinson
Erasmus W. Jones
Ernie Howard Pie
Ethel Turner
Ethel Watts Mumford
Eugenie Foa
Eugene Wood
Evelyn Everett-Green
Everard Cotes
F. J. Cross
Federick Austin Ogg
Ferdinand Ossendowski
Francis Bacon
Francis Darwin
Frances Hodgson Burnett
Frank Gee Patchin
Frank Harris
Frank Jewett Mather
Frank L. Packard
Frederick Trevor Hill
Frederick Winslow Taylor
Friedrich Kerst
Friedrich Nietzsche
Fyodor Dostoyevsky

Gabrielle E. Jackson
Garrett P. Serviss
Gaston Leroux
George Ade
Geroge Bernard Shaw
George Ebers
George Eliot
George MacDonald
George Orwell
George Tucker
George W. Cable
George Wharton James
Gertrude Atherton
Grace E. King
Grant Allen
Guillermo A. Sherwell
Gulielma Zollinger
Gustav Flaubert
H. A. Cody
H. B. Irving
H. G. Wells
H. H. Munro
H. Irving Hancock
H. Rider Haggard
H. W. C. Davis
Hamilton Wright Mabie
Hans Christian Andersen
Harold Avery
Harold McGrath
Harriet Beecher Stowe
Harry Houidini
Helent Hunt Jackson
Helen Nicolay
Hendy David Thoreau
Henrik Ibsen
Henry Adams
Henry Ford
Henry Frost
Henry James
Henry Jones Ford
Henry Seton Merriman
Henry Wadsworth
Longfellow
Henry W Longfellow
Herbert A. Giles
Herbert N. Casson
Herman Hesse
Homer
Honore De Balzac

Horace Walpole
Horatio Alger, Jr.
Howard Pyle
Howard R. Garis
Hugh Lofting
Hugh Walpole
Humphry Ward
Ian Maclaren
Israel Abrahams
J.G.Austin
J. Henri Fabre
J. M. Barrie
J. Macdonald Oxley
J. S. Knowles
J. Storer Clouston
Jack London
Jacob Abbott
James Allen
James Lane Allen
James Andrews
James Baldwin
James DeMille
James Joyce
James Oliver Curwood
James Oppenheim
James Otis
Jane Austen
Jens Peter Jacobsen
Jerome K. Jerome
John Burroughs
John F. Kennedy
John Gay
John Glasworthy
John Habberton
John Joy Bell
John Milton
John Philip Sousa
Jonathan Swift
Joseph Carey
Joseph Conrad
Joseph Jacobs
Julian Hawthrone
Julies Vernes
Justin Huntly McCarthy
Kakuzo Okakura
Kenneth Grahame
Kate Langley Bosher
L. A. Abbot
L. T. Meade
L. Frank Baum
Laura Lee Hope

Laurence Housman
Leo Tolstoy
Leonid Andreyev
Lewis Carroll
Lilian Bell
Lloyd Osbourne
Louis Tracy
Louisa May Alcott
Lucy Fitch Perkins
Lucy Maud Montgomery
Lydia Miller Middleton
Lyndon Orr
M. H. Adams
Margaret E. Sangster
Margaret Vandercook
Maria Edgeworth
Maria Thompson Daviess
Mariano Azuela
Marion Polk Angellotti
Mark Overton
Mark Twain
Mary Austin
Mary Cole
Mary Rowlandson
Mary Wollstonecraft
Shelley
Max Beerbohm
Myra Kelly
Nathaniel Hawthrone
O. F. Walton
Oscar Wilde
Owen Johnson
P.G.Wodehouse
Paul and Mable Thorn
Paul G. Tomlinson
Paul Severing
Peter B. Kyne
Plato
R. Derby Holmes
R. L. Stevenson
Rabindranath Tagore
Rahul Alvares
Ralph Waldo Emmerson
Rene Descartes
Rex E. Beach
Richard Harding Davis
Richard Jefferies
Robert Barr
Robert Frost
Robert Gordon Anderson
Robert L. Drake

Robert Lansing
Robert Michael Ballantyne
Robert W. Chambers
Rosa Nouchette Carey
Ross Kay
Rudyard Kipling
Samuel B. Allison
Samuel Hopkins Adams
Sarah Bernhardt
Selma Lagerlof
Sherwood Anderson
Sigmund Freud
Standish O'Grady
Stanley Weyman
Stella Benson
Stephen Crane
Stewart Edward White
Stijn Streuvels
Swami Abhedananda
Swami Parmananda
T. S. Ackland
The Princess Der Ling
Thomas A. Janvier
Thomas A Kempis
Thomas Anderton
Thomas Bailey Aldrich
Thomas Bulfinch
Thomas De Quincey
Thomas H. Huxley
Thomas Hardy
Thomas More
Thornton W. Burgess
U. S. Grant
Valentine Williams
Victor Appleton
Virginia Woolf
Walter Scott
Washington Irving
Wilbur Lawton
Wilkie Collins
Willa Cather
Willard F. Baker
William Makepeace
Thackeray
William W. Walter
Winston Churchill
Yei Theodora Ozaki
Young E. Allison
Zane Grey

CPSIA information can be obtained at www.ICGtesting.com
Printed in the USA
BVOW02*1853121214

379215BV00001B/2/P